COLD MOON RISING

A THRILLER

MICHAEL SLEDGE

*To my parents. For my mother, who took me to the library
and arranged for the bookmobile to make our neighborhood
one of its regular stops. For my father, who passed on his love
of reading and visiting bookstores every chance he got.*

CHAPTER 1

A beautiful, early spring morning in North Carolina greeted Donna as she stepped onto the porch. Still cooler than she really cared for, but a welcome change from the colder than average winter they had that year. She breathed in the fresh air and quickly made her way down the steps, across the drive, and picked up the paper lying in the grass.

She stopped for a moment and looked at a small flower bed she had made around the mailbox. The tulip bulbs she had carefully placed in the rich, dark soil would soon be splitting open and pushing up into the sunlight. Another sign that winter was over. Donna slowly rose up from her crouched position and began walking back towards the house. She had a busy day ahead.

A few blocks away, in a budget motel down Capital Boulevard, the foursome sipped cheap coffee out of the small Styrofoam cups that are common in such a place. They had spent the night there, checked in under a false name and paid with cash.

Nick was the leader of the group. Just over six feet tall and still in pretty good shape for his age, he had briefly played football for a Division 1 university. He hadn't been a star, but he had played. Studying wasn't his thing, so he dropped out after that first season and never went back.

Nick looked around at the rest of the group assembled in the room. Penny was his second wife, blond and good-looking in a trashy sort of way. She was younger than him by a few years. Whatever he said or did was fine with her. Aspiring to better things in life wasn't something she spent much time on.

Ray was not like Nick at all, at least not physically. Shorter and stocky, he had dark hair, a muscular frame, and rarely displayed emotion. He and Nick went back a few years. They had been involved in some things that didn't quite work, but they had developed trust in each other that was still holding together.

Nick hadn't known the fourth member for very long. Ray introduced them to Rose a few months back at a local bar. She was dark-haired also, and not really all that attractive. She had a thing for Ray and had kept hanging around, hoping it would turn into something long-term. They had been up late the night before, and the empty, cheap beer cans scattered around the room were a testament to that.

For hours they had argued, made plans, discarded plans, made new plans, and then finally agreed on how they would pull it off. They celebrated this accomplishment with a couple of shots each of cheap bourbon, then settled down for the night, agreeing before they turned out the one lamp in the room that they would go over the plan again the next morning.

Nick woke them all up by 9:00 a.m. After sending the women to the small lobby to grab coffees for the group, they all gathered in a sort of semi-circle in the room. Nick sat on one chair by the small desk in the corner. Penny sat on the edge of one of the two double beds, Rose on the other. Ray sat stoically on the floor, back against the wall.

Nick spoke first. "Let's run through the plan again."

And they did – three more times. Nick was determined to get it right. No more failures. He needed it to work.

The sign at the front entrance to the lot was new, and Eddie Johnson couldn't be prouder of it. Buy Here, Pay Here, it said. Right underneath that was the name of the business - Johnson Auto. Eddie sold used cars. Not the ones at the high end like Lexus or Mercedes – his were lower to middle end with some miles on them. Because his customers couldn't afford the high end. He had been selling cars for many years, working for others after he dropped out of college at the age of 20, then later for himself.

He hadn't gotten rich, but business was pretty good and getting better, especially since he had rolled out the Buy Here, Pay Here financing option. Now he didn't just make money on the sale of the cars themselves but was also getting a growing income from his part of the interest spread on the financing of the cars. Yes indeed, life was good.

It was a quiet morning on the lot. Too early for a lot of traffic and the weekdays were never as busy as the weekends anyway. After all, his customers were working class folks who were busy during the week. Eddie was holed up in his office at the back of the lot, feet up on his desk, shooting the breeze with Bill, his right-hand man and best salesman. As usual, they were in a sports argument.

"So let me get this straight," said Eddie. "You're telling me that there's absolutely no way the 1983 NC State national basketball champs could have a prayer of beating the 1982 UNC national champs team if they had played head-to-head. That's what you are saying?"

"That's exactly what I'm saying," snorted Bill. "Michael Jordan, James Worthy, Sam Perkins! Are you kidding me? That State team hit a completely insane lucky streak. Nowhere near the talent on the UNC team." And so, it went. Back and forth. Neither man won. How could they when facts don't matter anyway and it's all about your team loyalty? After another twenty minutes they tired of the argument and changed to religion. More of the same.

Finally, a customer broke up the fight by driving onto the lot in a beat-up Ford sedan. Bill could spot a sale immediately. He told Eddie to hold his last thought and strode out onto the lot to greet the man driving the sedan.

Eddie threw his feet on the desk and watched Bill through the plate glass window working the man like a champ. He was damn lucky to have Bill working for him. Never complained, worked as many hours as Eddie needed him too, and was as honest as they came. A real good guy.

Pretty soon, though, Eddie began to drift away with other thoughts. He was thinking about his wife, Donna. She was another treasure in his life. They had been married almost 20 years. No kids, but they had been happy together. He had some plans to show her how much she meant to him – a little getaway to Bermuda for a few days. He was going to surprise her at home later that day and take her out to lunch to spring it on her. Then he might be a couple hours later getting back to the lot if he got lucky.

Bill and the customer interrupted his daydream as they walked into the office. "Eddie, I want you to meet Larry Lee," said Bill. "He's got his eye on that red Chevrolet on the second row."

Eddie stuck out his hand. "Larry, pleasure to meet you, and I really appreciate you coming out to see us today. We're gonna take care of you and make sure you get what you need. Bill here is my best guy. You couldn't be in better hands."

Larry looked almost visibly relieved. "Thank you, sir, thank you a lot," he said. "I'm in real bad need of a new car and a friend told me you guys would treat me right."

"Well, he told you right," said Bill as he slapped Larry on the back. "Now let me get the key to that car and let's take her for a spin. Eddie, we'll be back in just a few. I know you need to leave in a bit."

"Take your time, take your time," said Eddie with a broad smile on his face. "The customer always comes first at Johnson Auto."

Bill and Larry walked out of the office, key in hand, headed down the track to another sale for Johnson Auto. Eddie turned back to his desk and decided to do a little paperwork before he left for home. Life was good.

Donna stepped out of the shower and quickly grabbed the robe hanging nearby. Even though she was alone in the house, she was too modest to just stand naked in front of the mirror as she applied her makeup to get herself ready to go out. Besides, it was cold in that bathroom, and the robe helped fight it off. She found herself checking off all the things she had to get done that day – make the deposit at the bank, dry cleaners, stop by the garden center and see what new flowers they had, grocery store, and the drug store to pick up her prescription refill. She couldn't forget that. Then she would go back home to clean the house. Maybe she could hire a cleaning service soon. Eddie's business seemed to be doing well, and the bank deposits he gave her were getting bigger these days. He seemed so happy now. On top of the world!

She looked in the mirror and frowned. "Damn," she whispered, fingering back the hair just above her ear. Another age spot had appeared. When had that happened, she wondered? It seemed like suddenly. She turned back to the business at hand, methodically applying her makeup, focused again on getting to her tasks of the day.

Nick scanned house numbers carefully as the plain brown work van he and the gang were in slowly turned onto the Johnson's street. Rose was driving with him in the passenger seat. Penny and Ray were in the rear of the otherwise empty van. Penny was holding a large arrangement of flowers, Ray a small handgun. Rose eased the van to the side of the street and looked over at Nick.

"You guys ready?" asked Nick.

"Let's do it," came the reply from Penny.

"Okay," said Nick. "Rose, pull slowly down the street and act like you are scanning the house numbers on mailboxes, looking for the right address, just in case anyone is at home and watching out. Penny, get up here in front. I'll sit back there with Ray. You know what to do from here."

Rose eased the van back onto the street, slowly rolling past the other houses. When she got to the address for the Johnson's, she carefully pulled into the drive and moved up close to the porch. As they stopped, Penny looked over at her and gave her a little smile. "Don't worry, hon. I got this. Me and the boys will be in and out, quick as a flash and with the cash! Ray, hand me the gun."

Ray handed her the gun, which she jammed down into the arrangement of flowers. She opened the door, quietly closed it, and moved up onto the porch. She stopped briefly in front of the door, swiftly looked up and down the street, then pushed the doorbell.

Upstairs, Donna jumped when she heard the doorbell ring. Who could that be, she wondered. Hopefully not another person soliciting for whatever. Did these people not get the message that no one wanted to be bothered at home anymore by door-to-door salespeople? And couldn't they read the neighborhood sign that clearly said No Soliciting Allowed?

She tried to ignore the bell, hoping they would go away. No luck. It kept ringing. She peeked out the front window of their bedroom, looking down into the driveway. Some kind of van. Must be a delivery of some sort. She pulled her robe tight and sighed. No avoiding it. She had better go down and sign for whatever it was Eddie had ordered.

Donna stepped out of the master bedroom into the upstairs hallway. From there it was just a few steps to the stairs, and she made her way down carefully so as not to trip and fall, feeling the coolness of the wooden steps under her feet as she went down. She glanced at herself in the hallway mirror to make sure she looked decent enough to open the door and greet a stranger, brushing back a few strands of hair as she continued to the front door.

She looked through the security peephole in the door, seeing a dark-haired woman holding what appeared to be a bouquet of flowers. Her heart leapt at the sight. Eddie had ordered something for her, it seemed, not for the lot or the house. She turned the lock and opened the door, smiling at the woman on the other side of the glass storm door.

"Are you Mrs. Johnson?" inquired the blond-haired woman, as Donna was easing the door open.

"Yes, that's me," replied Donna, "and I suppose those lovely flowers must be from my wonderful husband!"

"Why, yes they are," came the reply. "And I will be happy to bring them in and set them down for you."

The offer to bring the flowers in struck Donna as a bit odd and an immediate feeling of uneasiness swept through her. She glanced out into the driveway, immediately noting another woman sitting in the van.

"No, that's okay. I can handle it myself," she replied, reaching for the vase of flowers.

The blond-haired woman started to move towards the door. "Really, it's no bother at all," the woman said. "I'll just set them down and be on my way."

Donna instinctively began to close the door, glancing again at the van as she did so. Her brain registered two facts. First, the woman in the van was talking...to who? And secondly, the van was unmarked, without any kind of signage designating it as belonging to a flower shop.

Both Donna and the woman were holding the vase at this point. The woman released her right hand from the vase, still holding on with her left hand, and reached into the large bouquet of flowers. As her hand came up and out of the vase, Donna realized she was grabbing a handgun that had been hidden in the flowers. The woman moved her left hand off the vase and grasped the door instead, pulling it back open and trying to push her way through and force Donna back into the house.

Donna let go of the vase as well, and the flowers dropped to the porch floor, the glass shattering as it struck the bricks and concrete. She screamed and stumbled backwards into the house, desperately trying to pull the storm door shut and keep the woman from entering. The woman slammed the gun barrel down on Donna's hand grasping the door, causing her to cry out in pain and release her grip on the door.

As the woman yanked the door open wider and bulldozed her way in, Donna could see behind her, through the fog of pain she now felt in her hand, that the side door of the van was sliding open. Two men were emerging from the rear. The dark-haired woman was yelling at Donna now as they tumbled into the hallway. Telling her to shut up and get on her knees. Waving the gun in her face and threatening to shoot her if she didn't do exactly what she was told.

Donna was numb with fear at this point and the pain in her hand had brought her to tears. What was going on? What was happening to her and who were these people? What did they want? The two men had run up the steps and into the house, closing both doors once they were in. Donna fell to her knees, as requested, and managed to say in a halting voice, "What...do you want? Why are you doing this?"

"The money," said the taller of the two men in an icy, calm voice. "We came for the money."

"What money?" cried Donna. "I don't have any money. Just a few dollars in cash."

"Quit lying," he said. "I know damn well he keeps that money here, and you're going to give it to us. You do that, you don't get hurt. We leave quietly and you can get back to your life."

"You mean the deposit for the car lot?" sputtered Donna. "Is that what you want?"

The shorter man snorted. "We'll take that too, since you offered."

"No," said the taller one. "You know what I am talking about. Eddie keeps a stash of money here from his other business, and you are going to give it to us. Now, where is it?"

"I don't know, I don't know what you mean," she said. "All I know about is the daily deposit he gives me for the lot. I think...I think it's about $2,000 today. I'll give it to you."

"Liar!" the taller one said, and he slapped her in the face. "Tell me where you keep the other cash."

"I don't know what you mean, I swear it!" she sobbed. "He hasn't told me about that."

"Okay, we do this the hard way then. Tie her up", he said to the other man, then looked at the woman, "You keep an eye on her while we search the house. Shoot her in the leg if she screams."

The shorter man reached behind his back, pulling a short coil of rope out of his waistband as the woman shoved Donna to the floor, face down, and roughly pulled her hands behind her. He quickly curled a strand of rope around Donna's wrists, then yanked her by the arms and shoulders back into a kneeling position. Donna shuddered as she gazed into his face. Flat, black emotionless eyes stared back at her. She looked down at the floor, suddenly even more terrified if that was possible.

The taller one stepped towards her, yanking her head up by her hair, forcing her to look at him. "One more time," he said. "Where is it?"

"I don't know! I swear!"

"You better hope we find it soon," he spat back at her. "If we don't, we're coming back in here and beating you until you give it up." He turned to the other man and said, "You go upstairs and go through the rooms up there. I'll check out the downstairs."

He gave one more look at Donna, then walked down the hallway in the opposite direction, headed to the kitchen. Soon the banging and closing of doors and cabinets filled the house, each one seeming more ominous to Donna as she cowered in front of the woman. Tears streamed down her cheeks, and she wiped her nose on the shoulder of her robe since she was unable to move her hands from behind her back. Her hand throbbed with pain and waves of nausea came over her.

She looked up at her, pleading with all she had. "Please, please! You must believe me. I don't know about any other money. I would give it to you if I did."

"Save it, sister," she hissed back at her. "You better hope they find it quick."

"But" Donna started to reply, then quickly stopped when she raised the gun as if to strike her again.

"Just shut up," the woman said. "I don't want to hear you whining."

The search went on for a few more minutes. Occasionally, curses would filter down from upstairs. The slamming of doors got louder each time as the frustrations grew with the two men. Eventually, the shorter man came back down the stairs and into the hallway, calling out that he had found nothing but some jewelry, no cash. Shortly after that, the taller man came back into the hall, and it was clear that he was not happy.

"Gonna ask you one last time," he said to Donna. "Where is it?"

"I don't know," she wailed. "Please believe me! I don't know."

He slapped her roughly. "Where is it?"

Donna just sobbed loudly and didn't reply. He hit her again, and this time she fell to the floor clearly dazed from the blow. The woman yanked her back to her knees, gripping her robe tightly in her left hand.

He crouched down, looking directly into Donna's eyes. "Is it really worth this? The money? I know it's here and I know you are lying. This is going to get a lot more serious if you don't begin cooperating."

Suddenly the mobile phone in his back pocket buzzed. He pulled it out and glanced at the screen. He punched the answer button. "What?"

He listened a moment, then replied, "Damn, you sure?"

After another moment, he shouted into the phone "Stay close by," then shoved it back in his pocket.

"Hubby is making a surprise visit," he said to the woman. "Shut her up and drag her into the kitchen. He looked at the other man. "We'll jump him when he comes in the door."

"Front door or back?" asked the other man.

"You go to the back. I'll go to the front. Once we know which one he's coming in the other one of us can move towards that door. She's waiting down the street in the van, so he won't know if anyone is here. We should have the drop on him."

"Got it," he nodded as he headed to the rear of the house.

CHAPTER 2

Somewhere deep in the fog of sleep, Jimmy Quinn realized some kind of alarm was waking him up. He fought it, clinging to the dream he was having, although he honestly couldn't remember later what the dream was even about. He rolled toward the sound coming from his nightstand beside the bed, opening one eye to see that his cell phone was ringing. He reached for it, knocking it on the floor. It kept ringing.

Groping with one hand on the floor, he finally felt the phone under his hand and pulled it up to see who was calling. Susan, his ex-wife. He glanced at the clock beside him: 12:57 in the afternoon. What the hell did she want?

He punched the answer button and braced for the worst.

"Jimmy? Are you there?"

"Yep. Here. To what do I owe the pleasure of your call?"

"Are you still in bed?" Susan sneered. "Good Lord, it's almost the middle of the afternoon."

"No, Susan. I just got back from a five-mile run. That was right after I finished my Pilates class. And my personal trainer will be here in a minute. What do you want?" he asked sarcastically.

He had pulled a double shift the day before and then stayed out a couple of hours past when he should have after that, hanging out with some of his friends from the police department at a trendy new club in downtown Raleigh – The Brownstone. Not enough beers to be drunk but combined with the long shift it had made him almost comatose after he collapsed into bed the night before. He was off today, so he hadn't bothered to set his alarm.

"It's a courtesy call," said Susan. "A reminder about your daughter's dance recital tonight. 7:00 p.m. at the gym in the high school. She's counting on you to be there."

"Okay, right. I have it on my calendar. Wouldn't miss it," said Jimmy in return. "Tell her I will be there. And thanks for the reminder. I know you didn't have to do that."

"No problem," said Susan softly. "She is so excited. And she's looking forward to you being there."

"I will be there. Bye," Jimmy said as he punched off the phone and laid it back on the nightstand.

He rolled onto his back, staring at the ceiling, thinking about his daughter Chloe. He missed her a lot. She wasn't that far away, just over in Chapel Hill, about 25 miles. But he didn't get to see her that often, or her brother Jack. They both lived with Susan, and he knew that was best for them. Much more stable with her since his job kept him working various shifts and sometimes having to go in unexpectedly.

He and Susan had separated three years previous, with the divorce finalized around two years ago. She had taken a new position at the University of North Carolina as an associate professor of biology. It paid well and had been a promotion from her previous job at NC State. Jimmy himself was a detective with the Raleigh City Police Department. He had been a detective for several years now after spending a few years in a patrol car. He loved it, but it had taken its toll on his family life.

He glanced at the clock again. After 1:00 p.m. now. Could he drift back to sleep again? What was that dream he had been in when Susan called? He couldn't pull it out of his brain. It might have been sports. Might have been a woman.

Then the phone rang again. Uh oh, he thought as he glanced at the caller ID. Micky, his partner on the force, was calling. It probably meant he could forget about going back to sleep. "Is this my wake-up call?" he asked, laughing as he answered the phone.

"Jimmy, get your lazy ass out of bed. The criminals are working overtime, and you're over there frittering away the sunlight."

"It's my day off, Micky. How could you forget – it's yours too."

"Yeah, well that all looks good on paper, but Todd and Ben have their hands full on that shooting down on South Street, and the boss decided we needed some overtime."

"What's up?" asked Jimmy.

"Breaking and entering perhaps. Definitely an assault. Not sure yet. I am on the way to the scene. Dispatch will text you the address. Roll it out and meet me there in twenty minutes."

"Do I have a choice?" asked Jimmy sarcastically.

"Always," replied Micky. "Turn in your badge. Been wanting a younger partner anyway. Maybe a hot young female, eager to make a name for herself."

"Right," snorted Jimmy. "I'm on the way. Try not to screw up the crime scene before I get there." He clicked off, sighing deeply. No wonder Susan had left him. His work life was unpredictable. He rolled out of bed and headed for the shower, eager to find out what awaited him next.

Thirty minutes later, Jimmy was navigating a couple of streets off Capital Boulevard looking for East Lane Avenue. When he reached it, he could see the circus was already in full swing at the crime scene. Patrol cars, a crime tech van, media vans, neighbors standing in clumps at a distance. He had seen it so many times before, and it never failed to kick his pulse up a few notches. This was the beginning of the chase, and he loved it.

A young, uniformed officer was walking towards him as he eased the car over to the side of the street, just outside the cordoned off area surrounding the driveway and yard of the house. He wondered for the millionth time who had filed the patent for the yellow crime scene tape that was strung up as a flimsy, but very effective block to the unauthorized visitor to the scene. Whoever it was had made a killing – all pun intended – he laughed to himself, wishing it had been him.

"Good afternoon, sir," the officer said pleasantly.

"Back at ya," came his reply, glancing at the name badge the officer had on his chest. "Steve, is everything secured now? Have you seen Micky Bondurant yet?"

"Yes, sir, on both counts," came the quick response. "Detective Bondurant arrived and is at the house. Patrolman Wilson is talking to the neighbor who called it in, a Mrs. Wilson, just over on the other side of the lawn. Crime tech is beginning their work and the EMT's left a good while ago with the victim."

"Victim?" asked Jimmy. "How do you know you have a victim already? Maybe he is really one of the perpetrators."

The young patrolman blushed deeply, shifting his weight from one leg to another as the nervous reaction to Jimmy's question quickly sank in. "Sorry, sir. You're right. We don't know what happened here yet."

Jimmy laid a hand gently on Steve's shoulder, looking at him with a reassuring smile. "Steve don't be embarrassed. Making assumptions is how you start to solve a crime. Just be careful how quickly you voice them and who's around. The man they carted off probably is a victim – of some kind anyway. You and Wilson have done a fine job securing the scene. Thanks."

"Thank you, Detective Quinn. And thanks for the advice."

"No problem," said Jimmy as he turned towards the house, moving purposefully across the lawn and up the drive. He quickly scanned the scene in front of him. Decent, but not extravagant two-story house with a two-car garage. A well-kept lawn with several flower beds. Both garage doors open, with one space empty and the other occupied by a silver Toyota Camry with a few years on it.

Across the lawn, on the far side, he took note of Patrolman Wilson talking to an attractive older woman. The woman was obviously distraught. She must be the neighbor who discovered all this, he thought, remembering what Steve had told him. Funny how she and the patrolman interviewing her shared the same last name. That would be way too small a world if they were related.

Jimmy stopped as he reached the drive and watched a crime scene tech at work on the front porch. The door was open, and the tech was photographing something near the opening. He decided to learn about that later and walked through the garage to the entry door leading inside. He noticed a license plate frame on the back of the Camry with Johnson Auto engraved on it. He had seen that somewhere in town but couldn't quite remember where. Also for later.

He stepped through the open door and directly into the kitchen area of the house. The first thing he noticed was what a mess it was. Some kind of struggle had taken place there. The second thing he noticed was his partner, Micky Bondurant, pad in hand and shaking his head.

"So glad you could join us," said Micky. "Can I get you some coffee? Maybe a cup of tea?"

"Yeah. Thanks, Sherlock. And after that we can catch a movie. What do we know so far?"

"Not much," sighed Micky. "But this one might be interesting before it's over. The house belongs to Eddie and Donna Johnson. He runs Johnson Auto out on Capital. She does some work for the dealership from home. No other jobs. A neighbor," Micky paused as he glanced at his notes, "Rachel Wilson, lives a couple of doors down, came over after lunch and found Eddie in the kitchen. He was alive but pretty badly beaten up."

"Where did they take him?" asked Jimmy.

"Probably Wake," said Micky. "We can confirm that in a few minutes."

"What about his wife?"

"Well, that's one we will have to figure out. Suffice it to say she's missing right now."

"Neighbor know anything about that?"

"Nope. Once she looked in the kitchen and saw Johnson face down, she backed out and dialed 911."

"Huh. Tell me more."

"As you can see, the kitchen was the scene of some kind of fight. The neighbor says she saw Johnson's car drive up earlier, so maybe he came in and the wife clocked him with a bat. Or maybe he surprised some burglars."

"The Camry his car?"

"Wrong again, my friend. He drives a white SUV, Chevy Tahoe. You might have noticed it's not in the garage."

"Yeah, I did notice that. Not as dumb as you think I am." Jimmy grinned. "What else?"

"Blood. In the hallway downstairs. Not a lot, but enough. Smeared a bit as you move back towards this room, but it stops. No real signs of a struggle there, but when you look through the rest of the house you have to wonder if someone was searching for something. A couple of drawers open here and there and a closet door or two standing open. Maybe it matters. Maybe they just weren't really neat and tidy, these Johnsons."

"What's on the front porch?" asked Jimmy. "I saw the tech out there."

"Broken flower vase and some flowers. Most of it on the porch but some fragments of glass just inside the doorway."

"Hmmm, curiouser and curiouser."

"Yeah. That's about all we have so far. Techs are working the house over. Photographs and fingerprints. The works. I was just heading out to talk to the neighbor."

"You go ahead," said Jimmy. "I'm going to walk around the house a bit and then I'll join you."

"Okay. See you outside," said Micky, and he disappeared through the garage.

CHAPTER 3

Highway 98 runs through the heart of North Carolina. Calling it a highway is an overstatement by more modern standards, but when it was first built, the title was a better fit. It was a two-lane road, one for each direction, of course, and linked the town of Wake Forest to Highway 64.

Along the way lies the community of Bunn. Route 1609 winds through Bunn east towards what had, at one time, been a bit of a haven for people who liked to fish. 1609 crossed over the Tar River a few miles outside Bunn and then led straight over to Pine Lake. Both bodies of water had attracted casual and serious fishermen in the years past, but now the lake attracted more of the boating and water sports set. Pollutants had caused the safety of fish in the Tar River to come into question more recently, making that a less attractive option to the serious fishermen.

A mile from the Tar River, on the Pine Lake side, and right off Route 1609 stood the Lake Pine Motel. Lake Pine Motel had been erected in the late 1940's, just after the end of World War II, as the country began to flourish again and those coming back from overseas began looking for relaxation on the weekends.

They had argued about whether to bring her here or not. Ray had been the biggest holdout since the motel was, at the moment, the place he called home. In the end, he gave in because they didn't have any better options. His room was in one of the pods at the rear and was on the back side, a reflection of his innate desire to maintain his low profile. It was late in the afternoon when the van that had just hours before rolled up into the Johnson's driveway turned carefully off Route 1609 and came to a stop at the back of the Lake Pine complex.

Ray was driving and the passenger seat was empty, just in case someone was around and got curious about who was with him. He turned the ignition to the off position and shifted his weight so he could pivot and look to the rear of the van. "Okay, I am going to get out and just peek around the corners to make sure no one else is out. I'll open the door to my room. Move fast and get her in there," he said.

His three partners all nodded at him. As he was shutting the door to the van, Nick spoke to the two women. "Penny, you get on one side, and I'll grab the other and we'll walk her into the room. Rose, you open the door to the van for us and slide it back."

Donna lay on the floor of the van, unconscious from the dose of chloral hydrate they had forced into her earlier. That and the combination of what was probably a concussion from a blow to the head at her house had left her limp as a rag doll. At least for now. She had a nasty bruise forming on the side of her face, along with a deep gash on her arm that they had wrapped up with a towel. It looked like the bleeding from the gash had all but stopped for now.

Ray moved quietly from one corner to the next. No one was staying in the other two rooms on the back side of his block, so that wasn't a worry. Weekdays and nights weren't very busy at Lake Pine Motel. It was the weekends that provided just enough business to keep it open. Ray finished his check, waved at the van, and then quickly unlocked his room. Rose turned and whispered, "Let's go," and then slid the van door back.

Nick and Penny struggled to slide Donna to the opening. Nick jumped out first, then reached back and sat Donna up on the floor of the van, swinging her legs out. Penny stepped out and they both put a shoulder under opposite sides and lifted her straight up, her head rolling over to the one side. They walked rapidly across the parking lot and porch that wrapped all the way around the four sides of the pod, dragging her feet as they went.

Rose slid the van door shut, looking all around as she followed behind them. They laid her on one of the double beds in the room, and Ray closed the door and locked it as Rose came in. He reached over and drew the blinds shut for both windows beside the door and then turned on the lamp between the beds.

He turned from the lamp, stood fully erect and then looked down at Donna lying on the bed. When he looked up his eyes were cold, distant. He moved his gaze first to Rose, then Penny, and finally to Nick. "Okay, Nick," he said, "it's time for a full debrief on what the hell just happened to us."

For a moment Nick just stared at him. Then he softly said, "You're right. This has gotten serious. We never planned it this way. It just.... it just happened. We've got to come up with a new plan, a way out of this somehow."

"You're damn right," said Penny. "I didn't sign up for this. Christ, I need a drink."

"There's a bottle of bourbon on top of the fridge," said Ray. "And some glasses in the cabinet on the right of the sink. Pour us all a drink."

"Not me," muttered Rose. "I feel like throwing up as it is."

Penny walked to the fridge and then the cabinet, taking the bottle of bourbon and three small glasses with her to the table that stood in the kitchenette area of the room. She slumped down into one of the chairs, waving the others over to join her. They did.

"So, what exactly happened in the kitchen to get it started?" asked Rose.

"I was up against the wall beside the door leading to the garage, waiting for him to come in," said Nick. 'He started calling out for her as soon as he opened the door. He didn't see me at first. He was throwing some mail, or papers, or something on the counter as he was coming in. About that time, Ray stepped into the doorway leading to the hall. That got his attention pretty quick."

"Yeah. He looked at me and said who the hell are you and where is my wife," said Ray.

"That's when I spoke up from behind him and told him to freeze." Nick went on, "He asked what we wanted and again where his wife was. I told him she was in the hallway and if he just did what we said, no one would get hurt. We would leave them alone."

"And then he asked again what we wanted," said Ray. "I told him we wanted the money he kept in the house. He said he didn't keep money in the house."

"So, I called him a liar," said Nick. "Told him we didn't have time to play games and that he needed to just cough it up."

"And then he heard the wife cry out from the hallway," said Ray. "He started towards me, and I pushed him back against the counter. He came up off the counter, headed towards me again, and that's when Nick grabbed him from behind. The three of us got into it then, knocking things over and throwing punches at each other."

"Yeah, that's when the wife tried to get crazy on me," said Penny. "Tried to get up and run towards the kitchen. I just reacted. I hit her in the head with the gun. She fell and I think her arm caught the corner of a glass table. That was what opened up the gash on her arm."

"Is her husband even alive?" asked Rose. "Did you kill him?"

Rose had not come back to the house after calling Nick and alerting him that Eddie was on his way in. She had driven the van to a nearby fast-food restaurant, in a near panic to get away, and had waited there until Nick had called her.

"He was breathing," said Ray. "But he wasn't doing well. That's for sure."

"So, what happened next?" asked Rose. When Nick had finally called her, he had instructed her to meet them at a secluded parking lot on Falls Lake, just north of Raleigh. Her three partners had met her there, with Donna bound, gagged and groggy, in Eddie's car, a newer model SUV. They had transferred Donna to the van. Nick and Penny had joined her in the van, while Ray drove the SUV to another spot to hide it.

Nick sighed a long, heavy sigh. "He wouldn't stop. Ray and I kept yelling at him to quit, but I don't know. It's like he snapped and wasn't hearing us. He picked up a bottle off the counter – wine, I think – and swung it at my head. I ducked and he missed. Then Ray punched him from behind, hard, and he fell forward into the counter. That knocked him out."

"And then the debate started," sneered Penny.

"There was nothing to debate," shot back Nick. "Killing them both and leaving the bodies? That's not us. What the hell were you thinking?"

"So, how's it working out for us now?" shouted Penny.

"Shut up!" snarled Ray. "Both of you. You keep raising hell at each other in here and somebody might get curious and come see what all the fuss is about."

"You're right." Nick ran his hand through his hair. "We need to figure out what we do now. How long can we keep her here?"

"I don't know," said Ray. "A day? A week? Where are we going to take her to then?"

"What if he lives?" asked Penny. "Do you really think he would pay us ransom to get her back?"

"Maybe," said Nick. "Bastard must have a pile of money stashed somewhere. He can't go to the police. He's a crook. What kind of story can he give them? Yes, officer, my wife has been kidnapped by some people who are extorting me for my illegally gained fortune, and I need your help getting her back."

"And what if he dies?" asked Ray. "Then what do we do? Even if she really doesn't know anything about where his money might be, we can't just let her go. Can we?"

"Maybe we could," said Rose softly. "Just drop her off somewhere. Then we could leave. Move somewhere else."

"Really?" asked Nick with an exasperated look. "Just leave my kids. Never see 'em again?"

Back and forth it went between them. Sometimes heated and sometimes reasonable. It went on for about thirty minutes, until Ray finally stood up and said he had talked enough. Needed to clear his head.

"I'm gonna walk up to the office and talk to Bobby. See if I can catch anything on the news from Raleigh about what we did. We gotta make a plan when I come back, though."

Bobby was the owner of the motel. He had bought it about 10 years before, when it was supposedly on its last legs and all but bankrupt. The previous owners had been desperate to sell. Bobby retired after 40 years of working for the state department of transportation. He had no family. His wife had left him many years before because of his fishing addiction, which kept him away most weekends. Bored and with nothing else to do in retirement, he sold his modest house out in the country and plunked most of the proceeds down to buy the motel.

He wasn't much of a marketing wizard, but he began to cater to the fishing types and had managed to get enough of a regular clientele, combined with the occasional oddball like Ray and other transients, to make a break-even go of it with the motel.

Bobby wasn't a guy who talked much, so when Ray pushed open the door and walked into the office, he just looked up from his magazine and grunted a simple hello. The small color television mounted on the wall in the office played behind Bobby and Ray glanced up at it as he walked over to the coffee pot that was set up for motel patrons. The local news from Raleigh was coming on.

"What's shaking Bobby?"

"The usual. Nothing. Dead as always during the week."

"How's the weekend looking?" asked Ray. "Expecting a big crowd?"

"Probably not. Fish ain't biting."

"Too bad. Anything else going on?"

"Nope." Bobby looked back down at his magazine. Small talk time was over for him.

Ray sipped the cup of coffee he had poured, staring out the office window for a bit, contemplating the next move. None of the options were great, and it wasn't clear at the moment which ones were even viable. He was getting ready to walk out of the office, and he glanced at the news program as he moved to the door. He froze in his tracks but tried not to be too obvious at the suddenness of his stopping or his interest in the television. They were running a story on the robbery at the Johnson's with one of their young, fresh-looking reporters live on the scene. He stepped a little closer so he could hear the report.

"Police aren't saying much about what happened here on East Lane Avenue," the reporter said with the typical new reporter style, sincere but a bit exaggerated. "A neighbor apparently called in the 911 message shortly after noon. EMT's arrived and at least one of the residents was transported to Wake Med. We don't have information at this point on the condition, but we do know he was alive when they left the scene. We'll bring you more as the situation unfolds with a full update at eleven. Jim, back to you."

The news moved on to the next story, and Ray decided to move on as well. "Bobby, check you later man."

"Yeah," said Bobby, never looking up from his magazine.

Ray walked quickly back to his room.

CHAPTER 4

Jimmy pulled into a parking space in the visitor's lot at Wake Memorial Hospital shortly after 6:00 p.m. He and Micky had agreed to meet there after they left the crime scene on East Lane. Their priority now was to check on the status of Eddie Johnson, and if possible, interview him about what had happened.

He turned the ignition off and then sat and stared at the hospital. It made him think of his mother, Lisa Williams, and his family. His mother had always wanted to be a nurse, from the time she could first remember playing with dolls as a child. Pretending she was taking care of someone else was something she loved. She dreamed of going to college and getting a nursing degree, and then working in a hospital, maybe in Richmond, taking care of the sick, comforting their loved ones.

But she couldn't resist the charms of Michael Quinn, her high school sweetheart, and she dropped out of college her freshman year, pregnant with twins – Jimmy and his brother Tommy. She married Michael and they settled down in a small town in Virginia named Lynchburg. Michael went to college – Liberty Baptist – and got his degree in divinity while Lisa stayed home with the boys. They didn't have much money, but they had a lot of love. For a while anyway.

A few years later another child came, this time a girl. They named her Virginia but called her Gina. The years passed. Michael became the pastor of a small church, an evangelical, God-fearing congregation whose beliefs seemed to bring out of the best, or worst, of Michael, depending on how you viewed it. For Lisa, it eventually came to be seen as the worst, and she made the gut-wrenching decision that she had to leave. The boys were sixteen. Gina was eleven.

The boys learned to cope soon enough. Gina didn't. Too many visits to the emergency rooms because Gina had pumped herself full of drugs or alcohol or done something else destructive to herself. These were bad memories, of course, and Jimmy always felt some sense of guilt, wondering if there was anything he or Tommy could have done differently after their mom left that might have kept Gina from the path she had gone down. At least she was alive, even if her life was still a train wreck.

He shook off the memories and got out of the car. As he was walking towards the entrance, he caught sight of Micky pulling into the parking lot, so he stopped to wait. Micky pulled in a few spaces from Jimmy's car, then walked up to him with a grin.

"Did you sit in that car and think about your mom and sister for a while?" he asked.

"Of course. Can't stop living in the past," replied Jimmy.

"You need a shrink," said Micky. "Or to get laid. Or a wife. Or something."

"What I need is to get this case solved as quick as we can. I'm supposed to take some time off soon, and I know damn well you won't solve it while I'm gone."

"That's right, Sherlock" replied Micky. "I'd be lost without you. How did I ever make detective before I met you?"

Jimmy laughed, punched him playfully on the arm, and they both walked across the lot to the front entrance. Once inside, they turned right into the lobby, walking up to the reception desk. Micky flashed his badge and gave the elderly woman behind the desk his most winning smile. "Good evening," he said. "Need to know where to find a patient that was checked in this afternoon, Eddie Johnson. Can you tell me which room he is in?"

"Hello officer. Let me see what I can find." The receptionist turned to her computer screen, punching in data. She searched for a couple of minutes, frowning and then looked up at Micky, who said, "He was transported via EMT service this afternoon."

"Oh," came the reply. "If he went to ER, then maybe he hasn't been assigned a room yet. He might still be back there."

"Okay," said Jimmy. "Thanks. We'll walk back and check at the admission desk."

"Yes," she said with a smile. "I'm sure they can help."

"Thanks again," said Micky.

Jimmy and Micky walked down the hallway towards the emergency section, nodding and saying hello to the occasional nurse or doctor they recognized. They had paid more than a few professional visits to the site. Sometimes to visit victims, other times to talk to the perpetrator of a crime who managed to get themselves shot or cut up during the crime or the subsequent arrest by the police.

Wake Memorial was a sizable hospital, so it took them about ten minutes to wind their way back to the ER. They chatted about the crime scene as they walked.

"So, what do you think?" asked Jimmy. "Robbery? Love scene gone bad? Meth addict broke in and went crazy?"

"Probably not a meth addict. Wouldn't rule out the love thing yet. The wife is gone. The husband is in the hospital. Most domestic violence is not the wife on husband kind, so her abusing him is probably a long shot."

"Unless she had a reason to strike back at him, maybe," mused Jimmy.

"I don't know," said Micky. "Her car was still at the house, so she most likely was there when he came home. Now his car is gone and so is she. Odd that she would leave in his car and not her own, don't you think?"

"Yeah maybe. Unless she wanted it to look odd and took his instead."

"Perhaps she took it because it was bigger, and she needed the space to haul away something. Clothes. Food. Maybe she took off, running for the border after almost killing him," replied Micky.

Jimmy stroked his chin thoughtfully. "It wasn't obvious that she had cleared out the closet or the pantry, but I didn't look at those that closely. We should get a patrol car to go back and check that out. My guess is that will come up empty."

"Okay. I will call that in after we are done here," said Micky. "So, we know there was a struggle in the kitchen of some kind. That's where he was found, and a few things had been knocked around."

"What about the glass at the front door? What do you make of that?" asked Jimmy.

"Well, looks like it was a flower vase of some kind. Glass on the front porch. Some inside the door area of the house. Flowers lying on the porch as well."

"Easy enough to check and see if he sent them," observed Jimmy.

"Yeah. Already got somebody running that," replied Micky. "But that's kind of strange, don't you think? He sends her flowers, then shows up at the house, and she tries to put him away?"

"I don't know. Maybe he had been running out on her. She found out. He sends the flowers as part of his mea culpa. She's not buying the apology, and they get in a fight. That works, doesn't it?"

"So, she just threw the vase down on the porch in disgust? I don't know. Would you do that knowing someone's gotta clean that crap up?"

"True," said Jimmy. "That's not likely. But who knows? A woman scorned...."

They reached the ER reception area and walked up to the desk. There were a couple of patients standing there, talking to the reception nurses. One looked like she had a bad case of the flu or pneumonia. The other was holding his arm, wrapped in a towel, clearly in pain and sweating. Probably a broken bone, thought Jimmy.

They waited patiently, finally getting the attention of the third person, a staff member who had just come in. "Hi. How can I help you?" she asked.

Micky flashed his badge again. A concerned look crossed the staff member's face. Micky moved quickly to put her at ease. "Hello," he said cheerfully. "How's business?"

"Busy," she said rather curtly. "How can I help you?"

"Eddie Johnson. Transported here earlier today. The receptionist up front says he's not been assigned to a room yet. What can you tell me?" asked Micky.

"Sorry. Can I see that badge again?" she asked. "HIPAA rules are strict. I need to make sure you are indeed who you say you are."

"No problem," Micky said sweetly, holding the badge up closely for her to see. "We understand."

"Okay," she nodded, satisfied that Micky truly was a detective. "Let me check admissions." She peered at the screen, punched in a few things, scrolled down a time or two, then looked up. "Okay. Eddie Johnson is still here. He's out of OR and in observation awaiting transfer to a room. I can't allow you back to see him, but I can ask the attending or one of the nursing staff to come out and talk to you."

"That would be great," said Jimmy.

"Fine. Please have a seat in the waiting area and I will have someone out shortly."

"Thanks," said Micky. He and Jimmy walked over to the waiting area and sat down in adjoining seats.

"So," said Jimmy, picking back up on the thread they had left off. "Flowers and a broken vase out front. Struggle in the kitchen in the back. What about the blood in the hallway?"

"Don't know," replied Micky. "We're going to run tests on it, see what type it is and try to match to their medical records. Should know pretty soon."

"Let's say it's his," Jimmy said. "Why blood in the hallway if the struggle was in the kitchen and that's where they find him?"

"Good question," came the reply from Micky. "That would suggest the fun started in the hall and then moved to the kitchen."

"Maybe he crawled in there?" asked Jimmy.

"Maybe. Seems unlikely though given the evidence of a struggle in the kitchen. Unless it started there, moved to the hall, and then he made his way back to the kitchen."

"What if it's hers?" asked Jimmy.

"Ahh!" exclaimed Micky. "Then we have one of two things. She was hurt, but not bad enough to keep her from getting away. Or...."

"Someone else was in the house." Jimmy finished his thought for him.

"Yep," said Micky. "Either one works."

At that moment one of the ER physicians walked over to where Jimmy and Micky were sitting. They quickly got to their feet as she stopped in front of them. She was tall, around 5'10" and dressed in blue hospital scrubs.

"I'm Dr. Harrington," she said with a steady gaze at first Micky, and then to Jimmy. "I understand you are here to see one of my patients."

"Yes," replied Jimmy. "I'm Jimmy Quinn. This is my partner, Micky Bondurant. We are detectives with Raleigh PD. We are here to see Eddie Johnson."

"I see," came the reply. "And you were expecting me to just believe you are who you say you are?"

"Sorry. No. Here's my badge," said Jimmy as he slid his credentials out of his back pocket and held them up for her to see. Micky did likewise.

"Thank you. How can I help you?"

"What can you tell us about Mr. Johnson's condition?" asked Micky.

"I can tell you he's lucky and his head is going to hurt when he comes out from under the anesthesia. He took a rather nasty blow to his forehead. It doesn't look like he will suffer any long-term effects at this point, but we will have to monitor him for a while. Always the risk there could be some internal bleeding or swelling of his brain. We stitched him up and have him in observation on the step-down unit. Once he's awake and stable, we'll put him on a floor."

"Thank you, Dr..." paused Jimmy.

"Harrington."

"Thank you, Dr. Harrington. We would like to just ask him a few questions. Won't take long."

"Not now. He's out anyway, and he won't likely be able to respond or focus much for a while once he's awake. I suggest you check in tomorrow sometime."

"Well, that's disappointing," said Micky.

"Yeah, I'm sure Mr. Johnson would be pretty disappointed himself right now if he had any awareness of his condition," she replied. "Is there anything else I can do for you? Things are hopping right now, and I need to get back."

"Just a couple more questions," said Micky. "Was he conscious when he got to the ER? Did he say anything about what happened to his wife?"

"Don't know. I don't do intake. He was sedated when I went in to see him. Check with the intake nurse. Anything else?"

"Any other injuries to him apart from the head trauma?"

"Nothing that I observed," she said.

"Okay," said Jimmy. "I think that's all we need for now. Thank you very much for your time."

"My pleasure," she said smiling for the first time. "Always happy to help Raleigh's finest." She turned and made her way briskly across the waiting room, pushing quickly through the two double doors directly beneath a Hospital Personnel Only sign.

Jimmy turned toward Micky. "What do you think?"

"Personally, or professionally?"

"What?"

"Personally, I'm telling Jules when I get home tonight that I'm leaving her for a surgeon."

"You wouldn't make it out of the house alive, so that would be a stupid move," snorted Jimmy.

"Yeah, I know," signed Micky. "I guess I'm stuck with her."

"We should all be so unfortunate as to be "stuck" with someone like Jules," said Jimmy.

"You know I'm a one-woman man anyway. Personally, I think you should find a way to see that woman socially yourself," replied Micky. "Harrington. That's some kind of Irish name, right? You two might hit it off."

"I wish. She probably isn't interested in a street detective. Lawyers and accountants are probably more her speed. So, what about professionally? What are you thinking?"

Micky scratched his ear, shrugging his shoulders. "Not much. At least not much new. We already know he had a head injury of some kind. Responding officers noted that. And it's a damned shame he's not conscious. We're losing precious hours in trying to find his wife."

"Yeah. Pretty much what I was thinking too. We could go back to the house and see if the crime scene crew has found anything new."

Micky glanced at this watch. "It's after 6:00 p.m. Probably packed up and gone by now."

"Oh shit!" exclaimed Jimmy. "Chloe's recital is at 7:00 p.m. I had completely forgotten that. I gotta get out of here and over to her high school."

"Go," said Micky. "I'll call in and see if there is anything worthwhile, plus push them for the written case report. You want to talk later?"

"Yeah. I'll call you when I'm done."

"Sounds good. Don't kill someone trying to get over there. Traffic's gonna be a bitch this time of day."

"I know. Thanks, Micky."

"I'm going back to the ER. Something I forgot to ask about. I will update you tomorrow if it turns into anything."

"Sounds good", said Jimmy as he took off in a sprint down the hallway, headed back to the parking lot.

CHAPTER 5

The tension inside Room 46 at the Lake Pine Motel hung in layers. Not much had gone right for them so far. Penny sat at the table, occasionally taking generous swallows of the bourbon sitting in front of her. Nick stood by the windows, peering out through a crack in the curtains, wondering what to do next. Rose, true to form, was a nervous wreck. She sat in a chair close to the bed, chewing her nails and continually curling her hair around an index finger.

Donna lay on the bed, still unconscious, but emitting groans from time to time and showing signs that it wouldn't be long before she was present with them in the room. Her breathing was normal and except for the bloody makeshift bandage wrapped around her arm, a visitor might have taken her for just another member of the happy little gang sleeping off one too many drinks from the afternoon.

Rose broke the silence. "What are we gonna do, Nick?"

He didn't turn from the window, but just raised his head a bit, saying quietly, "I'm not sure."

"I still say we just kill her, dump the body in a pond somewhere and hit the road," muttered Penny.

"I'm not killing her," cried Rose. "I ain't no murderer!"

"No, you're just a thief and an accomplice to aggravated assault and attempted murder at this point," sneered Penny. "You won't become a murderer until hubby dies, and they manage to catch us with our heads up our ass in this motel waiting around for what's next."

"I wasn't in the house. They can't put that on me," said Rose.

"Yeah, right. They will probably let you go," laughed Penny.

Nick finally turned from the window, looking directly at Penny. "We're not killing anybody. We can figure this out."

Penny stared back at him. "Well, we better start figuring something out pretty quick. That chloral hydrate's gonna wear off soon and we're gonna have a live, screaming woman on our hands."

For the first time that day, a smile crossed Nick's face. He had made a connection in his mind to their next step. "Penny, did Ray tell you where he got that chloral hydrate from?"

"He didn't mention a name. Sounded like some loser friend from his army days. You think it's Drew?" asked Penny.

"Who else could it be?" replied Nick.

"Who the heck is Drew?" asked Rose.

"An old friend of Ray's from his war days. Guy was a med student who turned all patriotic and ended up in Ray's unit."

"Ok, so how does Drew figure into this?" asked Penny.

"Drew could look at that arm, probably stitch her up good as new."

Penny looked at Nick with obvious bewilderment. "And what, we're just gonna tell him to forget he saw any of this? What are we gonna say when he asks why we are holding her? Hell, what if she starts blabbing to him herself?"

"I think we can probably trust him to keep his mouth shut. Ray will know. We can discuss it with him when he gets back," said Nick.

"I don't know," said Penny, shaking her head. "Seems risky to me. Got any other ideas?"

"Not at the moment," shot back Nick.

Rose cleared her throat. Both Nick and Penny turned towards her. "What if we just dump her back at her house?" she asked.

"Well," Nick began. "There are a few problems with that. First, if the place isn't crawling with cops, it might be under surveillance, and they will spot us when we go to the house. Second, she's already seen us, so she might identify us to the cops after we leave."

"But wait, you said her husband's a crook. Won't that keep her from calling the police?"

Nick pondered that. "Possibly," he said. "But that could be a problem for both hubby and us if she decides to turn him in too. Last problem is maybe the worst – even if there are no cops hanging around and she and her man don't turn us in, it means we did all this for nothing."

"Better to have nothing than end up in jail," said Penny.

"I'm not throwing this away yet. We can figure this out. Ray might have some other ideas."

Rose returned to her nails and hair. Penny lapsed back into staring off into nothing while sipping more whiskey. Nick turned back to the window. Silence returned to the room, challenged only by the breathing and occasional noise from Donna.

Outside and across the yard, Ray was making his way back to the room. When Nick caught sight of him through the window, he could sense that Ray was moving with a purpose, not simply walking back to his room. He crossed the remaining distance quickly, then carefully looked around to both sides and behind him before he opened the door. No one around. Well, at least we have that going for us thought Ray, as he turned the knob and entered the room.

Nick spoke quietly. "What's up?"

"News story on Channel 6." he said in reply. "Cops and reporters crawling all over that house. They don't seem to know much. Or at least they aren't reporting much. They said he was alive when they left the house headed to the hospital."

"What about Drew?" said Nick.

"Say again? Drew? What about him?"

"That woman's going to wake up soon, and when she does, she's going to be in pain, and she'll still have that gash on her arm. Drew can sew that up, can't he?" asked Nick.

"Yeah. He can sew it up. Don't you think that's kind of risky, though? Involving somebody else in this?"

"I don't know," said Nick. "What do you think?"

Ray was silent for a few moments, staring out into space. "Well, it's an option. What else you got?"

"Nothing yet."

"Kill her and dump the body," said Penny flatly.

Nick just glared at her.

"That's a stupid idea," replied Ray.

"Thank you," said Nick.

"My idea was to just dump her – alive - back at her house," said Rose. "Forget this ever happened and just hit the road for Texas or Mexico. Or somewhere."

Ray just shook his head. "Bad idea...really bad."

"Thank you. Again," said Nick.

Ray walked over to the table. He poured himself some whiskey, then drained it in one gulp. Poured another and then looked at Nick. "So far, we have two very bad ideas and one that has some risks.

"Okay," said Ray. "Let's talk about Drew. What do you see the risks with him as?"

"Well, let's start with the big question. Do you trust him?"

Ray scratched his chin, then let out a long sigh. "Me and Drew, we went through a lot. Saw some pretty tough things. Gave us a bond that's been tight through the years." Ray nodded. "I trust him."

Penny spoke up. "But will he keep his mouth shut?"

Nick jumped back in. "Yeah, and not only that, is he going to want anything in return?"

Ray looked at Nick and asked, "Would you?"

"Hell, I don't know. That's not the point man. What about Drew? What would he want?"

"I don't know," said Ray. "Maybe nothing. Maybe a little cash to keep him going for a while. Maybe he just keeps a marker on us for something down the line."

The room grew quiet for a bit as they all stared off into the future in front of them. The refrigerator hummed along. Donna breathed heavily, still showing signs of starting to wake up soon. Rose shifted around uneasily in her chair, starting to twirl her hair again. Nick let out a heavy sigh and rubbed the back of his neck. For a long minute he stared at the woman they had kidnapped. Kidnapped! he thought to himself. This wasn't supposed to be the way it turned out.

He turned his gaze, one by one, on each of his partners. Finally, he spoke, "We don't have a lot of good options here guys. We can't kill her. We can't dump her off somewhere or back at her house. We need to get that cut sewed up. That's the humane thing to do. We can't take her to a hospital or an urgent care. I say we go ahead and contact Drew. Have Ray talk to him, see how he might react and what he might want. If Ray says it safe, we bring him out here and get the job done."

"Yeah," said Penny. "And then what?"

"We have to figure that out. Maybe the three of us can work out some ideas while Ray contacts Drew."

"Better make it fast," Rose said nervously. "I don't think she's gonna be asleep much longer."

"You're right," agreed Ray. "Somebody make sure that gag is secure, so she doesn't wake up the whole county when she comes to. I'm going to step outside and try to get Drew on the phone."

"Shit on a stick," muttered Penny. Nick and Ray just stared at her.

"You with this plan or not?" asked Nick.

Penny shook her head and took another. "You're right. We don't have options. Of course I'm in."

"Good," said Nick. "I need you on this. Ray, go do your thing brother. We have it covered here. We'll figure something out. Nothing we can do now but move forward."

The path leading Nick Rivers to this motel-from-another-era - the Lake Pine - had been one that was never quite clear to him. What seemed like promises and fresh starts often turned into disappointment and setbacks. The freshness in each new start never lasted long, going stale sometimes before Nick even realized things were not good. Kicked out of boarding school at age 14. Flunking out of college and a promising future in football. Marrying his sweetheart, Cristina, then seeing that crumble years later after their two kids were born.

Nick was remembering all this as he sat waiting for Ray to track down Drew. Penny had snuck out for a cigarette and a walk through the woods behind the motel. Just him and Rose left alone with their captive, who was beginning to show real signs of soon being fully aware of her surroundings.

Nick ran his fingers across his scalp. What would Cristina think of him now, he wondered. Breaking and entering. Assault. Kidnapping. He was a real criminal now. He looked across the room at Donna Johnson, lying on the bed and breathing shallowly. Wondered what she would think of him when she woke up. They couldn't kill her. He knew that much. She was of no value to them unless she was alive.

A sudden movement behind him caught his eye. He turned just as the woman on the bed hoarsely whispered. "Oh my God! Where am I?" Donna was awake.

CHAPTER 6

Donna Johnson looked down at her hands, taking in the duct tape that had been used to bind them together. After that she raised her head up, looking around at the shabby motel room she was in. Only then did the pain in her arm register. She looked at her arm, wrapped in makeshift bandages, blood spotting through. She looked at Nick. Screamed at him, "Where am I? Where is Eddie?"

Rose was closest to her and clamped a hand over her mouth, hissing at her "Shut up. Quit yelling!"

Donna struggled to try and get off the bed. Rose pushed her back down and she fell awkwardly as she tried to avoid landing on her injured arm. Nick took several quick strides and was standing by the bed, angrily staring down at Donna. "Look, you need to calm down. If you yell out again, we're going to tape your mouth shut."

Donna, fearful now, and cradling her injured left arm with her right, nodded. Tears began to flow as she sobbed softly this time. "Where am I? What have you done to Eddie?"

"Eddie's fine." Nick lied. "You, not so much. Your arm has a gash in it. We're going to sew it up soon."

"You're taking me to a hospital?" asked Donna.

Nick shook his head. "Hardly. We're going to do it here. You won't be going anywhere for a while."

"Where's Eddie?" she repeated.

"I told you, he's fine. You'll see him when we say the time is right."

"Am I a hostage?"

Nick snorted. "Yeah, something like that."

"Are you going to kill me?"

Rose joined in, "Not if you do what you're told and quit your damn screaming."

Nick glared at Rose. She shrugged and stepped away from the bed, taking a seat at the table. Nick pulled a chair next to the bed, deciding to take a gentler approach with their captive. "Look, no one wants you to get hurt any further. I know your arm must be hurting. We have someone on the way to fix you up. Then we can talk about what's next, okay?" he asked, trying to show a smile to Donna.

Donna nodded, hesitantly, and shifted on the bed a bit more. "Can I have some water?"

"Rose, some water please."

Rose got up from the table, rambled through a couple of the cabinets in the small kitchenette area of the room until she found a plastic cup. She filled it with tap water from the sink, then walked over and handed it to Donna. As she began to drink, Rose returned to her seat at the table and sat down with a heavy sigh. Her bluster from a few moments before was gone and the worried look had returned to her face. She looked at Nick.

"How much longer before Ray gets back?"

Nick replied, not taking his eyes off Donna. "I don't know. Shouldn't be much longer."

Ray had left the motel a couple of hours earlier after trying in vain to reach Drew on his cell phone, leaving several urgent messages over the space of about thirty minutes, none of which earned him a response. With the afternoon fading towards evening and the prospects of a long night ahead trying to deal with a woman who had a serious wound to her arm facing them, Ray decided to swing into action. He told Nick he was headed to Raleigh to find Drew. After a few brief minutes of arguing about the risks of Ray somehow being picked up by the police, they concluded the bigger risk was doing nothing. Ray said he would be in touch, then got into his pickup truck and headed out.

The drive back towards Raleigh was largely uneventful. Ray knew the conversation with Drew would be a tricky one. He trusted him to a point, but Drew could be unpredictable. When he had his alcohol and drug habits under control, he was solid. When they were not in check and money was tight, things became more unstable. Ray could only hope they were catching him at a good time.

He also knew that there needed to be something in this for Drew. Cash was usually a good option. The question was how much. And how soon. Ray had a few thousand stashed away, some in his truck, the rest back at the motel. That money was for his living expenses, though, and who knew how long it might be before they got any ransom payoff, if ever. He was sure Nick had stashed a little somewhere too, but probably not much more than he had.

He slammed his hand down on the steering wheel in frustration. He and Nick should have talked about this before he left the motel. He reached across the seat, grabbing his phone to call Nick. It rang just as he was starting to punch in Nick's number. It was Drew.

"Drew, where are you?"

"Ray, my man. What kind of greeting is that for an old friend? How about a good old-fashioned hello for starters?"

Drew sounded happy. Strong. That was a good sign his demons were at bay, thought Ray. He could hear music and voices in the background. "Drew, You're right. My bad. Hello. How ya' doing?"

"Never better. Never better. Shootin' the shit over a beer. How about you, Ray? You doing good?"

"Not bad. Look, I need to cut to the chase, though. I need some help with something. Someone with some medical skills."

"Sounds intriguing," laughed Drew. "Come have a beer with me and let's talk about it."

"Where are you?"

"Out at the Bull Chute."

The Bull Chute was a dive bar off Highway 1, between Raleigh and the town of Wake Forest. Not a place that Ray frequented, but one he had been to a few times, usually with Drew. He looked at his watch, mentally doing the math on how long it would take him to get there. It would suck up more time, but he didn't want Drew to drive himself out to the motel. Who knew how many beers he had downed and getting stopped by a county sheriff might not end well.

"I can be there in about 15 minutes."

"Good deal. Good deal." Drew had a habit of repeating phrases that could be annoying. "You take your time. I'll be sitting at the bar when you get here."

"See you then," said Ray, punching the disconnect button.

Twenty minutes later Ray walked into the Bull Chute. He spotted Drew quickly, seated at the bar, laughing and talking up a blond woman seated next to him. Ray had called Nick on the way, and the two had agreed on their offer to Drew. Drew spotted Ray when he was a few steps away, and he rose off the barstool to greet him. After handshakes, including with the blond woman, and a few pleasantries, Drew looked at the blond and said, "Hey babe, I'll catch up with you later, okay? My friend and I have a little business to talk over."

The blond woman shrugged, said maybe she would be around, then picked up her drink and headed to the other side of the u-shaped bar.

Ray took the barstool she had occupied, and they sat down. The bartender was quick to show up, and they both ordered draft beers. Drew got his usual Budweiser. Ray was a bit more of a discerning beer drinker and went for the Hell Yes Ma'am from a local brewer.

Drew got right to it. "What's going on man?"

Ray took a long pull on his beer before he answered. "How many of those have you had today?"

"This is number two. You my sponsor now or something?"

Ray shook his head. "Nope. But if you agree to help me, I just need you fully aware of what you're doing."

"Fair enough," replied Drew. "Tell me more."

"First, I need your word. This one stays with you even if you don't help."

Drew drank from his beer, wiped his mouth with the back of his hand, then turned slightly towards Ray. "How long you known me, Ray? You ever had a problem with me running my mouth?"

Ray drank more beer, ran his hand over his scalp and through his short hair. Sighed a bit, then turned a little towards Drew. "You're right. Sorry. Just a little wired up right now."

"Apology accepted," said Drew.

Ray drank more beer, looking around the bar before he set his glass back down. It was a weeknight and still relatively early, so there were only about a dozen or so people at the Bull Chute. He looked at Drew, lowering his voice and said, "We need someone with some medical skills. Got a woman who has a cut on her arm. Fairly deep and looks like it needs to be sewed up. Worried about it getting infected also."

"Should I ask why this woman doesn't just go to the ER?"

"You could, but I'd rather not say right now."

"Has she bled a lot? Still bleeding now?"

"No. I don't think so. At least she wasn't when I left."

"Well, that's good news. So, you need me to sew her up, maybe keep a check on her?"

"Something like that."

"Where is she?"

"Out at my place, Lake Pine Motel."

"She there by herself?"

"Nope. Got some friends staying with her."

They both grew silent for a few moments, each drinking more

of their beer. Ray could practically feel the wheels turning in Drew's head, calculating what he wanted in return for helping Ray.

Drew finished his beer and turned to Ray. "Okay. We need to swing by my place, get my bag."

Ray drained his own beer, taking a minute to process that Drew wasn't pressing for something in return. He began to feel a little guilty that he had expected Drew to bargain with him. He set his beer glass down, threw some money on the bar to cover their tab, then got up from the bar stool.

Drew got up as well and for a moment the two old friends stared at each other. Ray spoke softly. "I appreciate it, Drew. I'll take care of you on this."

"That's what friends are for," replied Drew.

The two men pushed their barstools up to the bar, then turned and headed out the door.

Drew lived in an apartment off Capital Boulevard, on the outskirts of the Raleigh city limits, less than ten minutes from the Bull Chute. Ray drove them there quickly, but carefully, and waited in his truck while Drew retrieved his medical kit. It wasn't uncommon for Drew to get calls from friends and acquaintances who needed medical care for cash and either had no insurance or didn't want to go to an ER or doctor. Ray knew he enjoyed providing the care and was pretty good at it. He managed to keep his kit well stocked for the kinds of things that could be handled outside a clinic or hospital.

Ray scanned stations on the radio while he waited, hoping for news about their home invasion. He had no luck and turned the radio off as soon as he saw Drew walking back towards his truck. Drew opened the door and placed the medical bag on the seat in between them, then got in and closed the door.

"Ready?" asked Ray.

"Ready," replied Drew. "Let's do it."

Ray nodded, put the truck in drive and moved out onto the street connecting back to Capital Boulevard. From there it would be a short drive to Highway 98 and another twenty minutes or so back to the Lake Pine Motel. Ray turned off 1609 into the parking lot of the Lake Pine Motel at precisely 9:00 p.m. Still only a few cars scattered around in front of the rooms. He glanced over at the motel office to see if Bobby was there. Dark inside. That's good, he thought. He pulled around to the back cluster and parked in front of his room. The lights were on inside with the blinds drawn shut. He turned the engine off and looked at Drew.

"What's inside?" asked Drew. "What should I expect?"

Ray cleared his throat. "She was still out of it when I left a few hours ago. Probably awake now. What I gave her has probably worn off."

"And what did you give her?"

"Chloral hydrate."

"Should have known," smiled Drew.

"Yeah. Gash is on her left arm. Friend of mine named Nick is here, plus two women."

"What the..." Drew started to ask before Ray held up a hand and cut him off.

"Better for you not to know, Drew. For your own good."

"Okay. I won't ask any more questions unless they have to do with taking care of the woman."

"Thanks."

Ray opened his door and stepped out of the truck, closing it softly behind him. Drew did the same. They walked up to the door, Ray in front, knocking and announcing quietly it was him. The blinds at the window next to the door were pushed back a bit, the face of a woman appearing and then quickly lost as the blinds fell back into place. The door swung open, and they walked inside.

Donna Johnson was sitting up on the bed, looking scared and exhausted, clutching her injured arm. Nick sat in a chair a couple of feet from the bed. Rose was the one who opened the door, and she was standing to the side, waiting to close it behind them.

Nick stood and walked over, laying a hand on Ray's shoulder. Looked him in the eye and said, "Glad you're back." He stuck his hand out to Drew. "Thanks for coming out. We really appreciate your help."

Drew shook his hand, nodding as he replied, "No worries. Happy to help an old friend. Mind if I go over and take a look at her?"

"Please," said Nick.

Drew walked over to the bed, pulling the chair up and taking a seat. He smiled at Donna. "Ma'am, I'm here to help, okay?"

Donna sat up a little straighter on the bed. "Who...who are you?"

Drew smiled again. "Let's just call me Jim, okay? I promise you that I know a thing or two about sewing people up. I'll take care of you."

Donna glanced over at Nick, who nodded at her encouragingly. She looked back at Drew, slowly nodding her agreement.

"Ray and I are going to step outside and talk a minute while you do your thing. She," he said while pointing at Rose, "will get us if you need us." Then he looked directly at Donna. "Remember what we agreed to earlier about yelling."

Donna nodded slightly, wincing as Drew started to unwrap the bandage on her arm. Ray opened the door and the two of them stepped outside.

Nick closed the door behind them, and they stepped off the porch to lean against Ray's truck. Nick spoke first. "Man, I need a smoke."

"Got a pack in the truck. I think I'll have one too." Ray opened the truck door, then the glove box. He fished out a pack of Marlboro Lights, took out two, threw the pack back in the glove box and slammed it shut. He rustled around under the seat until he came up with a book of matches, then closed the truck door and handed one of the cigarettes to Nick. After striking a match and holding it up for

Nick, he lit his own cigarette, leaning against the truck bed and taking a long drag.

After exhaling the smoke, he said to Nick. "You know, he didn't ask for anything. Not one damn thing."

"Huh. You surprised?"

"Yes. And no. Drew's an oddball. I can't quite figure him out sometimes. But if I was a betting man, well, he's going to want something back. Someday."

Nick took another drag. Looked up at the stars. "Yeah. Nobody does stuff for free anymore." Took another drag.

"You got a plan?" asked Ray.

"Sort of. Figured we'd hash it out a bit. Talk to the girls about it once Drew leaves."

"We can't all stay here in this room with her," said Ray. "Sooner or later Bobby is going to come nosing around and figure out something's up."

"Think he'd call the cops?"

"Hell, I don't know. He doesn't seem the type to get much into people's business."

"Yeah, but maybe he comes with his hand out too. Wants a little something to keep his mouth shut."

Ray took a last drag on his cigarette, throwing it down and grinding it out with his heel. "Yep. That's possible. So, what's your plan?"

"Well, we have to find out what kind of shape Ol' Eddie's in. Need to know if he's going to make it out of that hospital and when. Once he's out, then we need to make contact and let him know we have something of value. His wife. Let him know we need some cash, a lot of cash, for her safe return."

"How much cash are you thinking?"

Nick took a last drag on his own cigarette before answering. "How does one million sound?"

Ray let out a low whistle. "You think he's got that kind of cash?"

"Don't know."

Ray turned and looked at Nick. "What if he doesn't make it out of the hospital alive?"

Nick shrugged. "That wouldn't be very good, would it?"

Ray shook his head. "Need a plan for that too."

Nick nodded again. "For now, we need to split up. Two of us stay here with her. The other two head back to Raleigh and see what's going on."

"I need to stay here, just in case Bobby does come nosing around. Rose can stay here with me. Be better if Penny is with you. Somebody runs into you and starts asking where Penny is just gives us one more tale to have to tell."

"Exactly," said Nick. "You trust Rose?"

"Trusted her enough to bring her into this. Don't see much sense in putting her out now. Better to keep her close."

"Fair enough. After Drew leaves we'll clue them in on the plan, and then Penny and I will head back."

"Where is Penny, anyway?" asked Ray.

"You know how she is. She got restless. Said she needed a walk. Should be back any time now."

Ray shoved his hands in his pockets. "She better be careful. Don't want somebody seeing a woman walking around out here after dark."

"She can take care of herself."

"Not worried about that. Worried about somebody asking too many questions, maybe remembering later they saw her out here."

"Good point," replied Nick. "All the more reason to head back. Let's go in there and see if he's done yet."

Ray nodded. Both men turned towards the woods suddenly, hearing footsteps behind them. A few tense moments, then Penny appeared out of the wooded area.

"Drew's inside," said Nick as she walked up to the truck. "We got a plan. We'll talk about it once he's gone."

Penny shrugged. "Okay."

"Come on," said Ray. "Let's get back inside."

CHAPTER 7

Jimmy and Micky sat in a coffee shop in downtown Raleigh a couple of blocks from police headquarters, munching on bagels, sipping coffee, watching people move in and out of the shop. Micky set his cup down, wiped his mouth and looked at his partner. "Almost twenty-four hours now and no clue where she might be. If she ran, she could be in Miami by now. Or Aspen."

"If she was taken," replied Jimmy, "good chance she might be dead by now. Dumped in a ditch somewhere."

"True."

"That's it? True? That's all you have for me?"

"Yep. Whatcha got for me?"

Jimmy tore off a hunk of his bagel, shoving it in his mouth. Chewed for a minute, staring blankly out the plate glass windows. Thinking. Turned back and looked at Micky. "I don't think she ran. The flower vase on the porch makes me think someone else was there."

"You think Eddie came home, surprised whoever was there?"

"Maybe. Suppose she was running around on him. Her boyfriend comes over with some flowers for a little morning hookup."

Micky shook his head. "I don't think that works. Why is the vase shattered on the porch, like it had been dropped?"

"Maybe the guy is at the door, she's opening it up for him, Ole Eddie pulls up in the drive and startles them, so they drop the vase."

Micky shook his head again. "Two things. First, open your mind up a bit. Maybe it wasn't a guy. Maybe she had a girlfriend. Second, either way, it's the middle of the morning, broad daylight, and the lover...person...is coming in through the front door on display for the whole neighborhood?"

"Yeah. That might be a stretch."

"It's possible, though," said Micky. "Let's keep following it for a bit. What happens next?"

Jimmy sipped some coffee. "Loverboy doesn't want a confrontation with the husband, so he goes in the house and tries to exit out the back door to get away. Eddie jumps out of the car and runs in after him. Maybe Eddie doesn't even suspect it's a hookup. Maybe he sees the guy as an intruder."

Micky nodded. "Keep going. It's working so far. Except maybe the flowers. Wouldn't Eddie have seen those?"

"Maybe not. Or at least not enough to realize what they were. So, he runs in the house after the guy, catches him in the kitchen before he can get out the door."

"Crime scene notes did say the rear door was open," offered Micky.

"Right. So, there's a fight in the kitchen and Eddie comes out on the short end."

Micky smiled. "Then Donna and lover boy decide to just leave Eddie lying on the floor and run for it together?"

Jimmy's turn to smile. "Yeah. Maybe."

Micky twisted in his chair, taking out a notebook and flipped a few pages. "Blood on the floor and a table in the room next to the kitchen. How did it get there?"

"I guess that depends on whose blood it is."

"Eddie's," offered Micky.

More bagel for Jimmy. "At first there isn't any fighting. Eddie comes in, Donna introduces lover boy as the flower delivery guy who just came in to put the flowers down and he's going to be on his way in a minute."

"Wait," said Micky. "That won't work. You just said a minute ago that Eddie chases him into the house."

"Yeah, maybe I was wrong!" laughed Jimmy. "Anyway, at first there's no fisticuffs. Maybe yelling a little. Who the hell are you? That sort of thing. Eddie gets suspicious and starts pushing it a bit. They haven't made it into the kitchen yet. Things get heated, some shoving starts and the guy, or gal, pushes Eddie down into the table where he cuts his arm."

Micky picked it up from there. "The guy starts out through the kitchen and Eddie gets to him before he hits the door. Things turn ugly, Eddie loses Round 1 and out they go. Technically, it works."

"What do you mean 'technically'? It works. Period."

"What if it's Donna's blood, not Eddie's?"

Jimmy shifted in his chair. Scratched his arm. Drank some coffee. "You're a real pain in the ass sometimes, you know that? You ruin all my best theories."

Micky raised his cup in salute, grinning across the table. "You're welcome."

Undeterred, Jimmy pressed on. "Okay, it's Donna's. Eddie gets hot and shoves her. She falls and cuts her arm on the table. Lover boy jumps to her rescue and the fight spills into the kitchen. Same result. Eddie goes down. They run out." Jimmy picked up his own mug in salute, looking smugly across the table at Micky.

"Touche," Micky said thoughtfully. "And if it's the guy's or gal's blood, does that change it up? Maybe not, although I am having a hard time with a gal theory."

"Um, that was your theory," interrupted Jimmy.

"Yeah, I know. I was just being open-minded. The hallmark of a great investigator, you know. You should give it a go more often."

"Right," snorted Jimmy. "I'm making a note of that right now. What's the problem with your gal theory?"

Micky's turn for more bagel. Chewed a minute, followed by coffee. "Eddie took it pretty hard according to the doc at the ER."

"You went back and talked to her again last night?"

"Yes. After you left for the recital. I wanted to get a little more on the extent of his injuries. He took quite a few punches it seems. Some abrasions to his face. Some kind of blow to his head. Probably would have been a strong woman with some fighting skills to knock him up that bad. I'd say the odds are more against that than for it."

"Did he have any cuts?"

Micky's chance to look smugly across the table at his partner. Shook his head.

Jimmy just laughed, setting his mug on the table. "Ya jerk. You knew this all along, while we were playing 20 questions on whose blood was in the hall?"

Micky smiled. "I like watching you spin your webs. Makes it more fun to tear one or two of them down."

"Ass," was all Jimmy could say.

"I know. I'm sorry. Couldn't help myself."

"Well, at least we know it's not Eddie's blood. It probably doesn't matter whose it is. She's gone. He's in the hospital. Where do we go from here?" asked Jimmy.

Micky stood up, threw his napkin and a couple of dollars on the table. "From here, I go to the men's room, and then we head out to Eddie's car lot. Let's get to know a little more about Eddie before we head over to the hospital and ask him some questions. That sound good?"

"Yep. Thanks for leaving the tip. Now pay the bill, too, for withholding information on me. I'll grab the car. See you outside."

Thirty minutes later, Jimmy eased the car into a parking spot outside the Big Lots on Capital Boulevard, across the street from Johnson Auto. On the way over, the two of them had debated whether to just go straight in or sit and observe things first. Micky's vote carried the day, and they decided to watch the lot for about twenty minutes and then go talk to any employees who might show up or already be there.

"You know, they have some good stuff inside those Big Lots stores. Great deals," said Jimmy.

"Really? When's the last time you were in a Big Lots?"

Jimmy laughed. "Well, I can't say I have been honestly."

"You just know because some of your cheap-ass friends shop there?"

"Hey, hey! Easy there with the judgments my man. My friends are just careful with their money. Didn't grow up in a fancy neighborhood like you."

Micky rolled his eyes, then pointed across the street to the car lot. "Looks like someone's going in."

They sat and watched as a man, average height and build, blond hair, stepped out of a late model Chevy Tahoe. He walked up to the bars that served as a gate blocking entry to the lot, fished some keys out of his pocket, and unlocked the gate, pushing it open by swinging the bars off to either side.

"Decent sized car lot," observed Micky. "Must have close to a hundred vehicles sitting over there."

"Yeah. Our man Eddie looks like he's doing okay."

"Company," Micky said, alerting Jimmy to turn his attention back across the street. An older model Jeep was pulling past the gates, the man inside raising his hand in greeting to the first guy as he rolled by. The blond man returned the greeting, then got back in his Tahoe and drove across the lot and behind what looked to be the main office building, which sat about three rows of cars deep from the entrance. The guy in the Jeep had parked beside another building that looked like it might be for storage and a couple of bays for working on the cars.

"Think they're going to open? Business as usual?" asked Micky.

"Kind of looks that way, doesn't it?"

"Yeah. Maybe they don't know yet."

"Maybe."

They sat there longer. Idle chit-chat. Watching the lot. Occasional comments about the clientele at the Big Lots. One other person had driven up on the car lot, a woman who had also pulled around behind the office. There must have been a back door because Micky and Jimmy never saw anyone enter the building but could see that lights had been turned on inside.

Jimmy glanced at his watch. Cracked his knuckles. "Okay. We go in Big Lots and shop for treasure, or we go across and do some real work. Your call."

"Tough one," said Micky. "Not getting paid to shop today, as much as I love it. Let's go charm our way into more info on Eddie and Donna."

"My man," smiled Jimmy, putting the car in gear and rolling out.

Jimmy parked the car in a spot directly in front of the office building. As they got out, they both turned to look up at the sign on the front of the structure: Johnson Auto. The Walking Person's Friend.

"Wordings a little awkward," said Micky.

"Yeah."

The blond man opened the door to the office, stepping onto the covered porch that ran the length of the building. A few rocking chairs sat on either side of the entrance, with a chair railing on the very front. The man walked the couple of strides across the porch and then down the set of wide, wooden steps, a look of concern etched on his face.

"I'm Bill Sandford," the man said to Jimmy and Micky. "I'm guessing neither one of you is here to look at cars."

"I don't know," replied Jimmy. "My pal here could use some new wheels. Got some nice ones to choose from here. But, yeah, he probably needs to save that for another day. I'm Jimmy Quinn, Raleigh PD. This is Micky Bondurant."

A look crossed Sandford's face. "Micky, huh? Don't meet too many Black guys named Micky," he said somewhat nervously.

"He's Irish. Black Irish," grinned Jimmy.

Micky snorted, shifting his feet a bit. "Yeah. Black Irish. From New Orleans. Bondurant's a popular name among the Irish down there."

"Hey, no offense meant. That was kind of a dumb thing to say, I suppose. We're all a little rattled here this morning. Please forgive me. I guess you must be here about Eddie."

"None taken," said Micky. "So, you know about the Johnsons?"

"Yeah. Eddie never came back after lunch yesterday. I wondered about it for a couple of hours. Couldn't get him on his cell phone. Then we saw the breaking news report on Channel 5. Pretty shocking."

"How about we take a seat in those rockers and talk for a bit?" asked Jimmy.

"Sure. That's fine. You guys want some coffee?"

"Thanks. Never a bad time for coffee," said Micky.

The three of them went up the steps, Bill going inside to grab the coffees. Micky and Jimmy settled into a couple of the rockers to wait for Bill's return.

"Black Irish? Really?"

Jimmy broke into a broad grin. "Pretty clever, huh?"

"Black Irish," said Micky. "I'm about as Irish as you are African."

"He's got a point, though. Micky is not that common a name among Black men. Bondurant, either."

"You should travel more. Get down to Nola. There's a few of us down there."

They fell silent. Slowly rocking, watching traffic pass by on Capital Boulevard. Finally, Bill opened the door, one coffee in each hand, kicking it shut behind him as he came out.

"Sorry. It wasn't quite ready. Lila is moving a little slow this morning."

"No worries," said Jimmy.

Bill handed each of them a cup, then shook his head. "I didn't think to ask. Cream? Sugar?"

They both shook their heads. Bill sat down in a rocker on the opposite side of the doorway, turning it so he could face the detectives. "How can I help?"

Micky sipped his coffee. Nodded his head with approval. "Gotta say, that's better coffee than I expected at a car lot."

"Coffee Culture brand. Eddie can't stand bad coffee."

Micky continued, "You said Eddie never came back from lunch yesterday."

"That's right. Occasionally, he'll go home to have lunch with Donna. Their house isn't too far from here." Bill suddenly ran his hand across his head, a look of deep concern returning to his face. "Any word on Donna yet? That woman's a saint. Been awfully good to me over the years."

"Nothing yet," replied Micky. "You said he goes home occasionally. Anything unusual about yesterday?"

"No, I don't think so," said Bill, looking across the lot. He stared out for a moment, then turned back to Micky. "Yeah, you know there was one thing. Eddie was planning a little surprise vacation for him and Donna. I think maybe he was going to spring it on her when he got home. Have her start packing her bags. They were supposed to leave tomorrow."

Micky glanced over at Jimmy, who could read his thoughts. – I told you she didn't run out on him – clear as day on Micky's face.

Jimmy jumped in. "So, how about their marriage? Pretty solid relationship?"

"Yeah," said Bill. "I mean, they had an occasional spat, but don't we all? They have been together for many years. Seems solid to me."

"Any problems lately that you know of?"

Bill paused a moment, scratched a spot on his face, "No, I can't say that I have seen anything or heard Eddie mention any problems."

"They have any enemies of any sort, arguments with neighbors, an angry customer here at the lot?" asked Micky.

"You think somebody was trying to get even with Eddie?" returned Bill.

"Maybe."

Bill looked at them. "I can't really think of anything like that at the moment. Even if that's the case, where's Donna?"

Jimmy nodded. "Great question."

A look of confusion came suddenly to Bill's face. "Could Donna have attacked Eddie, or had something to do with this?"

"Another great question," said Jimmy. "You think that's possible?"

Bill stared at his shoes. "I guess almost anything is possible, but if I had to bet, my money would be Donna didn't do this."

"What makes you so sure of that?" asked Micky.

"Donna just doesn't have any violence in her. She's not a pushover either, though. I've always thought of her as one of those typical tough southern type of woman. The ones who are polite, gracious, defer too much to their men in public. And underneath all that, a stiff backbone and a real stubborn streak when they need it."

"Maybe Eddie did something to stiffen up her backbone," offered Micky.

"Like what?" asked Bill. "Running around on her? I don't think so. I don't know when he would have had time for that. If he wasn't at home with her, it seemed like he was always out here. He doesn't have much of a social life apart from her or this business."

Jimmy decided to shift gears in the conversation. "Tell us about the business. About the folks who work here."

"Well, other than Donna doing the books, there's just the three of us – me, Lila, and Otto. We're all full-time employees. I handle sales and work with customers. Along with Eddie, of course. He's a damn fine car salesman."

"Seems that way," said Jimmy, looking out across the lot. "Looks like a pretty successful operation you guys have built."

Bill blushed a little. "Don't give me too much credit. I do my part, but this business was started by Eddie. I guess he opened it about ten years ago. I've been here just over five. He started it from scratch.

Maybe had 10-20 cars to begin with. Left his job as a sales manager at the Ford dealership in Wake Forest. Wanted to have his own place."

The office door opened, and the woman Micky and Jimmy had seen earlier stuck her head out.

"Bill, a call for you." She looked at the other two, a warm smile on her face. "Good morning, detectives. Can I get you more coffee?"

"No thank you" came simultaneously from both.

"You know who it is?" asked Bill.

"Mr. Rezavik," replied Lila.

"Fellows, I hate to do this, but can you give me a couple of minutes?"

"Sure, no problem," said Micky.

Bill got up from his rocker quickly, then stopped and turned just in front of the door. "And forgive my poor manners. Guys, meet Lila. This is Jimmy Quinn and Micky Bondurant."

"Pleased to meet you," said Lila as Bill walked by her and inside the office. "You sure, no more coffee? Maybe a donut?"

"Thank you. Very kind of you but my partner just doesn't need the extra calories," said Jimmy, nodding his head towards Micky.

"You could bring Jimmy a couple, though," retorted Micky. "As you can see, he gave up on his self-image a long time ago, so what's another 400 calories for a man like him?"

Jimmy chuckled. "Lila, we'd like to ask you a few questions when we are finished with Bill. Will that be okay?"

Lila's face became serious quickly. "Of course. It's just awful. Mr. Johnson's such a kind man. I can't imagine who would want to hurt him. And Donna. A saint. She has been so good to me and my baby boy."

"Thank you," said Jimmy. "We're doing all we can to find out what happened."

"I'll be right in here when you need me," said Lila. She turned and went back inside, closing the door gently as she went.

Micky looked over at him, stretching his legs out, slouching a little in the rocker. "What do you think, Sherlock? Are you learning anything?"

"Not yet. How about you?"

"All American story so far. Man builds a business from scratch, marries a saint. Nothing to see here, folks. At least according to the Bill and Lila Report."

"I've seen this show before," said Jimmy. "There ain't no all-American story out there. That's only on TV."

"Right you are, my man. Right you are," Micky replied softly.

They sat quietly, waiting for Bill to return. After a few more minutes, just as Jimmy was starting to get restless, the door opened, and Bill stepped back onto the porch.

"My apologies," he said as he sat down across from the detectives. "Where were we?"

"I think you were telling us about the business, how it got started. Tell us about the last few months. Any changes worth noting?" asked Micky.

"Not really. Things have been pretty good."

"No financial problems of any kind?"

"Not that I can see. Some months are a little slower than others, of course. But even the slow months are a lot better than they used to be," replied Bill.

"What made them get better?" asked Jimmy.

"Well, I think it's because of the financing program Eddie put in place. That was maybe a year and a half ago, something like that. It's called Buy Here - Pay Here in the industry."

Micky nodded his head. "I'm familiar with that. You do all the financing here, write the paper yourself for the customer. Cut out the bank. Right?"

"You got it," smiled Bill. "Customers love it. Keeps them from having to hassle with a loan officer at the bank."

"Doesn't it cost them more? Higher interest rates?" asked Jimmy.

Bill frowned a little before answering. "Yeah, I suppose that happens in some cases. Lots of other times, though, the guy - or gal - wouldn't even qualify at the bank. So, then they are stuck with some rip-off personal loan financer, or worse, they can't get financed at all." Bill had brightened back up at this point. "Good for us. Good for the customer."

"I guess you might have a point," offered Micky. "Any other changes you can think of we should know about?"

"No. I just can't see how this whole thing with Eddie and Donna has anything to do with the car lot."

"Okay," said Jimmy, standing up and fishing a business card out of his pocket, handing it to Bill. "If you think of anything else, be sure to call us."

Bill and Micky stood up as well. "Mind if we talk to Lila a few minutes?" asked Micky.

"Sure," replied Bill. "Why don't you guys come inside for that?" Bill opened the door, motioning them in ahead of him.

Well done, thought Micky, as he quickly surveyed the interior of the office building, following Bill just inside the door. The furnishings were nice, but not extravagant. Exactly what was needed to make Eddie's clientele the most comfortable. It showed he was successful, but not too successful. Making a profit but not gouging his customers.

There was a small reception desk at the front where Lila sat. To the right, a couple of bathrooms, a small waiting area with chairs for customers and a coffee station. Micky noticed the signs on the bathroom doors said "We Don't Care" instead of Mens and Ladies. Surprisingly progressive, he thought. In the back corner was a larger desk with a nameplate for Bill on it. To the left side was the only office with a door, presumably for Eddie. Adjacent to that was what appeared to be another small room, probably for storage, guessed Micky. Another door beside that served as the exit to the rear of the building. "Nice looking place," he said, looking at Bill.

"Thanks. Clean and comfortable. That's all we need."

Lila looked up from some paperwork. "Hello again, officers. Ready for more coffee yet?" she asked with a smile.

"I'm good," replied Jimmy. "Maybe just a few questions if that's okay."

"Of course. Pull up a chair, or we can sit over in the waiting area."

"Let's do that," said Micky, wanting her to be comfortable.

"Lila, I'm going to go out back and check on Otto. Buzz me if a customer shows up on the lot," said Bill, heading for the rear door.

"You got it, Bill," she replied. Lila stood from her desk, smoothed her dress down with both hands, then took a seat with Micky and Jimmy in the small waiting area. She crossed her legs, settling into the chair before she spoke. "I just can't believe all this has happened. What is the world coming to? Not even safe in your own home in the middle of the day!"

Jimmy nodded his head. "You mentioned earlier how much you thought of the Johnsons, especially Donna. You called her a saint, I believe."

"Lord, yes," said Lila. "She is always so kind, but she was especially good to me right after I started to work here. When my momma took sick she looked after Nico on more than one day to help me out."

"Nico?" asked Jimmy.

"Yes, sorry. Nico is my son. My mother keeps him during the day. She went through a battle with cancer last year, spent some time in the hospital, so of course she couldn't keep Nico for a while. I tried to find daycare on a temporary basis, but there was nothing I could really afford. Donna stepped in and insisted that he could stay with her until Momma got better."

"You must be very grateful," said Micky. He could see that Lila was the type who might tell them fifteen stories about Donna, most of which probably would be of little benefit in their investigation, so he decided to focus her on Eddie first. "How long have you worked for Eddie?" he asked.

Lila thought for a moment. "I guess almost two years now."

"What's he like to work for?"

"He's been good to me. Gave me a chance. I didn't really have any experience in the car business or helping out in an office setting. Most of my jobs before this were at restaurants or bars."

"Noticed anything unusual lately about Eddie, or Donna? Anything different going on here at the car lot?"

Lila paused again, thinking. Pursed her lips and smoothed her dress again. "No. Things have been pretty good. The paperwork and the files were kind of a mess when I first got here. But I straightened all that out with a little help from Bill. He's so nice, too."

Jimmy jumped in. "Bill mentioned that business had been good, especially since the new financing program was put in place."

"Well, that has made a noticeable difference," said Lila. "Sales volume has sure increased. Even more paperwork to organize."

"So, how's does that work?" asked Jimmy. "The financing part. Does the business here have the cash available to buy the cars and then hold the note until the customer pays it off?"

Lila shook her head. "No. That would take an awful lot of cash. We have a deal with a third-party finance company. They underwrite the loan for us and then advance the proceeds from the sale, minus the interest on the loan. We get that later, as the customer is paying it off."

"Got it," Jimmy nodded. "So, a bank like First National, or US Federal? Something like that?"

"Not for us. Eddie made a deal with a group out of Wilmington, Hanover Limited. In fact, that was one of their partners who called for Bill a few minutes ago, Mr. Rezavik."

Micky made a few notes in the small journal he kept for each of the investigations they worked on. "You do all the paperwork and the accounting out here?" he asked Lila.

"Most of it," she replied. "Donna does some of the accounting work. Maintains the journal entries in the system and closes the books each month. She also does all the tax stuff for our outside accountants. She's been teaching me some of that lately." Lila looked down at her hands, then quickly reached up to wipe away tears starting to fall. Micky handed her a tissue from a small box on a nearby table. "If something bad has happened to her," she said as she wiped her face, "I just don't know what we'll do. I don't know what Eddie will do."

Micky reached over to lay a reassuring hand on her shoulder. "Lila, we promise you we are doing all we can to find out what happened. We don't have any evidence that she has been hurt. Is there anything else you can think of that might help us? Anything at all?"

Lila shook her head again, more tears welling up in her eyes. Jimmy slid a card across the table towards her. "If you think of something, or something unusual happens that you think might be connected in some way, just call us at the number listed there. Thank you for talking with us."

Lila stood, and the men followed suit. "Do you need to talk to Bill again now?"

As if on cue, the rear door opened, and Bill came back in the office.

"We were just wrapping up with Lila," said Micky. "Maybe just a few minutes with your other employee. I believe Otto is his name?"

"Looks like you might have to come back for that. Otto just got an urgent call from his brother. He had to run out for a bit," said Bill.

Micky handed Bill another of their business cards and told him to have Otto give them a call when he returned. Jimmy thanked them both again for their time, reminded them to call if they thought of anything that might aid the investigation, and then he and Micky left the office. They were both silent until they got in the car, Micky speaking first as he cranked the car and put it in reverse.

"Learn anything?"

"Eddie's a swell guy, good to work for. Donna's a saint. Bill and Lila got nothing to hide. That about sums it up?"

Micky laughed as he pulled into traffic on Capital Boulevard. "Can't get anything by you, can they?"

"Nope. Except maybe Otto. We need to check in with him. Should we read anything into him getting an urgent call?" Jimmy making air quotes with his fingers as he said the word urgent.

Micky checked the side mirror, easing over a lane, before speaking. "I don't know. Probably not. Benefit of the doubt and all that."

"Yeah. You're probably right. So, what's next detective?"

"Back to the office to check on the lab work from the crime scene. Lunch at Tres Caminos. Pay an afternoon visit to the hospital. See how Eddie is doing,"

"Tres Caminos, huh? You forgot to mention an afternoon nap in your plans. I get sleepy every time we eat there for lunch."

"Maybe it's the margaritas, not the food," grinned Micky.

"Who can eat Mexican without a margarita?" asked Jimmy.

"Sounds like we have a plan," replied Micky.

CHAPTER 8

Jimmy and Micky arrived at police headquarters downtown shortly after 11:00 am. Micky sat in his desk chair, flipping through the pages of the crime scene reports. Jimmy was perched in a side chair, slouched down, legs extended out in front of him.

He stared at Micky. "Well? What's it say?"

Micky glanced up, pushing his reading glasses down on his nose a bit. "It says you owe me $20."

"Oh, yeah? How's that? It's his blood from the hallway, isn't it?", Jimmy smirked.

"No, dumbass. It's hers."

"Right. Exactly like I said it would be."

"You're a piece of work," laughed Micky.

"Any other news in those pages?" asked Jimmy.

"Nothing that I can see from just skimming through it. I asked Janie to email copies to both of us. We can read the rest of it later today. I think there is one more section from one of the lab techs who was on the scene that hasn't been added yet."

Jimmy sat up straighter in the chair. For the millionth time he picked up a small, framed picture Micky kept on his desk. It was from his wedding day. He and his wife, running down the steps at the end of their reception, guests lined up on either side, throwing rice at them. "Tell me again why this woman married you?" he asked Micky, shaking his head.

"I'm the total package. Not much more complicated than that," Micky said, opening a drawer and shoving the crime scene report into a folder.

Julia Reynolds, his wife, was an attorney in Raleigh. Those close to her called her Jules. Many who had been on the other side of the fence from her through her career had less flattering nicknames for her. After graduating from law school in her native Pennsylvania, she had taken a job in the public defender's office in Raleigh. She made a name for herself there, then moved into private practice a few years later after a serious incident with a particularly violent client who came too close to taking her life.

Jimmy set the picture back on the desk, remembering his own wedding day. He and Susan had been that happy once upon a time as well, he thought. "I was the total package, too, you know," he said as he got up from the side chair.

"Yes" said Micky. You were the total package," emphasizing the word were. "I, on the other hand, am still the total package."

Jimmy snorted. "A legend in your own mind. Let's go get that margarita you promised me. We can work out our questions for Eddie over some chips and salsa."

Micky stood up as well, closing the desk drawer with the files. "An excellent idea. Except the margarita, of course. I can't remain a total package by sipping those at lunch."

Jimmy and Micky decided to walk to Tres Caminos from their office. It was only about 10 minutes, a few blocks down on Fayetteville Street. As they walked, they once again remarked on the changes that had taken place over the years. How vibrant the downtown scene had become compared to a couple of decades before. New restaurants, shops, the shiny new civic center, a renovated and revived Memorial

Auditorium, traffic flowing again, drunk and loud millennials on a Tuesday night.

True to his word, Jimmy sipped a margarita over chips and salsa while the two of them talked about the interview with Eddie at the hospital. They didn't linger once the food was gone and quickly walked back to Micky's sedan afterward. It was about a ten-minute drive to the hospital. Wake Memorial sat just off New Bern Avenue.

Micky parked in the surface lot at the rear where spaces were designated for emergency room transport and patient vehicles. He stuck their official "Police Business" sign on the dashboard before he closed the door and locked it.

"Really?" asked Jimmy. "You think people take one look at this ride and suspect it's anything other than a cop car?"

Micky smiled. "Keeps the car thieves away. There's half a box of donuts in the back. Don't want those to get lifted."

"Remind me to have one when we come back out," replied Jimmy. "It will be just the thing to settle that burrito in my stomach."

Micky laughed, pushed the button on the key fob to lock the doors, and they walked across the lot, down the sidewalk, and entered the rear doors of the building. They knew it was very unlikely Eddie was still in an ER bed, but they had decided to speak to the physician who had treated him upon arrival the day before. Micky had called earlier to make sure Dr. Harrington was in that day. He flashed his ID to the staff at the reception desk, told them who they were looking for, and they were directed to make themselves comfortable while they waited, which they did in a couple of chairs adjacent to the reception desk.

Twenty minutes later, a nurse in standard blue scrubs walked out of a set of doors behind them towards the exit. He stopped when he was adjacent to Micky and Jimmy, just a few feet away. They were heads down, reading magazines, a bit startled when the nurse called. "Hey, you guys here to see Dr. Harrington?"

Jimmy looked up. "Yep, that's us."

"Okay. You're going to need to put on these gowns," he said. "They tie in the back."

"Funny," said Micky.

The nurse laughed. "I was born with a funny bone. What can I say? Go through those doors I just came out of, a few yards down on the right is a small conference room. Blinds on the windows. You can't miss it. She should be in there." He waved at them, turned and headed out the door.

Jimmy turned to look at Micky. "Actually, that was kind of funny."

"Yeah. A riot. Come on."

They put their magazines back on the small table, got up and walked to where the nurse had instructed. Dr. Harrington was seated in one of the four chairs around the small round conference table, papers piled in front of her. She was writing something on one of them as they stood in the doorway. Micky knocked lightly on the door that stood open.

She looked up, her frown turning into a smile when she recognized Micky. "Good morning detective," she said. "Nice to see you again."

"And you," replied Micky. "We appreciate you giving us a few minutes of your time. You remember my partner, Jimmy, I presume?"

She stood, walked over with her hand outstretched. "I do. Nice to see you as well, Jimmy. Please close the door and have a seat," she said as she turned back to the chair she had been sitting in. Micky took the chair to her right. Jimmy closed the door, then sat to her left. She had picked up her pen and was scribbling on the paper again. "Just one moment, if you don't mind. I want to finish this thought."

"No worries," said Jimmy.

They sat quietly for a couple of minutes, gazing around the small room, posters on every wall with various notices of hospital rules, privacy rights, and who to call if you had a complaint. Outside they could hear an occasional laugh or a groan of someone in pain. The doctor finished what she was writing, quickly signed her name at the bottom, then closed the folder and placed it on top of one of the stacks. She took off a pair of reading glasses and placed them on the table. "Okay, thanks for your patience. How can I help?"

"We have more questions about the patient you treated yesterday. Eddie Johnson," said Micky, flipping open his notepad, ready to jot down anything that would potentially be helpful.

"The man who was attacked in the home invasion, right?" she asked.

"Well, we're not sure yet exactly what happened, so it might be a bit early to call it a home invasion," said Jimmy.

"Oh," she said, turning to look at him. "I guess we should be careful about repeating what we hear on television. Or from the police," she smiled sweetly.

Micky grinned at Jimmy. "I might have mentioned to her when we spoke yesterday that it kind of looked like an invasion."

"He's still learning," Jimmy deadpanned in response as he looked back towards Dr. Harrington. "Anything new you can tell us about his condition?"

She picked up another folder and flipped it open. She hesitated for a moment, eyes scanning, then flipped a couple of pages deeper. "Mr. Johnson was unconscious when I first saw him. He had clearly been involved in something where he ended up with several abrasions and a significant blow to the head. We put him through all the standard protocols, especially for head trauma, put him in an observation bed overnight, and he was transferred to a floor late this morning. That's about all I can tell you without further privacy release from the patient. Is he a suspect of some kind?"

Jimmy shook his head. "No, not a suspect. At least not now. Can you tell us if he said anything about his wife or what happened at his house?"

"No, there is nothing I can share with you there. He was either unconscious or very drowsy during my time with him last night and earlier today. I don't recall him talking at all."

"How about his recovery?" asked Micky.

"Probably too early to say," she replied. She looked down at the folder again, flipping back to the first page. "Notes from just before he was moved indicate he was conscious. That's a good thing." She looked back up at Micky. "I'm afraid there's not much more I can tell you."

"Can we talk to him?"

"You would need to discuss that with the attending on the unit. Dr. Powers is probably over there today. I can have someone call over for you, see if he can speak with you."

"Thank you," said Micky. "Much appreciated."

"Anything else I can do for you gentlemen?"

"No," said Jimmy. "This has been very helpful."

She stood and smiled at Jimmy. "Not sure I gave you much that could be considered helpful. Good luck with your investigation."

Both men stood as well, shook hands with the doctor. Micky opened the door and walked into the hallway. Jimmy followed, then turned a moment to look back. "Harrington. That's Irish right?"

"That's what I've been told," she replied.

"Good info to know," he said.

"Be careful how you use it," she said in response, turning back to sit down at the table.

Jimmy carefully closed the door, turning to follow Micky, who shook his head and grinned at Jimmy. "Doctor 1, Detective 0."

"Yeah, maybe. But at least I might be in the game. Let's go see if we can have that chat with Eddie."

The neurology unit was in the west wing, third floor. They made their way down the halls and up the elevator, discussing Jimmy's chances of a successful date request with Dr. Harrington as they went. They also reviewed a few of his spectacularly unsuccessful dates in recent months, most of which made Micky laugh. Meanwhile, the doctor had called the neurology unit and spoken to Dr. Powers, advising him of what she had discussed with them and that the two were en route to see him.

They arrived at the unit, showed their badges to the reception desk staff, and asked to see Dr. Powers. After just a minute or two, Powers walked up and introduced himself. He was an older man, probably in his sixties, with graying hair and a rather serious look about him. He led them down a hall, asking them the purpose of their visit as he stopped outside the closed door of one of the patient rooms on the unit.

Micky explained what had happened the day before at the Johnson's house, noting that his wife was not there and presumed missing. He noted the concerns they had about whether she had been taken and the urgent need to speak to Eddie regarding the events that had occurred in the house. Powers nodded, indicating he understood what they needed.

"He was pretty banged up," he said. "He's conscious right now, but probably a bit groggy from the meds we have him on for the pain. I need to limit you to about five minutes or so and I will need to observe while you talk to him."

"Thanks," said Jimmy. "But I am curious. Why do you need to observe us?"

"Not you," Powers replied. "Him. Seeing how he's responding to your questions will help give me a sense of where he is cognitively."

"Oh, got it," said Jimmy. "Only thing we ask is that whatever we discuss remains confidential for now since this is an active investigation."

Powers nodded his assent, opened the door and the three of them walked into the room. Eddie was lying on the bed, halfway between being fully flat and sitting up. His eyes were closed, but he seemed to be breathing normally. Various tubes and monitoring devices ran from his arms, chest and head. A nurse was standing next to a counter in the room, writing something on a chart on the wall. She turned, a smile on her face that quickly turned to a puzzled look when she took in all three of the men coming into the room.

"Hi, Janet," said Dr. Powers softly. "These guys are detectives with

Raleigh PD. They want to talk to Mr. Johnson for a few minutes, ask him some questions."

The puzzled look quickly became a smile again. "Okay. I was just finishing up. I will be back at the station if you need me." Janet left the room, closing the door softly behind her.

Micky and Jimmy walked over to the foot of the bed and Powers came around to Eddie's left side. He glanced at one of the monitors before speaking. "Mr. Johnson, it's Dr. Powers. Are you awake?"

Eddie stirred slightly, but his eyes remained closed. Jimmy could see a large bruise on the right side of his face, along with some bruises and abrasions on his right arm. Other than those and being pale in color, there were no visible signs he was injured.

Powers glanced at the monitor again, then laid one hand softly on Eddie's left arm. "Mr. Johnson, it's Dr. Powers. Can you hear me talking?"

This time Eddie's eyes opened. They seemed unfocused at first, looking in the general direction of the end of the bed before turning towards Powers. His gaze remained steady on the doctor, and he nodded his head slightly.

"Mr. Johnson, you are here at Wake Memorial Hospital. Do you remember coming here?" asked Powers.

Eddie nodded once more, his eyes opening a bit wider.

"Good. These gentlemen are policemen. They want to ask a few questions. Do you feel up to that?"

Now Eddie turned his eyes to Micky and Jimmy. "Yes," he said hoarsely. "Can I maybe get something to drink first?"

"Absolutely," replied Powers. He reached over to a tray table close to the bed, poured water from the small container into a cup with a lid and straw and held it for Eddie to take a few sips.

"Thank you," he said when he was finished. To Micky and Jimmy, "Where's my wife? Where's Donna?"

Dr. Powers stepped back from the bed, making room for Jimmy

to walk up closer to Eddie. Micky did likewise on the other side of the bed.

Jimmy spoke first. "Mr. Johnson, what can you tell us about what happened?"

Eddie was becoming more alert now, shifting on the bed, trying to sit up further. Jimmy asked if he wanted the bed raised and Eddie nodded. "Where's Donna?" he repeated. "Is she okay?"

"She wasn't at your home when the EMTs arrived," replied Jimmy. "We don't know where she is now. You were unconscious when the paramedics arrived. What do you remember about what happened?"

Eddie was clearly becoming distressed now. "If they hurt her..."

"If who hurt her?" asked Micky.

Eddie turned his head towards Micky's side of the bed. "There were two men...I think...in the kitchen when I came in the back door. I came home early for lunch to surprise Donna."

"Do you know who the men were?"

"No. Never seen them before. I asked them what they were doing in my house. One of them, a taller guy, said I needed to stay quiet so no one would get hurt. He said they were there for the money. The other guy had a gun in his hand, pointed at me."

"Was your wife at home?" asked Micky.

Eddie lay back on the bed, closing his eyes, resting for a moment.

"Mr. Johnson are you okay continuing to discuss this?" asked Dr. Powers.

Eddie nodded, eyes still closed. "Yeah, just give me a minute."

"Take your time," said Jimmy.

He spoke without moving his head, eyes still closed, a look of pain on his face. "I remember yelling, What money? What are you talking about? Then I shouted for Donna, asking them where she was. She yelled out my name from the next room, calling for me to help her." He was silent again for a few moments, eyes still closed.

Jimmy looked over at Dr. Powers. Powers held up one finger signaling to give Eddie a minute. They both nodded their assent.

A couple of minutes passed and then he opened his eyes again, looking at Jimmy. "I remember yelling something else at the taller guy. I don't remember what. I started to push by him to get to Donna. The other guy grabbed my arm. I turned to punch him and then all hell seemed to break loose, the three of us going at it in the kitchen." He stopped again, closed his eyes, a line of tears trickling from the corner. "If they have hurt my Donna, I swear..." he said softly trailing off to being quiet and still again.

"Is there anything else you can tell us at this time?" asked Jimmy.

Eddie shook his head, barely moving but enough to indicate he had nothing else to give. Dr. Powers stepped forward. "I think that's enough for now."

The detectives stepped away from the bed and all three men stepped out into the hallway.

Micky spoke first. "Thanks for letting us have a minute with him."

"Yes," replied Powers. "I hope that was of some benefit. He didn't give many details."

"Well, we have more now that we did," said Jimmy. "That's a start. When do you think we can speak to him again?"

"Hard to say. He was more alert and responsive than I expected, frankly, but still, he took quite a blow. Leave me a number where you can be reached. I'll have someone call you."

Micky handed him a business card. They all shook hands, with the detectives once again offering their thanks, then Powers walked off to his next patient.

Jimmy looked at Micky. "Now what?"

"Easy. We go find those two guys," he said with a grin as they headed to the elevator.

CHAPTER 9

"Heard from Pop lately?" Jimmy asked his brother. The two of them were out for dinner, downtown at one of Jimmy's favorite restaurants, a place called Jiddu. In Lebanese, Jiddu is the equivalent of the English word grandpa. The restaurant had been started by a brother-sister duo and named for their beloved grandfather who had immigrated to the United States in the 1950's, eventually settling in the Raleigh area.

Tommy Quinn was Jimmy's older - by only a few minutes as Jimmy often reminded everyone – fraternal twin. Tommy owned a security services firm based in Wilmington, down on the coast a couple of hours southeast of Raleigh. He was in town overnight for a business trip and the two brothers were taking a long overdue opportunity to see each other and catch up on their lives.

Tommy gave a little smile, taking a sip of his wine before answering. "Yeah. A couple of weeks ago, maybe? Same old Pop. We spent half the time talking about fishing, the other half about God. How about you? Talked to him or seen him this year?"

While neither son had a very close relationship with their father, Tommy's was the better one and they both knew it. He had managed to let go of much of the anger towards his father from their childhood. Jimmy was still sorting it out, twenty plus years later.

Their father, Michael Quinn, was a pastor in the mountains of Virginia, the shepherd to a small flock of ardent evangelicals at a church he had founded on the outskirts of Lynchburg in a town named New London. The boys, along with their sister Gina, had been raised there, getting out as soon as they could. Their mother, Lisa, had gotten out even sooner. Unable to stay with Michael and his strident beliefs, she had fled when the boys were in high school. They had long since reconciled with her as they fully understood what she had faced as the wife of a Bible thumping, bordering-on-snake-handling zealot of a preacher.

Jimmy shook his head in answer to Tommy's question. "It's been a couple of months, maybe three," he said. "I'll have to say we were able to have a civil conversation. The old man is softening up some."

"Really? How so?"

"Well, he talked about fishing, of course. You know how much I like that," he said sarcastically. "But when it came to the God-talk, it was mostly about some new things he had been reading. A couple of guys named Reza Aslan and Rob Bell."

"Huh," grunted Tommy. "And how do you remember their names so clearly? You go out and buy their books too?" Tommy asked this with a sly grin, knowing that Jimmy held his own keen interest in spiritual things.

"Maybe," Jimmy laughed. "If I did, I'll mail them to you when I'm finished with them."

"Don't bother. Me and God are getting along just fine."

The two men settled quietly into their own thoughts for a few minutes, each recalling memories from their days in New London. The earlier years of their lives hadn't been too bad. In fact, they had lots of fun exploring the hills around their community, hiking or fishing in the mountain streams, playing youth sports with their friends. Both had been decent athletes, but ones who approached it in different ways.

Tommy was disciplined, practiced hard, and worked out rigorously. Jimmy was all heart and unstoppable when it was game time but cared little about the preparation or practice. Tommy had eventually gotten a partial scholarship to play baseball at a Division III school in North Carolina. He still looked like he could walk on the field and compete, and in truth probably could. Jimmy had also gone to a small college in North Carolina, but the only sports he played were intramural and the occasional weekend softball tournament.

As their early years faded into being teenagers, life at home became more restrictive. Their father's rules – God's rules he proclaimed – would keep them safe, on the right path. Keep them holy, not like the sinners all around them.

When their friends begged them to go to the movies in Lynchburg, the boys constantly had to come up with excuses to cover the embarrassment they felt at trying to explain why their father wouldn't let them go. Most of the programs on television were also forbidden as they teemed with violence and sex. One day Jimmy challenged his father to explain why those shows were so bad when clearly the Old Testament in their bible was chock full of one violent story after another. Not to mention all the sex in there. After a lot of shouting back and forth, their father had simply said this was the way God wanted it, and Jimmy didn't need to understand it.

Jimmy was reflecting on that day when the waiter, thankfully, showed up to take their order for dinner.

"How's it going so far?" he asked. "Questions about the menu, or the specials?"

"Well, Robert my friend," Jimmy said, calling the waiter by name. "I want you to meet my illegitimate brother Tommy. He's in town for the night. Thought I would treat him to one of the best meals he could get up here."

"Pleased to meet you, Tommy," Robert said. "Glad to have you here. What can I tell you about the menu?"

"Jimmy raves about the salmon, but I kind of have my eye on the shawarma. How's that?"

"That's one of my favorites. Beef plus lamb. Comes with a grilled tomato tahini sauce. You don't like it, I'll bring you the salmon."

"Sold," said Tommy, folding his menu and handing it to Robert.

"And how about you, Jimmy? The salmon?"

"You know it," replied Jimmy. He picked up his wine glass and looked at his brother. "Another one for you?"

"Sure"

"Refill the wine, please, and bring us the roasted red pepper hummus to get us started."

"I'm on it," said Robert, taking the menu from Jimmy as he turned back to the kitchen.

"How about Mom?" asked Jimmy. "You talked to her lately?"

"I have. Just yesterday."

"What's new with her? I haven't talked to her in a couple of weeks."

"She said the restaurant is doing well now. She hired a new chef a few months ago, a woman who had been up in Charleston. She's revamped the menu, they're doing another night of live music. Even thinking about expanding the bar." Tommy smiled as he set his wine glass back down on the table. "It's good to see her doing so well."

"Yeah, I agree with that," said Jimmy. "She deserves it after all the crap she's been through."

Their mother, Lisa, lived in Savannah, Georgia. She had arrived there via a second marriage about twenty years earlier. That marriage had gone okay for a while, until she eventually discovered that Paul, the husband she so adored, had a thing going on the side. Paul had several things going on the side as it turned out. Affairs with other women, one of which was Lisa's best friend, who just happened to be the wife of a very successful divorce attorney in town. Lisa and the lawyer joined forces and took good old Paul to the cleaners. Lisa was generous with sharing the proceeds of the settlement and a life-long friendship with Daniel Evans, Esquire was born. Nothing romantic, but Dan still provided whatever legal advice she needed, and Lisa had eventually introduced him to the woman who became his second wife.

Lisa had spent several years in the restaurant business before she met Paul. She decided to jump back in after the divorce was finalized. Not that she needed the money, but she craved the work and the distraction. She bought an existing establishment, one with middling success, on the waterfront in downtown Savannah. It had been successful for the last few years, enough to keep the doors open and keep her busy.

"How's Matt doing?" asked Jimmy. Matt was Lisa's love interest, a local jazz musician who was a Savannah native.

"Seems to be okay. I don't know how you make it being in jazz. Does anyone buy that stuff anymore?"

Jimmy snorted into his wine glass, laughing at his brother's obvious disdain for the genre. "Seriously bro, are you kidding me? Peter White, Chuck Loeb, Stanley Jordan. Ever hear of Norah Jones?"

"Nope. Not familiar with any of them. If it ain't country or it ain't rock, well, it ain't worth listening to," replied Tommy.

Jimmy laughed and shook his head. They grew silent again for a couple of minutes, sipping their wine, checking out the rest of the crowd, occasionally nodding to each other when they spied a particularly attractive woman.

Robert broke the silence, strolling up to the table with a plate in each hand. "Salmon for Mr. Regular," he said, sitting one plate in front of Jimmy. "And the shawarma for our newest regular," as he put the other in front of Tommy. "Gentlemen, what else can I get for you at the moment?"

"I think we're good," replied Jimmy. Tommy nodded, and the waiter wheeled away to another table. Jimmy raised his glass, looking across the table at his brother, "To your health."

"To your health," said Tommy, raising his own glass in return, as both said at the same time, "Slainte."

Silence fell around their table again as they started in on their meals, a comfortable space for them both even as they sat amongst the bustle and laughter, the clinking glasses, the noises from deep in the kitchen. Jiddu stayed full, regardless of the night of the week. Jimmy finally broke the silence. "How's the shawarma?"

"As advertised. Salmon?"

"Good. Try some."

Tommy reached across with his fork, taking some of the fish as Jimmy offered up his plate.

"That's tasty."

"Try the shawarma?" he asked, offering up his own plate.

"Don't mind if I do." Jimmy chewed a moment, swallowed, then said," Damn, all these years and I have been missing out on that!"

"What can I say?" said Tommy, shaking his head. "You're always following behind me."

Jimmy laughed. "How's business?"

"You know," replied Tommy. "Steady. Good."

"Try not to elaborate so much, Tommy."

Tommy's turn to laugh. "Actually, things are going well right now. I'm looking at opening up a new office."

"Really? Where?"

"Here."

"No shit," said Jimmy. "You serious?"

"Maybe. That's why I'm in town. I looked at some office spaces today. Tomorrow I will meet with a woman who could be my person to get it open."

"Damn, bro. Moving into the big city, adding some female leadership to your team. That's awesome."

Tommy smiled. "We'll see. Lots to figure out before it's a go."

"How's Jenny?" Jimmy asked next. Jenny was Tommy's wife.

"She's good too. Market is booming on the coast, so she stays busy."

Jenny owned a small but growing real estate firm in Wilmington that focused on properties in the historic downtown section as well as mid to upper tier homes not in the beach areas.

Robert appeared again. "All is well? More wine?"

"Yes, and yes," replied Jimmy.

"I'm good on wine," said Tommy.

"And the shawarma?" asked Robert.

"You can leave the salmon in the kitchen. It's all you said it would be."

"Excellent. I'll check on you again in a bit."

"How about work for you?" Tommy asked his brother. "Catching all the bad guys?"

"Not quite. Working on a new case in the last couple of days. Home invasion. Husband roughed up pretty good. Wife is missing."

"Yeah. I saw something about that online. Any leads?"

"Slow so far. Took us a day or so before we could talk to the husband. He doesn't remember a lot. Came home early for lunch and found some guys in his house. Got into a tussle with them and took a blow to the head. Wife and the guys were gone when the EMT's and patrolman arrived, of course."

"You think she's in on the deal or she's a gone girl at this point?"

"I don't know. Too early to say. He seems genuinely upset that she's missing, so they must have been tight in their relationship. Nothing yet to suggest she was in on it and trying to have him whacked. Plus, he's still alive."

"Yeah. There's that," agreed Tommy.

Jimmy pushed his plate back as he took the final bite of his salmon. "Dessert?" he asked Tommy.

"Naw. I'm good. Go ahead if you want."

"Nope. I'm good too. I talked to Gina a couple of days ago." Gina was younger by three years and had not fared as well in the wake of their mother's departure as her brothers had. She had been headed into her teenage years when Lisa left. The brothers had done the best they could to support and protect her. Their father had tried, but his mothering skills at that point were almost nil. Gina started sampling drugs and alcohol by the time she was fifteen, discovering she had a taste for both. She kept it mostly under control until her sophomore year in college. She dropped out of Virginia Tech when the partying got to be more regular than going to class.

"How is she doing?" asked Tommy.

"Still sober. For now, anyway," Jimmy replied. "She started a new job not long ago. Still waiting tables mostly, but she'll be doing some hostess work at least one night per week. Says the owner wants her to learn how to run the whole front end."

"She still liking living in that armpit of a city?"

Jimmy laughed. "How do you really feel about Washington? Yeah, I think she does. Plenty of distractions up there. Helps her forget about the past."

Tommy shifted in his chair, drank the last of his wine. "Plenty up there to drag her back into the past, too. We better stay close to her. She's still fragile."

Jimmy nodded. Drank the last of his own wine and glanced at his watch. "You're going to turn into a pumpkin soon, Cinderella. We better get you out of here and headed to bed."

Tommy looked at the time on his phone and nodded. "Yep. Dinner is on me," he smiled. "My civic duty to help our poor, struggling civil servants."

"Liar. You want the tax write-off."

"Well, there's that too," he laughed as he slipped his credit card inside the check sleeve.

Minutes later both men were on their way, Tommy taking the short walk a few blocks to his hotel, Jimmy to the parking garage nearby to retrieve his car. Jimmy had ignored his phone for the most part during dinner, but now he checked his text messages as he walked. One from each of his kids, a couple from friends about weekend plans. The last one was from Micky.

Meet me early for coffee. Looks like Eddie might be going home tomorrow.

Huh, Jimmy thought. That's fast. Maybe things will start moving now. They needed a break of some kind. He put his phone in his pocket, pace quickening a bit, a fresh smile on his face. Let's see what tomorrow brings, he thought.

CHAPTER 10

Jimmy pushed his way through the crowd inside their favorite coffee hangout, Jubula Beans, knowing he would find Micky seated at a table in the back. Sure enough, he was there, flipping through crime scene reports and munching on a bagel. Jimmy took a seat and reached across the table for the second cup with the lid still on it.

"Just the way you like it," said Micky without looking up. "Black and strong. Like me."

Jimmy smiled. This was part of their routine. Micky was always there at least half an hour ahead of him, table secured, thoughtful enough to get his coffee for him so he didn't have to stand in line. Sometimes Jimmy wondered if that was more about Micky not having to wait on him than actual kindness. It was both he concluded. And the black and strong joke? That never got old for either one of them.

"Thanks, man. You're the best."

"Goes without saying. How's Tommy?"

Jimmy took a sip of his coffee. "He's good. Thinking about opening an office here."

"Really?" Micky set the papers down and looked at Jimmy. "You mean I might have a chance to solve some crimes with a real investigator for a change?"

Jimmy laughed. "He's security, not investigation. You're stuck with me."

Micky gave an exaggerated sigh, chewed some more bagel and shook his head. "Can't figure out what I did wrong to deserve this fate."

"Enjoy it while you can. One day they will promote you to the big chair, leaving poor little me out here on my own."

"Not if we don't find this woman and the guys who broke in," said Micky. He pushed a report across the table to Jimmy. "Here's the recap of all we know – or don't – so far."

Jimmy took a minute to scan the first couple of pages. Most of it he was already familiar with since the two of them took turns keeping the log up to date. The newest information included preliminary results from the fingerprint testing the crime scene team had done in and outside the Johnson's home. Most of it was of little help. Lots of unique prints noted, but almost none of them matched any records of criminals in the system. Except one.

Jimmy looked up from the report to see Micky sipping his coffee, grinning at him over the top of the cup.

"Otto Sutter," said Jimmy. "That's the guy that works at the car lot? The one who left for the urgent call when we were there?"

"I'm guessing he's the one," replied Micky. "Might not mean shit, though. Guy works for Eddie, he's probably been in that house more than a few times, fetching things for the lot or sipping wine at the company holiday party."

"Yeah," said Jimmy, "but it's less interesting that his prints are in the house than the fact that he has a record. He do any time?"

"Couple of years on some drug charges. Arrested one other time for an assault charge, reduced to disturbing. Couple of DUIs before that. Could all mean nothing."

Jimmy picked the report up and read it for a minute. He put it back down and shook his head. "He wasn't in that kitchen. Eddie would have recognized him, right?"

"Unless he was masked."

"Eddie didn't mention masks when we talked to him."

"I guess we keep Otto on our list of interesting coincidences for now then. So, Eddie's going home today?"

"Good chance of it. I checked in with Doc Powers late yesterday to see how he was. Doc said he had made remarkable progress. Still sore and banged up, but his brain seems okay and he's pushing to be released. They will run him through some more tests this morning, and if they look decent, he'll check out before dinner."

"Time to pay him another visit?" asked Jimmy.

Micky smiled. "Who do you think is taking him home?"

Jimmy nodded. "Nice. Doing our civic duty. So, what else do we know at this point?"

Noting their scarce list of clues did not take very long and they lapsed into silence, pondering the case while they finished their coffee and bagels. Jimmy finally broke the silence.

"What about gloves? Eddie mention those?"

"On the intruders? No, I don't remember him saying anything about that. If I had to guess, though – which in fact I am – they probably had some on. We can ask him about that later today."

Jimmy drank the last of his coffee, stretched his legs and arms out, then looked at his watch. "Okay, we've exhausted all these paltry clues. What now?"

"Thought you'd never ask. Let's go back to the car lot. Shake the Otto tree and see if anything falls out."

"Got nothing else. Good idea."

Bill was out on the car lot with the first customer of the day when Jimmy and Micky rolled up in front of the office. He waved when he realized who they were, then asked his customer to excuse him for a moment. He was walking across the paved lot as the two detectives got out of their car.

"Gentlemen," he called out, "good to see you again. I hope you bring good news with you." Bill smiled broadly, though somewhat apprehensively as he shook their hands. "I talked to Eddie briefly this morning and he says he may get released today."

Micky smiled back. "That's what we heard as well." He decided to withhold any information that they were taking Eddie home. He wanted to see how closely Eddie stayed in touch with his crew. It didn't take long to find out.

"He said you guys were escorting him home," said Bill. "Turned me down flat on my offer to come get him."

"Happy to help," said Jimmy. "It will give us a chance to talk to him a little more about what happened."

Bill's face suddenly grew heavy with concern. "What about Donna?" he asked. "Any news on her?"

"Nothing yet," replied Micky.

"That's too bad. Well, what can we help you with today?"

Micky glanced around the lot, then looked specifically back at the garage area before answering. "Just finishing up our standard interviews of people close to the Johnsons. We missed Otto the other day. We thought we might speak with him this morning."

"Sure thing," said Bill. "He should be in the garage if you want to head on back. I need to finish up with my customer if that's okay."

"Of course," replied Jimmy. "You go ahead and take care of business. We can find him."

"Thanks, guys. Let me know if you need anything else before you leave." With that, Bill turned to walk back across to where his customer was looking over one of the several pickup trucks on the lot.

Micky looked at Jimmy, then clasped him on the shoulder. "Let's go see what Mr. Sutter has to say for himself, partner." Jimmy nodded and they made their way around the office building towards the garage.

They found Otto in a classic position for mechanics, lying prone on a creeper, mostly underneath a car. Otto must have heard their footsteps when they entered the garage as he was just starting to roll out from under the car when they came up. He cleared the side of the car and looked up at the two of them.

"Otto Sutter?" asked Micky.

"Yeah. That's me. Who's asking?"

"Micky Bondurant, Raleigh PD. This is my partner, Jimmy Quinn. We're the detectives investigating the home invasion at the Johnson's. We'd like to ask you a few questions."

Otto sat up on the creeper and picked up a small towel he had laid on the floor. He methodically wiped his hands on the towel, then stood up to face the two men. He was average height, and had his long black hair pulled back in a ponytail. The beard on his face was maybe a week old and several tattoos ran up and down his muscular arms. He looked Micky in the eyes and said, "Sure."

"Thanks. How long have you known the Johnsons?"

"A year, maybe a year and a half."

"And how long have you worked for Eddie?"

"Same. That's how I came to know them."

"How would you describe their relationship?" asked Jimmy.

Otto took a moment to consider the question, tucking his shirt back in his jeans as he did. "Hell, I don't know. Okay, I guess. It's not like I hang out with them or anything,"

"Any reason you can think of that someone would want to hurt Eddie or Mrs. Johnson?"

"Naw," replied Otto. He reached in a shirt pocket, pulled out a pack of cigarettes, holding them out to Jimmy and Micky. "Want one?"

Both men shook their heads. Otto fished a lighter out of his pants pocket, fired up the cigarette, taking a long drag and blowing the smoke up towards the ceiling. "I thought the whole thing was just a robbery," he said.

"Maybe," Micky said. "Donna's missing, though. Kind of makes us think there might be more to it than that."

"Maybe she beat Eddie up and ran," offered Otto.

"Hmm. You think that's possible?"

Otto took another drag on the cigarette. "Hell no. She ain't no pushover, but I don't see her getting the drop on Eddie."

Jimmy shifted the questioning. "How about out here at the lot? Things been okay? Any unhappy customers, maybe looking to get even on a bad deal?"

Otto snorted. "Doubt it. Bill and Eddie kiss everybody's ass that comes on the lot. Especially the ones who buy a car."

Jimmy could see that they weren't going to get much that was useful from Otto, so he moved towards wrapping things up. "Okay, anything else you can think of that we should know?"

Otto smiled. "Yeah. It wasn't me."

Jimmy looked at Micky, then back to Otto. "You are thinking that we suspect you in some way?"

Otto laughed this time. "Come on, man. Cut the crap. I know you're investigating every angle you can come up with. I got a record, so you probably already seen that. Know about my criminal past." He threw his cigarette down on the concrete floor, grinding it out with his heel.

Micky nodded. "Yeah, we saw that. Just so we can check the box, where were you that morning?"

Otto smiled again. "Right here. Working for the man. Just ask Bill."

"We'll do that," replied Micky.

"Anything else?" asked Otto. "I got a lot of work to do."

"No. That's all for now," said Jimmy. "Appreciate your time."

"Sure thing," replied Otto. He turned back towards the car he had been working on, picking up his wrench and kneeling back down on the creeper as Jimmy and Micky walked out of the garage.

Once outside and the door behind them closed, the two men paused and looked at each other.

"Well?" asked Micky.

"I don't know. What would his motive be? And if Bill confirms he was here, then he would have to have a crew working with him."

"I don't know either. He's probably clean in all this, but I have to say that was odd how he outed himself as an ex-con. Don't see that happen much."

"Nope. Let's talk to Bill."

Bill wasn't on the lot when they walked around the front, so they checked in the office. Lila expressed delight at seeing them but quickly became crestfallen when she learned they still had no news about Donna. She let them know Bill was out on a test drive with a customer and should be back soon. After telling her they would wait out on the porch, she insisted on making them coffee, which they both gladly accepted. Jimmy also could not resist a slice of the banana bread she had made and brought to work that morning.

They were rocking on the porch and talking about sports, and the case, when Bill and his new customer pulled back in. They parked right in front of the office and walked up the steps. Bill looked hesitantly at Jimmy and Micky. "We just have one quick question for you," said Jimmy.

"Maurice," Bill said to the man with him, "if you don't mind, I just need a quick minute with these gentlemen. If you will go inside, Lila can start the paperwork with you, and I'll be right in."

Maurice nodded his head and entered the office. Bill turned back to Jimmy, more than a little concern etched on his face. "Okay. How can I help?"

"Otto," said Jimmy. "Where was he the day of the crime?"

Bill thought for a moment. "Right here. That was Tuesday and we got in some cars from Wilmington, so he was here all day checking them out."

"Okay. That's all we need for now. Thanks."

"You think he's involved in this?" Bill looked really concerned now.

"No," replied Micky. "Just checking out what he told us. Don't have any reason to be suspicious about him at this point."

"Should we be?" Jimmy asked.

"Umm. No. No. I don't think so," replied Bill, who was clearly thrown off now.

"Alright," said Jimmy. "Thanks again for your time. See you later."

The men all shook hands again, then Jimmy and Micky got into their cars and left the lot.

Otto lay on the creeper, staring up at the transmission casing underneath the car after Jimmy and Micky walked out. He was a suspicious man by nature, and he was wondering just what the hell was going on with the break-in at the Johnson's. Something about it felt wrong to him, like it might not be just a random robbery attempt.

The detectives had put him on high alert now. Not that he had anything to do with the invasion. That would have been stupid. No, it was having the cops snooping around the lot and poking in his business that had him rattled. What if they started asking questions about other things? Things at the lot, not just things about the Johnson's and their personal lives.

He thought about calling his friends down in Wilmington, letting them know what was going on. He had a burner phone in his backpack on the tool bench that he used to stay in touch. What if this was nothing to worry about, though, and he got them stirred up for nothing? By now they probably already knew about what happened, he reasoned, so maybe best to lay low and see what developed.

In the end he chose staying quiet as the safest play. He might push Eddie a little bit, though. See if he had any idea of what the thieves were after at this house. This probably had nothing to do with his and Eddie's little sideline venture, but if it did, Otto needed to make sure it was contained there and didn't spread into other activities he was involved in. Nothing more he could do right now, he thought, so he picked his wrench back up and started in on the car.

Micky's cell phone rang as he and Jimmy were heading down Capital Boulevard after leaving the car lot. He glanced down and saw the number was from Wake Memorial, picked it up and hit the button to answer. "Micky Bondurant," he said, after he turned on the speaker phone option so that Jimmy could listen in.

"Good morning, detective. It's Eddie Johnson calling."

"Eddie, good morning. How ya feeling?"

"Been better detective, but good enough to get out of here. Listen, change in plans. I really appreciate the offer to take me home today, but Bill's going to send Lila out to get me."

Micky looked at Jimmy, a little puzzled by the change. "Look Eddie, we don't mind. It's not a hassle at all to come pick you up."

"I know, I know," Eddie replied. "And I really do appreciate it, but you know, Lila, she wants to do something to help and she's pushing Bill to let her come get me. She's such a sweet girl. I don't want to hurt her feelings, you know?"

Micky looked at Jimmy again. Jimmy just shrugged and mouthed. 'We'll go talk to him later.' Micky nodded. "Okay, Eddie. I get it. No worries. We'll come by later and check on you. Okay?"

"Yeah, yeah. That's good," Eddie replied. Then his voice took a more serious tone. "What about Donna? Any news? Any ideas yet on where she might be?"

"No. Nothing yet, Eddie, but we are on this as hard as we can be. We'll turn something up soon," he said.

The line went silent for a few moments before Eddie replied. "I don't know what to do next," he said in a halting voice. "I just don't know what to do."

"Nothing you can do right now," said Micky. "Go home. Try to get some rest and get stronger. That's the best thing you can do for Donna right now. We'll come by later and walk you back through what happened, see if you can remember anything new that might help us. Okay?"

"Yeah," Eddie replied softly. "Okay, I'll let you know once I'm there and settled."

"Good deal," replied Micky. "Take care, Eddie. We'll see you soon."

As he lay in his hospital bed after just talking to Micky, Eddie was deeply uneasy. Physically he was turning out to be in much better shape than expected. The diagnosis for a concussion had held, but it looked to be remarkably milder now. In the last twelve hours his ability to think and his awareness of his circumstances were almost fully normal. His body was banged up a bit, and the side of his face advertised that he had gotten the worst of a very unfriendly encounter. Dr. Powers had deemed him strong enough to go home but was urging him not to return to work for a few days. Eddie was already planning to ignore this advice.

Then there was the fact that his wife was missing, and the police had no clues as to where she was, whether she was even alive, or who had invaded their home and beaten him so badly. As much as he loved his work and had poured himself over the years into building what was becoming a successful small business, Donna was his life. He simply could not paint a vision of the future that did not have her at its center.

Eddie had been playing scenarios over and over in his head to try and come up with motives for what had happened. As troubling as they all were, however, there was another path that could be even more of a nightmare. One which led him to worry about exactly what Otto might be up to. Eddie could not imagine that the break-in was somehow tied to their secret venture, their own little partnership in crime. If it was, it led to a host of other questions and a growing sense of guilt for Eddie that somehow his own greed might be factoring into harm to his wife.

He would need to walk a very fine line with the detectives, giving them all he could to help them find Donna. But was he willing to confess his crimes if it came to it in order to find her? That might lead to a different kind of life without her, one behind bars for a while. And then perhaps on his own whenever he was freed, scorned and abandoned by her for what he had done.

Eddie had to find out what Otto knew as quickly as he could, but he couldn't risk that by calling him. He needed to see his reaction, to read what was going on. Plus, the cops could trace his cellular calls and that might blow back on him later. Perhaps he could get Otto to come by his house later, after the detectives were gone. He would think of some plausible reason to ask him over and have the request go back to the lot through Lila.

Feeling a little less worried now that he had some action steps, Eddie settled back down on the bed to rest until Lila arrived with fresh clothes for his ride home.

CHAPTER 11

Jimmy turned left onto East Lane Street shortly after Eddie called Micky from the hospital. They had debated the significance of Eddie opting for transport home by Lila versus them and concluded there was nothing to it. They also re-hashed the conversation with Otto but came away with no further insights or new ideas. Jimmy suggested, since they were sort of in the neighborhood anyway, that they drop by the home of the Johnson's neighbor who had called in the crime scene and look for fresh clues with her.

"What's the house number again?" asked Jimmy.

"8704. Two doors down on the same side."

"Gotcha."

A few moments later Jimmy spotted the correct address and turned right into the driveway of Rachel Wilson. Rachel was walking from the rear of her property as Jimmy put the car in park. She was pushing a wheelbarrow with bags of mulch to the front of her house. A look of concern etched her face as the detectives pulled into her drive, not realizing who they were. This gave way to a more relieved look as she recognized Micky once he got out of the car. Micky had spoken to her very briefly the day of the crime.

Rachel Wilson was a strikingly elegant woman, her long auburn hair with a few streaks of gray tucked up under the hat she wore to protect her fair complexion from the sun's rays. Retired from a long career as a high school English teacher in Wake County, she was also a widow having lost her husband Charles to a stroke a few years before. She lived alone now in the Cape Cod style home she and Charles had built two decades ago on East Lane Street. The two children she and Charles had raised, both married now with young kids of their own, lived out-of- state. Rachel spent much of her time visiting with them and traveling with friends and had only recently returned home after an absence of a couple of months. She parked the wheelbarrow in front of her porch, then turned to greet the two men.

"Mr. Bondurant, was it?" she said with a smile, extending her hand toward Micky.

"Yes, ma 'am," replied Micky. "Good to see you again, Mrs. Wilson."

"Please, call me Rachel," she said," All those years of teaching made me weary of being Mrs. Wilson."

Jimmy offered her his own hand. "Hi, Rachel. I'm Jimmy Quinn, Micky's partner."

"It's a pleasure to meet you, Jimmy." She took her hat off, then brushed some mulch off her pants before speaking again. "I hope you two are bringing good news about Donna and Eddie."

Micky shook his head. "A little. Eddie should be coming home today."

"What about Donna?"

"I'm afraid we don't have any good news on her. At least not yet. We were hoping we could ask you a few more questions, perhaps turn up something new that would help us."

Rachel nodded. "Certainly. Let's have a seat on the patio. Can I get you gentlemen something to drink? Some water? Coffee? Perhaps some iced tea?"

Both men declined. Rachel indicated she would go in and get some water for herself while they made their way to the patio at the rear of her home. She found them comfortably seated at the patio table when she walked out the back door. Taking a seat across from them, she laid her hat on the table in front of her, then removed the cap from her bottled water. She took a large swallow and set the bottle on the table.

"That was just the thing I needed," she smiled. "Now, how can I help?"

Micky had his notebook turned to the section with her statement on the day of the break-in. After glancing down at it for a moment, he looked up at Rachel. "We'd like you to walk us back through what you saw and did Tuesday morning, but first, please tell us what you know about the Johnsons."

Rachel brushed her auburn hair back and shook her head. "My goodness, that was just Tuesday morning? Seems it's been more than just a few days with all the police and news people over there. Not to mention the neighborhood chatter that has been almost nonstop it seems."

She paused and looked over towards the Johnson's house, thinking about where to start. "Let's see, my Charles died four years ago. That first year was hard. So lonely. Donna and Eddie moved in the week of the one-year anniversary of his passing. I remember it being tough to put on a friendly face to go and welcome them because I was so down and depressed. And yet it was good at the same time to have new people close by." She looked at Micky and Jimmy. "Does that seem odd?"

"Not at all," replied Jimmy. "It must have been difficult."

Rachel drank more water. "Indeed. It was a trying time. Anyway, I remember that I baked a loaf of banana nut bread - my grandmother's recipe - and took it over the day after they moved in. Donna was so...what's the word I want? Warm, I suppose. She had such a warm and inviting manner to her, you know? She sensed immediately that I wasn't myself, even though she didn't know me. By the end of my visit, I had spilled everything about Charles' death, how lonely I was. I wept like a child, releasing so much grief I had been holding."

"How about Eddie?" asked Micky. "What was he like?"

Rachel reflected a few moments before answering. "You know, I never thought about it, but I would have to say the way Eddie was that first day is pretty much how he has always been, around me anyway."

"How so?" prompted Micky.

"Well, he was gracious and kind. A very nice guy. But sort of in and out of conversation, or the room. Always off working on something in his head and then checking back in. Does that make sense?"

"There, but not there," offered Jimmy.

"Yes, you could say it like that."

"This next question is a bit delicate," said Micky.

"You want to know about their marriage," said Rachel. "Were there any problems."

Micky and Jimmy both looked surprised. "Yes," said Micky.

Rachel smiled a bit wistfully. "Remember, I'm a retired English teacher. Literature is my thing, and many a volume has been written about relationships that end in tragedy."

"Any reason to suspect that here?" asked Jimmy.

"No," she replied firmly. "I don't think so. Eddie may be a little less than fully engaged with the rest of us at times, but there is no doubt regarding his feelings for Donna. She's a saint, he knows it, and he loves her dearly."

Micky jotted down a few notes before continuing. "What about the last few weeks or months? Anything unusual you have noticed? Strange visitors perhaps?"

Rachel thought for a moment, then replied, "Nothing that stands out. I just returned last week, though, after seeing my kids and taking a trip abroad. But no, I can't say I have seen or noticed anything when I have been here."

Jimmy nodded, deciding to move them to the events of Tuesday. "Thank you, Rachel. The background on them is helpful. Can you walk us through Tuesday again?"

"Sure. My morning was a typical Tuesday morning. I'm an early riser, so I was up by 6:00 a.m. I had some coffee, checked the news, then did a yoga workout. After that I wrote for a while." She smiled modestly here. "Finally working on that great novel every English teacher promises to write. After writing for maybe a couple of hours I was trying to decide what was next. Donna had mentioned over the weekend that she would be going downtown to Logan's on Tuesday to get new flowers to plant. She has quite a green thumb!"

"Yes, their yard is beautiful," said Jimmy.

"It is," she replied. "I was debating whether to go with her and then work in the yard later or just ask her to bring me back whatever she thought would be best for my yard. She loved to surprise me sometimes with an unusual flower or shrub to plant." She paused and drank more water. "Anyway, I decided to ask her to surprise me. I called their house but got no answer. Tried her cell phone and no answer there either, so I decided to have lunch and then try her again after that."

"Was it unusual for her not to answer?" asked Micky.

"Hmm, not particularly. But she usually calls back quickly. Maybe another 45 minutes to an hour passed and still no call back, so I decided to walk over. I thought she might be out working in her yard." Rachel paused here for a moment as she remembered what she had seen that day. "The first thing I noticed was the glass on the front porch and the flowers. I rang the front bell a couple of times, then knocked loudly. No response came so I decided to walk around back. The garage door was open, so I walked through that to the entry door into the kitchen. I knocked again there and when I still got no answer, I tried the doorknob to see if it was unlocked. Donna's car was in the garage and at this point I think I began to sense somehow that something was wrong."

She paused again, emotions coursing through her as tears welled up in her eyes. Taking a deep breath to steady herself, she continued. "I opened the door and called out for Donna. No answer came, so I pushed the door open and stood in the doorway, calling a bit louder. Then I saw Eddie's feet were sticking out just beyond the island as he lay on the kitchen floor. Of course, I didn't know at first it was Eddie.

I rushed into the kitchen and around the island. He was lying there, unconscious. I wasn't even sure he was breathing."

"What did you do then?" asked Jimmy.

"I think I screamed. Then I yelled for Donna but of course got no answer. I walked quickly through the rest of the house looking for her, then came back to the kitchen and called 9- 1- 1."

"What did you notice about the house?" asked Micky.

"Well, there had clearly been a struggle in the kitchen. Some papers, maybe a wine bottle, were on the floor. The table and a couple of chairs were out of place."

"Do you remember anything unusual about the rest of the house? Any signs of struggles there?"

Rachel shook her head. "No, but I was so distraught from finding Eddie that I think I was in shock. I don't recall anything being strange."

Micky checked his notes. "Did you go into the master bedroom when you were looking for Donna?"

"Yes, I'm sure I must have."

"Crime scene photos show the drawers to a dresser pulled open. You didn't notice that?"

"No, I'm sorry. Was there something important about that?"

Micky shrugged. "Not sure yet. We think they were searching the house for something before Eddie came home and surprised them."

"You said 'them,'" she responded. "You think there was more than one person?"

"Seems likely," Micky replied. "Are they collectors of anything rare that you know of?"

"No."

"How about jewelry? Did Donna wear a lot of expensive jewelry?"

Rachel thought for a moment. "No. Nothing excessive. She has a nice anniversary ring Eddie gave her last year, but other than that, no. Flashy is not her style."

Jimmy was sensing there wasn't much more she could give them.

"Rachel, is there anything else you can think of that seems unusual or odd? Strange cars in the neighborhood that day maybe."

Rachel shook her head. "I'm sorry. I wish there was more."

Jimmy handed her his card and thanked her for her time and her willingness to speak to them. He and Micky got up from the table and headed back to their car, leaving her there pondering what they had discussed. They were opening the doors to their car when she came running around the side of the house, calling out to them.

"Wait, wait!" she said. "I do remember something. Your question about strange cars just clicked for me. There were two that morning that I saw, both within a few minutes of each other after I finished my yoga session. I was cooling down and just happened to be looking out the front at the yard, thinking about what I needed to do out there. I saw a red Trans Am ride by. An older one like from the 1970's or '80's. You don't see those much anymore."

Micky was taking notes as she spoke. "Did you notice the occupants of the car? How many were inside?"

"At least two. May have been more in the back. I don't remember."

"How about the other car?"

"Actually, it was a van, not a car. An old one, kind of beat up a little. Like one of those work vans a painter might drive. Pretty sure it was brown. Yes, it was brown."

"Occupants?"

"Hard to say. It didn't have windows other than on the front doors. There was a woman driving. I do remember thinking that was a little odd."

"What about markings on the van?"

She thought for a moment. "Nothing. It was just plain brown. I watched it go past my house, then I moved away from the window. That's all I remember."

"Rachel, thanks. If you recall anything else, you have our numbers."

They said their goodbyes once again and Rachel stood in her driveway and watched as they backed out.

CHAPTER 12

"Are you sure there is nothing else you need before I go?" Lila asked Eddie.

They stood just inside the front door of his house. Lila, as promised, had come to Wake Memorial that afternoon to take him home. He was sore and his head hurt a little, but he was happy to be out of the hospital with their constant poking and prodding, waking him up all night long. No way to really get any rest there.

"No, Lila. I'll be fine. You've done more than you should have."

Lila reached to hug him tightly, tears spilling down her cheeks as she said, "We are just a phone call away, Eddie. Not going to rest until Donna is home safely and you're all healed up."

"I know you won't," he replied, the emotion in his voice genuine, tears welling up in his own eyes. "You should go now. Get home to your son. He needs you too."

Lila let go and nodded. "I'll call you in the morning."

Eddie closed the door behind her, locking it as he stood and thought about what was next. He was tired and worried about Donna. He looked at his phone. Three voice mails from the detectives, probably wanting to know if they could come by yet. He looked at his watch. Not far from 6:00 p.m. Maybe he could put them off until tomorrow. Right now, he needed to talk to Otto.

He was smart enough to know that cops could look at cell phone records. Placing a call to Otto immediately after Lila left might come back to haunt him one day, so his next call would be to Bill. He punched in Bill's number and waited for him to pick up.

"Eddie? Is everything okay? Lila get you home and settled?"

"Yeah, yeah," he replied. "I'm good. She's an angel. Took good care of me. I'm calling to check on you."

Bill laughed. "Check on me? Are you for real? I'm fine. How are you feeling?"

"Banged up still. Head hurts a little, but I'm going to be okay."

"What about Donna? Any news on her?"

Eddie was silent for a few moments as the reality of the fact that Donna was missing came back to him again. "No," he said softly. "No, nothing yet."

"The detectives have been by here a couple of times," said Bill. "Nice guys. They seem pretty competent."

Eddie perked up at this. "Yeah? What did they want to know?"

"Well, kind of general stuff, I guess. Had I noticed anything unusual? Was the business doing okay? You and Donna getting along? That kind of thing."

"They talk to Lila too?"

"Yes. Otto also. They had to come back a second time for Otto. He had to leave the first time they were here. Something urgent with his brother."

Eddie was silent again. He knew that Otto wasn't on speaking terms with his brother, so he suspected he had just used that as an excuse to avoid talking to the detectives. "How about the lot?" asked Eddie.

"All good," replied Bill. "A little hectic covering all the customers without you here, but we're doing okay. You take whatever time you need. Focus on finding Donna. We got this for now."

"Thanks, Bill," his appreciation genuine. "I'll see how tomorrow goes. Probably do me good to be out there rather than sitting in this house 24-7."

"Do what you need to Eddie. Anything else for now?"

"No. That's all. Thanks, Bill. I'll call you soon," he said. Eddie hit the button to end the call. He decided to have a drink to settle himself down a bit before calling Otto. His doctor probably wouldn't like that given the pain meds he was taking, but what the hell. Doc Powers wasn't here to hassle him right now. He walked into the family room and poured a generous portion of Blanton's bourbon into one of the tumblers they kept on the bar. He took a sip and let the warmth roll down his throat and into his belly. He stood there, staring at nothing, and savored a few more sips before he walked into the kitchen.

He sat on one of the bar stools at the island, putting the tumbler down in front of him. The confrontation there a few days before was playing on a loop inside his head as he tried to remember everything that they said. It had all gone down so fast. Nothing he could remember gave him any clue to why they had chosen to break in on Donna that morning. It had to be either completely random or connected somehow to him and Otto.

Eddie took another sip of bourbon and contemplated what he and Otto had been doing over the last fifteen months. Of the 40 million vehicles sold annually in the US, over 200,000 have their odometers illegally rolled back. The vehicles are often sold for thousands more than they are worth. Johnson Auto, thanks to the technical know-how of Otto, and the sleight-of-hand paperwork wizardry of Eddie, was in the roll-back business. Not in a huge way, 5-6 cars per month. Keeping it small scale was part of how Eddie was able to sleep a little easier at night.

Of course, it started as only one for a couple of months, then two, then three. The more they did, the easier it got. He reflected on how it had started. After closing one Friday night, he and the staff hung around for a bit to drink a glass of champagne in celebration of a sales milestone Eddie had set for Bill and himself. After about an hour Lila left, then soon after that Bill. Eddie and Otto found themselves drinking bourbon by themselves on the front porch of the office, shooting the shit and getting to know each other better.

Otto had been working for Eddie for about three months at that point. He had been a referral from Eddie's financing partners in Wilmington. Eddie's prior mechanic had abruptly quit on him, and Otto's name came to him so quickly it almost seemed like a divine intervention. Eddie had, in fact, said more than one prayer of thanks for Otto coming his way. As they sat with their feet up on the porch railing that night it was Otto who had first raised the odometer scheme. Not directly, of course, but he slyly worked in a question or two to test Eddie on the topic.

Eddie knew the practice was out there but had never considered doing it himself. Other than occasionally smoking some weed and consistently breaking the speed limit, Eddie was a law-abiding citizen. Otto told him that night how much additional money per car was available and left it at that. Over the next few weeks, he disclosed to Eddie that he possessed the tools and knowledge to reset odometers. Eventually Eddie came to him, proposing that they just try a few, splitting the profits, and see what happened. Otto said yes and just like that, their little criminal enterprise was born.

Eddie thought for a minute about whether he should talk to Otto over the phone or in person. If it ever came to tracing cell phone calls, his cover would be he had called Bill and then Otto to check on the business. He decided it was more suspicious if somehow it was discovered Otto had come to his house. He drained the last of the bourbon in his glass and punched up Otto's cellphone.

"Yeah," was all Otto said when he answered.

"Otto, it's Eddie."

"Yeah."

"How are things at the lot?"

"Fine."

"Thats good," said Eddie. "Listen, I think we need to talk."

"Yeah? What about?"

Eddie took a deep breath, wishing he had poured another bourbon before he called Otto. "You know, about our deal."

"What about it?" asked Otto.

"I'm worried it's related."

Otto was quiet for a few moments. "Related to what, and what's that got to do with me?"

Eddie laughed nervously. "Seriously? How does it not have something to do with you?"

"Listen, Eddie, maybe we should talk tomorrow, in person."

"How about tonight? Why wait until tomorrow?"

"I kind of have something planned."

"This is important, Otto."

"I don't know. Maybe I could come by later if it ends early enough."

"Okay, that would be great. Text me later."

"Sure."

Eddie put his phone down on the counter. He stared at it for a while, feeling the panic settling into his bones about Donna, about his deal with Otto, about how to handle things with the detectives. He really needed that second bourbon, so he got up and poured a double.

Out at the car lot, Otto put his phone in his pocket after ending the call with Eddie. He leaned against the car he had been working on, an ironic smile crossing his face. He thought about the conversation with Eddie. Then he replayed the visit from Jimmy and Micky. He too had started to wonder if somehow the break-in and Donna being missing was related to their rollback scheme. He knew that he had not been talking to anyone about it. Other than it being a generally stupid thing to do, it wouldn't be wise for the brothers in Wilmington to find out he had a side hustle going on, much less one where Eddie was his partner.

Had he slipped up somehow and inadvertently mentioned

something to someone? He thought about that for a while, but nothing came to him. Had to be Eddie, then, if it was related. But had they actually made enough cash so far for it to be worth someone, and not just someone but at least two people, to break into Eddie's looking for it? Otto did some math in his head. He couldn't really be sure that Eddie was splitting things evenly with him. He never showed Otto any of the paperwork. Otto hadn't kept up with his total share. He had stashed some away, maybe about forty-grand. The rest he had blown on booze and gambling, a few toys at his apartment. So far, he had gotten what, maybe $75,000?

He pulled out a cigarette, lit it and thought about that number. If Eddie was hiding his share, would he keep it all in cash at his house? If Eddie was stiffing him somehow on the deal, then obviously his share would have been even higher. $100,000? $150,000? He blew smoke up towards the ceiling, wondering now if he could trust Eddie at all.

He glanced at his watch. It was past closing time. Bill must still be working on something in the office since he hadn't come out to say goodbye. He thought about poking Bill a little, see if he knew anything, then decided to leave that for now. Best to talk to Eddie first. He threw his cigarette down on the grimy concrete floor, grinding it out with his heel. After storing his tools for the night, he cut off the lights, locked the door to the garage, then got in his car and left the lot.

Back at the Johnson's, Eddie's phone rang as soon as he finished pouring the second bourbon. He glanced at the incoming number. Micky Bondurant, the detective. Should he see them tonight or put them off? He looked at his watch. Starting to get late in the day. Hell, maybe they would put it off. Then he thought about Donna. No, he had to talk to them. Donna was out there somewhere.

"Hello, detective," he said into his mobile phone.

"Eddie, it's Micky Bondurant. How are you feeling?"

"You know, my head hurts, my body aches. My wife is missing. Not that great actually. The bourbon is helping though."

"You go easy on that, Eddie. We need you clear-eyed when we talk. And speaking of that, how about tonight? We can be there in fifteen minutes."

Eddie took a generous swallow of the bourbon. "Come on. I'm not going anywhere."

"Great. See you in a few," said Micky, punching off the line.

Eddie sat and waited for them to arrive, polishing off his drink. Thought about having one more, then decided he agreed with Micky. He needed his wits about him, not just to help them find Donna, but to make sure he didn't say something stupid.

Thirty minutes after the call ended, the three of them were seated in the family room. Eddie was drinking water now. Micky and Jimmy had accepted Eddie's offer of a beer. Technically their shift was over, and they wanted to put Eddie at ease, making things a little more casual.

"Eddie, thanks for seeing us," started Jimmy. "We know you had a long day."

"Whatever we need to do to find Donna, and to find these guys," replied Eddie. "Have you made any progress?"

"Not much," said Jimmy. "We want to walk back through the whole thing in detail. Plus, we have some other questions for you. We need to fill in some background."

"Okay. Where do you want to start?"

"Let's start with you coming home at lunch that day. That something you normally do?"

Eddie shook his head. "No, not normally. I'll do it once in a while, on special occasions, I need to pick up something, or Donna needs something. Things like that."

"Anything special about Tuesday?"

Now Eddie smiled a little. "Yeah, actually there was." He paused and cleared his throat. "Our anniversary is coming up this weekend.

I had planned a surprise trip to Bermuda. We were going to leave Wednesday, and I was coming home to tell her, surprise her."

"So, she didn't know you were coming home that day?" asked Micky.

"No. Like I said, I wanted to surprise her."

"Do you remember what time you arrived at the house?" asked Jimmy.

Eddie thought for a moment. "It was before noon. Bill had a customer that morning and I waited until he finished the paperwork. I probably left the lot around 11:30 or so."

"Did you make any stops along the way?"

"No. Came straight here."

Eddie's Chevrolet Tahoe SUV was missing, so Jimmy asked him where he had parked that morning.

"I parked in the garage, like normal. I got out of the Tahoe, hit the button to close the garage door, then walked into the kitchen."

"Notice anything odd?"

"Nope. It was locked, like it normally is."

Micky consulted his notes from the brief interview with Eddie in the hospital. "You said there were two men in the kitchen when you walked in. What do you remember about them?"

Eddie closed his eyes, thinking back for a few moments. After taking a sip of water, he said, "Yeah. There were two. One of them was shorter, stockier. He was closer at first, nearer to the door. He's the one that had the gun in his hand."

"What can you remember about him? What was he wearing, his hair?"

"Dark pants, probably jeans. He had on a lighter colored shirt. Short sleeves. I remember he had tattoos on one arm, but I don't remember what they were. Maybe a snake? Dark hair that was short, maybe a buzz cut, sort of military style."

Both Micky and Jimmy were taking notes at this point. "You mentioned that the other one said something when you came in."

"Yeah. When I saw them, I was pretty surprised, and my first thought was Donna. I asked him who the hell they were, yelled at him." Eddie paused to reflect further on what had happened. "You know, now that I remember, the way he answered me, it was so calm."

"What did he say?" asked Micky.

"He said it didn't matter who they were, it only mattered what I did next. That pissed me off, so I yelled at him again. Asked him who they were and what they were doing in my house. He said they were there for the money. I said 'What money? What the hell are you talking about?'"

Micky prompted him to keep going. "Then what happened?"

"The shorter guy spoke up then. He said I knew damn well what money they were talking about."

"Do you keep cash in your home?" asked Micky.

"Occasionally we might have a deposit from the car lot here if I didn't drop it by the bank or Donna didn't go to the bank that day. It's mostly checks, but sometimes there might be a few thousand in cash in there." Eddie drank more water, his mouth a little dry from the bourbon. He thought about the cash he had stashed away in a safe deposit box at the bank, his share from the last few cars they had rolled back the odometers on.

"Who would know you might have some cash here, other than your employees?"

Eddie scratched his head. "Well, nobody in particular, but maybe anybody could guess that might happen since I own a car lot."

"Okay, that makes sense. What happened next?"

"I told them there was no money here. Then I asked them where Donna was. They said not to worry about her, that she was going to be fine if I gave them what they came for. That's when I yelled out for her and started to try and push past the taller guy."

"What do you remember about him?"

"He was lean, muscular. Kind of looked like he might have been an athlete. He had dark hair too, kind of a good-looking guy I suppose.

A little darker skin, maybe like he's an Italian of some kind, maybe Mexican."

"What was he wearing?" asked Jimmy.

"I think his pants were olive colored. And they were cargo style, you know, with the pockets on each side. I remember noticing those just before I blacked out on the floor. Weird, but I remember saying to myself I liked his pants. He had on a long-sleeved shirt of some kind. Blue maybe."

"Tell us about the fight in the kitchen."

"Yeah, that started when I tried to go around him," said Eddie. "He grabbed my arm to stop me. I yelled for Donna again and that time she yelled back."

"What did she say?"

Eddie choked up a little. "She yelled for me to help her. I shoved Guido and that's when all hell broke loose. The other guy came at me from behind. I think I got in a couple of good punches, but they had me outnumbered. They hit me in the head with something, and I went down pretty hard. I remember seeing his pants, the other guy's feet and then it all went black."

All three men were silent for a minute as Jimmy and Micky finished writing their notes and thought about their next questions. Micky spoke first. "Anything else you can recall?"

"No. Seems like I can vaguely remember Rachel coming in. Then a little when the medics got here. Sorry, that's about it."

"Where do you think Donna was when she called out?" asked Jimmy.

"I hadn't thought much about it, but she was probably in the hallway off the kitchen. Or maybe in the dining room?"

"If she was calling out, do you think they had her tied up in there?" asked Jimmy.

"I don't know."

"What if there was a third person?" mused Jimmy. "Somebody holding her or threatening her with a weapon if she moved?"

"That's a possibility," agreed Micky.

Eddie nodded his agreement. Jimmy asked Eddie to walk them through the house and point out the specific places he thought Donna could have been. They did this for a few minutes, talking over the new theory of a third intruder. In the end they concluded it was a possibility they couldn't rule out, but also one they couldn't just assume. They made their way to the family room again where Micky and Jimmy decided it was time to wrap things up for the night. Eddie was visibly tired and becoming less engaged with them.

Jimmy closed his notebook and stuck his pen in its binding, then looked intently at Eddie. "One last question, Mr. Johnson. Anything you want to share with us that could shed any light on why this happened and what these guys were after?"

Eddie shifted his stance, unsure exactly how to take Jimmy's question. Was he challenging him directly? Was he getting suspicious? He took a deep breath, blowing it out slowly, then he shook his head, letting all the emotions in him come out as a display of his concern for Donna.

"No," he said firmly. "There was no stash of money here. I don't know how they got the idea we were a good house to rob. Donna and I don't have any enemies that I know of, so I don't think it was about that. I don't understand why they would have taken her if they were after money. I swear, if they hurt her..."

Micky put a hand on Eddie's shoulder. "We're doing all we can, Eddie. We think one of the possibilities is this has turned into a kidnapping."

Eddie had not considered this. "What?" he exclaimed. "A kidnapping?"

"It's possible. If that's the case, you're going to hear from them soon. If you do, call us right away. Don't try to deal with it on your own. Understood?"

Eddie was clearly shocked now at this new turn of events. "Yes," he stammered. "Shit. That never occurred to me."

"We'll be in touch," said Jimmy. "You try and get some rest."

Eddie nodded his head. The men shook hands, saying their good-byes for the night. He closed the door behind them and sank into a nearby chair. Kidnappers demand ransoms, he thought. Could this be real? But why had they chosen him? He wasn't some kind of millionaire. Was Otto in on this? They had to talk. Tonight.

CHAPTER 13

It had been a long and mostly boring day at the Lake Pine motel. Donna was fully cooperative. She was too scared to do anything else. Rose read old magazines and tried to nap. Ray had taken the van and gone through a fast-food drive through nearby to bring back lunch. Kidnapping was becoming tedious.

Ray glanced at his watch again for perhaps the one hundredth time that day. It was almost five. Time for the early news on the Raleigh channels. He stood up and looked at Rose. "I'm going up to the office. See what's on the news."

"Can I go too?" asked Rose sarcastically.

"Sure," said Ray. "Make yourself a nametag and come on up."

Rose stuck her tongue out at Ray and went back to her year-old copy of People magazine. Donna found none of it amusing and continued to sit silently staring at the windows, wondering what lay on the other side of the curtains.

Ray closed the door quietly behind him. Out on the porch he paused to look around. Still no other guests on his side of the building. That was good, he thought. No one to nose around in their business. They didn't have to worry about cleaning staff either. Not that Bobby invested much in that for the motel, but Ray was paying by the week and had negotiated a few bucks off the rate in exchange for skipping the cleaning service each week.

He shoved his cellular in his back pocket, then walked around the building and started across the common area between the buildings. There was a young woman playing with her toddler in a sand box on the other side of the quad. Other than that, not a soul in sight. He wondered how much longer he would have to worry about it. He liked action, doing something. Sitting and waiting drove him nuts.

He pushed the office door open and found Bobby, alone as usual, head stuck in a book, television running behind him. He looked up and grunted a gravelly voiced howdy.

"Hey, Bobby. What's news?"

Bobby just pointed at the television and took a sip of his afternoon Jack and Coke cocktail. "All the news you want. Right there."

"How's the coffee?" asked Ray.

"Old. This ain't Starbucks."

"No shit. I'll have some anyway. See what's happening in the big city."

"Suit yourself," said Bobby, diving back into his book.

Ray poured himself a cup of coffee and sat down in one of the two chairs by the coffee table. He took a sip. Bobby was right. It was old coffee. He was only halfway paying attention to the television as he waited for any news on their break in. Fifteen minutes in he was about to give up when he got what he came for.

"An update on a story we first broke for you on Tuesday," said the news anchor. This, of course, was a bit of a ridiculous statement since every news show in Raleigh had "broken" the story that day. "We told you about a break-in and assault out on East Lane Drive late Tuesday morning at the home of Eddie and Donna Johnson. Let's go live for an update from police headquarters. Kat, what can you tell us?"

The picture changed to a reporter set up on the sidewalk outside the Raleigh police department. "Charlie, here's what we have learned. At least two men forced their way into the Johnson's home while Mrs. Johnson was there. Her husband came home and apparently surprised the intruders. Eddie Johnson suffered wounds and a concussion and was taken to Wake Memorial. Johnson spent a couple of days there and was released this afternoon."

"Good news there," said Charlie the anchor. "Any word on Mrs. Johnson?"

"Police remain rather tight lipped about Mrs. Johnson's status, Charlie. They are only saying that the investigation remains active at this time. Anyone who saw anything unusual in the neighborhood is encouraged to contact the police. Charlie, back to you."

As the anchor moved on to the next story, Ray was careful to sit quietly and pretend to continue watching. No need to create any memories for Bobby of him leaving at the end of this story. His mind was not so quiet though. It was mapping out plans and ideas to discuss with Nick as soon as the broadcast was over. He glanced at the clock on the wall next to the television. Nine more minutes until it ended.

Bobby spoiled his immediate plans by announcing he had to go to the bathroom and asking if Ray would watch the front for a few minutes. Ray reluctantly said yes, praying that Bobby only had to pee. Five minutes later, restless and ready to head out, he realized Bobby might be a bit longer.

He stood and stretched, drained the last of the coffee from the styrofoam cup and threw it in the wastebasket. As he did, he heard a car pull up. He turned to look out the door and saw an older model Jeep had parked in front of the office. The door opened and a man, dressed in jeans and a flannel shirt got out. The man reached his arm through the rear window and Ray noticed a dog sitting on the rear seat. After a few words to the dog the man came in the office.

"Howdy," the man said to Ray.

"Evening."

"Bobby still running this joint?"

"Yeah. He went back to the bathroom. Should be out in a minute."

"Good. You work here?"

"Nope."

"Just here for the amenities?" the man laughed as he asked the question.

"Something like that," Ray replied, eager now for Bobby to return.

"Yeah. me too. My dog loves the fresh baked treats. I'm partial to the spa myself." He laughed again. "We come here a couple of times each year. Do a little fishing, some hiking over in the state park."

"Sounds nice."

At that moment Bobby walked back into the office through a nearby hallway. "Pete," he exclaimed. "Been wondering where the hell you were. Figured you finally died off!"

"Not yet, you old codger. Still a lot of life left in these bones."

Ray decided to make his break. "I'll be seeing you, Bobby." Before Bobby or Pete could reply he pushed the office door open and walked out.

Pete watched him walk out, then turned back to Bobby. "One of your regulars now?"

Bobby scratched his head. "I guess you might say that. Been here a while now. Mostly keeps to himself."

"What's he do?" asked Pete.

"I dunno. Not my business to ask folks what they do."

Pete grinned and shook his head. "You never change, old friend."

"People want fun and games they can take a cruise. I just run a vintage motel with no frills."

"That's for damn sure. My usual room available?"

"Yep. How long you here for?"

"Two weeks. Got a little business to tend to this trip. Finally sold that piece of land out on Highway 98. Sale closes next week."

"Good for you. Here's your key," said Bobby. "Room service shuts down at 10:00 p.m."

Pete took the key and laughed. "I'll be sure to order by 9:00 p.m.! Sam and I will probably turn in early tonight. Long drive today."

"Sleep tight. Call me if you need something."

"Will do," replied Pete as he walked out of the office to his jeep.

Ray was retrieving a pack of smokes from the van as Pete drove around his building and parked in front of a corner room in the adjacent building. He had stopped on his walk from the office to talk for a moment to the young woman with the cute toddler. He nodded at Pete as he drove by, then quickly went into his own room.

Rose looked up as he closed the door. "Any news?"

"Yeah. Got some good news, and maybe some bad news. Good news is that our friend went home today."

Rose expressed the relief bottled up inside her. "That is really good news. And the bad?"

"New neighbor in the building next to us. Looks like he might be staying a while."

"Definitely not good news," said Rose. "Not good at all. We're going to need to be very careful. Stay low and keep her quiet."

"Yeah, we will," replied Ray. "But we can't do this setup for an extended period of time. Too risky. Still too cramped, even with them gone."

"That's for damn sure," muttered Rose. "What time is that doctor guy coming back to check on her?"

Ray glanced at his watch. "Won't be long. He said between 6:00 p.m. and 6:30 p.m. I need to talk to Nick. Going to do it in the bathroom. Keep an eye on her."

Ray walked into the small bathroom and closed the door to keep his conversation with Nick out of reach to Donna. Nick answered the second ring and Ray quickly updated him on the events of the last hour.

"How long can you keep things under wraps out there?" Nick asked.

"No way to know for sure. Maybe another hour. Maybe a year. Too many possibilities."

Nick was silent for a moment. "Yeah, I can see that. Got any ideas?"

"Yep. Remember that old cabin down east?"

"The one we used to stay in when we went duck hunting? Sure."

"I can take her down there. Lay low until it's time to trade her for the money."

Nick was silent again, processing the idea. "That's an option I suppose. Got any others?"

"Turn ourselves in."

This time Nick laughed. "I guess that's an option, too. Gonna pass on that one though. What about Rose?"

"Sending her back home. I can't stay cooped up with her much longer."

"I can see that too," said Nick. "Maybe it won't come to it, but the cabin idea is good with me. Right now, we need a plan to get in touch with Mr. Johnson about the ransom."

Nick and Ray talked for another ten minutes, finally settling on a plan for Nick to get in touch with Eddie about their demands. They also sketched out some ideas for how to exchange Donna for the money but agreed that needed more work. Ray could see that Drew was trying to reach him, so he told Nick he would call back later that night and finish up their plans. He punched up the call with Drew.

"Drew, where are you?"

"About five minutes out," he replied. "How's my patient?"

"Seems okay. Listen, some guy has checked into one of the rooms in the other building. Seems like the real chatty type. Keep it low and quiet when you get here."

"Gotcha. There in a few," Drew said as he hung up.

Ray ended the call on his phone and walked out of the bathroom. Rose looked up as he came out, questions on her face. "Well?" she asked.

"Drew will be here in a minute. We can talk while he's looking at her."

Rose just nodded and went back to her magazine.

Ray looked over at Donna, who was looking back at him. "You be nice while he's here, okay?"

Donna nodded. "I need to go to the bathroom."

"Rose, untie her legs."

Rose gave a heavy sigh of irritation but got up and did as she was told. They had put an improvised restraint on Donna with some chain and a padlock that secured one leg to the bed. They had decided this would allow them to get some sleep at night without risking her slipping out on them. Rose grabbed the padlock key from the top of the small fridge in the room and removed the restraint. Donna rubbed her ankle where the chain had been, mumbled thanks to Rose and walked into the bathroom, closing the door behind her.

Rose was waiting for Donna, shackles in hand, when she came out a few minutes later. She walked meekly over to the bed and sat down as Rose secured the lock. Ray stood at the window, peeking through the blinds as he waited for Drew to arrive. He turned and looked at Donna with indifference, then back out the window. A few moments later he saw Drew pulling in and he moved to the door. Three light knocks came, and Ray opened the door slightly.

Once he was sure it was Drew, he opened it enough to allow him in.

"Good to see you," said Drew as he pulled his jacket off. "How's it going?"

"Swell," said Ray. "Never better. Anyone out there?"

"Yeah. Your new neighbor was out. It looked like he was unpacking his Jeep. He didn't look my way though."

"Good. Make it quick with her. The less time you spend here the better." Drew nodded and walked over to Donna.

Ray motioned Rose into the bathroom to bring her up to speed on their plans. Rose took it all in without much comment. She was relieved when Ray told her he would go to the cabin without her if it came to that. Spending a few days in a cramped motel room with him was taking the shine off her infatuation. She was starting to regret getting involved in all this, but she did press him a bit on the ransom. Wanted to know what her cut would be. Ray coldly told her they hadn't worked that out yet and she shouldn't be counting her chickens before they hatched.

"I didn't do all this shit for nothing," she said to Ray. "I deserve a fourth of the money."

Ray couldn't help but laugh a little. "Don't get your hopes too high on that much, kitten. You didn't come up with this or plan it, and you damn sure didn't go in that house with us."

"You better not try and screw me over," Rose hissed angrily. "I've done my part."

"Look, no one's going to screw you over. We're gonna take care of you. Okay?"

"Yeah, okay. You better. That it? Anything else I need to know?"

Ray shook his head and opened the door for the two of them to leave. Drew was wrapping a fresh bandage on Donna when they came out. Almost on cue, there was a loud knock at the door. Everyone froze and then instinctively turned to look at Ray. He held one finger up to his lips to motion them all to be silent. He held his breath and waited. The knocks came again.

Ray walked up to the door. "Who is it?"

"It's another guest," came the reply on the other side. "I saw your friend go in a moment ago. He dropped something out here on the porch. Looks like some medical supplies of some kind. Thought you might need it. Everything okay in there?"

Ray turned and glared at Drew, who mouthed back a silent apology. He stared at Donna also, easily getting the message across that she had better remain quiet. Donna didn't like the odds at the moment and kept her mouth closed.

"Yeah. All good. Just leave it on the chair out there. I'll get it in a few."

"Sure thing. I'm over in 37 if you need anything. Name's Pete."

"Okay. Thanks, Pete."

Everyone in the room remained quietly frozen in place for a couple of minutes. Pete's footsteps gradually faded away and Ray exhaled. "What the hell?" he asked, looking at Drew.

"Sorry, man. I had three or four packs of gauze in my hand. One of them must have slipped out."

"It's done now," snapped Ray. "Hurry up with her and get out of here. Don't let that guy stop you to talk on the way out. I'll call you later."

"Gotcha. Will do."

Drew turned back to Donna, hurriedly finishing the process of wrapping her arm. Ray, brooding about what had just happened, poured himself a shot of bourbon and threw it back. He poured another more generous serving to sip on.

Rose tried to get back into her magazine, but she was worried they were going to have to bail out of the motel now. Any distance away from Ray and the gang probably lessened her chances of seeing a payday. Of course, she had the leverage of going to the cops, but who knew how that would turn out for her. And she wondered what Drew's angle on this was. Surely he was in it for something now as well.

Drew's voice brought her back to the room. "Okay. It's done. She should be good with that bandage for a couple of days and I'm leaving you with extras and some tape. Make sure she takes those antibiotics. Sorry again about the slip up. Call me later."

Ray nodded and opened the door, looking around the parking lot for Pete. No sign of him so he stepped aside and motioned for Drew to come by him. "Thanks, man."

As he shut the door, Rose looked up. "What now?"

"Time for a road trip," he said softly as he punched in the numbers to give Nick the news.

CHAPTER 14

Bill felt a minor surge of panic as he drove up to the gate at Johnson Auto just before the lot was to open for business. The gates were standing open. Had he forgotten to close them up last night when he left? He had worked until almost eight, then rushed out to get to dinner, his mind on things at home. He put his truck in park and stepped out to examine the chains and padlock that were used to secure the gates. No sign of forced entry. He looked across the lot towards the office building, noticing a light burning inside. Shit, he thought, maybe he had left the gates open. He hoped he had remembered to lock the office door at least.

He got back in his truck and pulled onto the lot, parking in his usual spot to the side of the office. As he got out, he scanned the rest of the lot, looking to see if any vehicles might be missing. None that he could tell. That's a relief he said to himself as he walked up the steps. Another panic surge came as he tried the door handle. Unlocked. Cautiously, he pushed the door open. Hearing sounds, he looked over towards Eddie's office and was surprised to see him behind the desk, his head buried in a report. Bill hurriedly walked over and stood in the office doorway.

"Eddie! What the hey man?"

"Morning, Bill. Can't sit at home all day staring at the walls. Thought I'd come out here and harass you."

"Good to see you, but are you sure you are up to this?"

Eddie sighed and laid the report down on the desk. "To tell you the truth, I'm having a hard time focusing on the words. And I can feel a headache starting to rumble around."

Bill nodded. "Yep. Concussion will do that to you. Used to happen to me back in my football days. Maybe leave those alone for a while," he said, pointing to the reports.

"Yeah. I guess so."

"Any word on Donna yet?"

"Nothing. Cops came over last night. They think it might be a kidnapping."

"No way!" Bill sat down in one of the side chairs across from Eddie and listened as he recounted the detectives visit the night before. He would occasionally interrupt him to ask a question. The gravity of what had happened was starting to settle on him for the first time. How could someone kidnap Donna? He could see the exhaustion now in Eddie. The deep worry that was on him like Carolina humidity in the summer. Relentless. Making it hard to breathe.

After a while, Bill got up and refreshed their coffees. He offered to run out and get breakfast for Eddie, but he declined. Bill settled back in the chair and asked Eddie about the break-in and what had happened at their house. After this retelling, they fell silent, faces lost in their coffee cups.

Mercifully, Lila burst through the door. She let out a squeal of delight when she realized her boss was in his office and rushed in to hug him. "Eddie Johnson! What are you doing here in this office? You better get home and take it easy for a couple of days."

This brought a smile to Eddie's face. He told Lila how he couldn't stay at home. She badgered him about following doctor's orders. Back and forth it went for a while. Bill found an opening to slip out to his desk to attend to some paperwork. Lila eventually ran out of steam and left Eddie's office. She settled in at her desk and started on that morning's paperwork.

Eddie sat alone in his office, alternately staring out the window at his employees and then off into nothingness. He was there, but he wasn't. He wondered if Otto was in the garage yet. Otto rarely checked in at the office when he showed up, preferring to skip the social banter that typically started the day. He liked to just get straight to the solitude of the garage and the hands-on of his work.

Eddie thought about the conversation with Otto the night before, after the detectives had left. Otto refused to come over, but they did talk over the phone. Eddie pressed him on whether he had told someone about their rollback scheme. Otto had flatly denied it and pressed back. After a few more minutes of heated back and forth they settled down into an uneasy truce and pledged to let each other know if anything came up that they felt might be tied to the crime. Otto offered what seemed a genuine hope that Donna came back safely and they ended the call. Eddie had sat for a long time after the call wondering if he could trust Otto. Now he sat in his office wondering the same thing, asking himself over and over how he might find out for sure. No answers came his way, so he just sat there, waiting for what was next.

A few miles away, Jimmy Quinn was also waiting for what was next. He had decided it was time for a bike ride, something he had not done since the previous spring. Jimmy wasn't a serious biker, but he could knock out a 20-mile ride easily. At least he hoped he still could. Riding gave his mind room to wander, and he was looking for a creative spark while he rode, something to connect more of the dots surrounding Eddie and Donna Johnson.

Jimmy had chosen to ride the portion of the Greenway known as the Neuse River Trail. The trail ran beside the river for miles, and the combination of water, woods and fresh air was just what he needed. He parked his Jeep Wrangler that morning in a small lot not far from the dam. After stretching for a bit, he hopped onto the familiar feel of the bike's saddle and headed south.

As he rode, he clicked through all they knew so far, which still wasn't much. Eddie had no obvious suspicious traits, and their marriage by all accounts was good. Otto had a history of criminal activity, but his alibi was rock solid and there was nothing else at the moment that tied him to it. If it was simply a breaking and entering robbery, then it was either random or someone who knew about Eddie's business and was hoping to find a lot of cash.

Jimmy thought more about this last possibility as he made his way under the Highway 1 overpass. With a second, and maybe even a third person involved, they must have been after a lot of cash to make the risk worth it. Could they really have been after car business cash? The way Eddie described it a few thousand dollars was a big cash day since most of the sales involved checks or money orders. Not much money to split three ways. He couldn't rule this out, but it seemed like a long shot.

Jimmy sipped some water from the bottle stashed inside the bike's water bottle cage. He was starting to warm up now. He thought about the random robbery angle. This didn't feel right either. Multiple people in broad daylight was risky. They had to be desperate or have some idea of a big payout inside.

He was so deep in thought on this one that he almost ran his bike into a woman running on the path in front of him. She heard him coming and looked back in time to step off the path. She stopped running, hands on hips, glaring at him as he came to a stop to turn and apologize. He was already yelling "Sorry, my bad" as he was turning around. Surprise covered his face when he recognized her as Dr. Harrington from their visit to Eddie in the hospital.

She laughed out loud when she, too, recognized Jimmy. "Do you want me to end up in my own hospital?"

Jimmy walked his bike sheepishly a few yards back to her. "No. Oh my god. I'm so sorry. No excuse for that. I could have hurt you badly."

"And yourself. Thinking about work instead of what you're doing?" He nodded.

"Well," she said, "that's not a good idea when you're hurtling along at twenty miles an hour with other people around."

"Yeah. Working on this case in my head. Getting out here helps me think." Jimmy moved his bike off the path as two other bikers came riding through. "How about you? Just out here for the exercise?"

She smiled. "No. It helps me think about some things too. But I do like the exercise part. You do a lot of biking?"

Jimmy sighed. "I did when I was younger. Gave it up when the kids came along. I just didn't have time. Today is my first time out since last spring."

Dani kneeled to retie her shoes. "Used to do a little biking in college. Gave it up when a friend got hit by a car one day." She stood and looked up and down the trail. "Probably less chance of that happening out here."

Jimmy saw an opening. "Maybe we could ride together sometime. Out here."

"Maybe," she said, a coy smile on her face. "Right now, however, I need to finish up this run so I can get to work."

"Yeah. Look, I'm really sorry I almost hit you."

"Thanks. Don't be too hard on yourself. It might all work out in the end," she replied, with a mischievous smile on her face. With a wave of her hand, she turned to run back the way they had come, leaving Jimmy standing there with a grin on his face.

He stood and watched her fade around a bend, then he got back on and started pedaling. Was her comment about things working out in the end an invitation to ask her out, or was she just yanking his chain? Only one way to find out, he concluded, and he resolved to call her later that day.

The adrenaline from his chance encounter with Dani Harrington layered on top of the adrenaline from the case and soon he was flying back down the trail. He picked the thread he had been working on back up, the idea of it being a random robbery. He pondered that some more and decided that it just didn't fit. Not many break-ins like this ever ended up being random. There was a connection somewhere.

Was it possible Eddie, or even both the Johnsons, could be in the drug business? They hadn't considered that angle. The crime scene team hadn't seen any evidence of that, but they hadn't searched their house for that purpose. They would need probable cause and a search warrant for that, and Jimmy and Micky wouldn't have anything to give a judge right now but a hunch, so the search warrant was out for the moment. Still, he would talk to Micky about this angle.

Rachel Wilson had recalled seeing two cars in the neighborhood that morning that weren't familiar to her. He discarded the red Trans Am and focused on the brown van. Micky had someone running DMV checks for all older model brown vans registered in Wake County. They would sort through those but running them down would take a while.

He came back around to Otto. Maybe they should dig further into Otto, shake him up some more and see if anything fell out. He decided to ask Tommy to nose around a little in the Wilmington area, see what he might come up with. This was where Otto had lived before coming to work in Raleigh.

Jimmy realized that the last half mile to his Jeep was now in front of him, so he put aside detective work and cranked up his pace. Minutes later he wheeled into the parking lot, breathing hard, but happy, and pulled up beside his Jeep. He removed his helmet and leaned his bike against the car to stretch. After that, he drained the last of his water bottle and hoisted the bike back on the rack.

It hit him as he fastened the last strap. Doorbell cameras, he suddenly thought. What if one of the neighbors had a doorbell cam and had footage of the brown van? They would get a patrolman out checking this today. Maybe they could catch a break and clearly identify the van or its occupants.

Jimmy finished loading up the bike and cranked the Jeep to head home for a shower. As he drove, he punched up Micky and brought him up to speed on his thoughts from the morning. They agreed to meet in their offices later that morning to look at the DMV info on the van. He hung up and turned up the volume on the radio, excited from his progress and feeling good from the ride. Oh, and Dani Harrington, he remembered. How much better could this morning get!

Otto drove into the car lot twenty minutes past his normal start time, sporting the dry mouth and aching head that comes with a hangover. He had stayed up long after the call with Eddie the night before, sorting through options and what-ifs.

He had a good thing going with the Rezaviks and the car lot. Eddie bought a few cars from them at wholesale every month, and they came to the lot for Otto to inspect and make minor repairs as needed before they hit the lot for sale. What Eddie didn't know is they each came with an extra feature, bags of fentanyl laced cocaine and heroin. Otto's job was to remove them and pack them up for transport to a drop for the Rezavik's dealer based in Raleigh. The drop place changed frequently. He would pick up bags of cash left at the drop in exchange for the drugs. While he never saw the dealer, he felt the eyes of someone watching him every trip, making sure he didn't leave with the drugs and the money.

He would keep the bags of money hidden in his apartment until he got instructions from the Rezaviks on where to leave the bags of cash, another drop that frequently changed. Having a few million dollars hidden in his possession wasn't unusual. Neither were the urges to take the money and run. But they would find him. He knew that. So, he kept going. The money they paid him for his services was growing, wired to an offshore account after each successful drop.

After finally passing out on his couch around three, he slept like the dead until the resurrection of his alarm clock came at its appointed time. He had laid on the couch debating whether to go in or not. No sense in creating any suspicions, so here he was, steeling himself to make it through the day. He thought about popping a painkiller for his head but decided against mixing business and pleasure. A bottle of Tylenol awaited him in the garage.

He glanced into the office as he drove towards the garage in the back. Eddie was walking by the front windows. Bastard probably came in to keep an eye on me, he thought. Well guess what, Edward, I'm here to keep an eye on you, he muttered to himself as he pulled into his space by the garage. He got out of his truck and slammed the door shut, immediately regretting it as the noise bounced off his skull. After some black coffee and the brake job he needed to finish up, he would call his friends in Wilmington. Just before passing out last night, he had decided it was better to keep them informed about events with Donna. Who knows, he thought, as he pushed open the garage door, he might just need their help before all this was over.

CHAPTER 15

Ray was already awake and staring out the window when Rose opened her eyes. Through the part in the curtains, she could see the first faint stirrings of daylight. Ray had his back to her, and he occasionally sipped from a cup he was holding. She lay there silently, staring at him. A week ago, she thought she was starting to feel something for him. Now she wasn't so sure.

Rose turned her gaze away from Ray and it landed on Donna, who lay in the other bed softly snoring. Rose marveled at how the woman could sleep. She had been kidnapped, for Christ's sake. If it were her, she started to think - then shut it down. No, she couldn't go there. It wasn't her. Nope. She was playing the role of the kidnapper today, not the victim.

She brushed her hair away from her face and sat up in bed. Ray heard her movements and turned to look at her. He nodded and turned back to the window. Rose sat there and thought about what was next. Ray would leave with Donna that morning, headed to God knows where down east. Some cabin, but he wouldn't say exactly where. He had told her the night before that it was for her own good. Best she didn't know.

She was supposed to return home. Home to her crappy apartment.

Home to her boring, dead-end life. Home to search for another job, probably waiting tables again in some half-ass meat-and-three dive. Home to wondering if she would ever see any payday from this stupid mess she had gotten herself into.

She looked at Ray again. Made up her mind right then that she didn't have any feelings for him. At least none that were romantic. He was decent enough in the sack, she thought. But hell, there were plenty of guys for that. Maybe it was for the best that she was headed back to Raleigh. She could close this chapter and move on. Resolute now, she pulled her hair back into a ponytail and threw the bed covers off, rising into that next chapter.

Otto fastened the last lug nut tightly against the wheel rim on the Toyota Camry, then reached over and hit the button on the lift to lower the car to the garage floor. The coffee and the Tylenol had worked their magic, and he was feeling almost human again. Time to call his friends in Wilmington, he thought. After peeking out the garage door to make sure no one from the office was headed his way, he took out his cell phone and punched in the number. Bruno Rezavik answered on the fourth ring.

"Rezavik here."

"Morning, Mr. Rezavik. It's Otto. Otto Sutter."

"Otto, to what do I owe this great pleasure?"

Otto cleared his throat. He always got a little nervous talking to Bruno. He and his brother were dangerous men, but especially Bruno Rezavik. He was more of the muscle, his brother Anton the brains.

"Well, there's something going on up here that I thought you might want to know about."

"Yes, what is it?" Bruno asked.

"It's Eddie. And his wife. Someone broke into their home. Beat Eddie up pretty badly. Donna is missing."

"I see. This sounds most unfortunate. How is Edward? He is still alive?"

Otto cleared his throat again. "Oh, yeah. Eddie's alive. In fact, he is back at work today."

"And his wife? What of her?"

"They are not sure. She's been missing since it happened. There's a couple of detectives involved. They have been snooping around out here."

Bruno was silent for a moment.

"Mr. Rezavik?"

"Yes, yes. I am here, Otto. These detectives, they have talked to you?"

"Uh, yes. They have. They don't have any reason to suspect me of anything. I wasn't in on this. That would be stupid."

"Yes. That would indeed be stupid," replied Bruno. "To be involved in other criminal activity given your history, and your, umm... how shall I say this, your other extracurricular activities."

Otto swallowed hard. Should he come clean now about the rollback business? Or just let it stay hidden and hope it never came to light? They might let it slide if he promised to shut it down. Then again, they didn't like being lied to. He decided to keep his mouth shut, and to make sure Eddie did the same.

"Otto, is there anything else you wish to tell me?"

"No sir. That's it. Just thought you both should know."

"Yes. It is good that you called me. Keep me informed, Otto. Especially of the activities of these detectives."

"Yes sir. I will," said Otto. "Goodbye sir", he added, but Bruno had already ended the call. Otto pocketed his phone, then walked over and leaned against the Camry. Should he try and get closer to Quinn and Bondurant to find out what was going on, or just lay low? Regular contact with the police wasn't a normal thing for him to consider. Maybe he should stay closer to Eddie instead, find out what to pass along to the Rezaviks that way. After their heated call the night before, he needed to smooth things over anyway. He couldn't have Eddie mistrusting him. Not right now.

Bruno Rezavik placed his phone on the huge, two-sided desk that he shared with his brother, Anton. They shared the desk by choice, not necessity. For much of their early years, growing up in war-torn Yugoslavia, they had been forced to share everything out of necessity. Food, clothing, a small bedroom, and eventually the slaughter of their parents and sister. An uncle in the United States had managed to get them visas to come over and they arrived in their late teen years, settling at first in Virginia and then later moving with their uncle and his family to Wilmington. Bruno was the older, by a year, and had always played the role of protector to his little brother. Not that Anton needed it anymore.

The desk they shared sat in an office constructed in one of the several warehouses they owned. The warehouses held the many products of their import business, which provided them with a very comfortable living. They had branched into other business ventures in recent years, including the loan origination service they provided for Johnson Auto and many small auto dealers like them scattered across the Carolinas and Virginia.

Anton looked up from the papers on his side of the desk, carefully studying his brother's face. He arched his eyebrows, prompting Bruno to speak.

"That was our friend in Raleigh," he said. "It seems there has been some unfortunate events that have struck the Johnsons."

"Yes, what has happened?" asked Anton.

"A home invasion. Edward was injured. His wife is missing."

"Hmm. That is unfortunate. Do the police have suspects in custody?"

"It would seem not yet. Edward has recovered enough to return to his business, though."

Anton took his reading glasses off and set them on the desk in front of him. "Surely our friend Otto is not involved in this."

"Surely not," agreed Bruno." It would be most unfortunate if he were. I do not believe him to be that foolish."

"Still, we must keep our minds open to that possibility. See what more you can find out. We must call our friend Edward and offer our sympathies. I shall do that this afternoon."

Bruno nodded and turned to his computer to search for news of the event in Raleigh. His brother put his glasses back on and returned to the business at hand after making a note on his calendar to call Eddie.

Leaving the Lake Pine motel to head down east had proved to be a little bit of a logistical challenge, thought Ray. One that had required Nick and Penny to come back out to help. The only vehicle they still had at the motel was Ray's pickup truck. That surely wouldn't do the trick to take Donna away. She had to be tied up and gagged to ensure she didn't try and run or scream, so having her sitting in the front of his pickup as he drove the three plus hours to the cabin was a non-starter.

He and Nick had debated which was the better alternative, the stolen van they had used the day of the break-in, or the now also stolen Chevy Tahoe belonging to Eddie they had taken when they left the Johnson's home. In the end the Tahoe seemed less likely to give him any mechanical problems, so it had won out.

As he closed the rear doors of the Tahoe, he reflected further on the choreography it had taken to get from the room at the motel that morning to the point of departure. First, Penny had to drop Nick off at the spot where they had hidden the van. Then they had to deal with Ray's pickup truck. Ray had informed Bobby he would be away from the motel for a while, so they couldn't leave his truck parked there without potentially drawing further attention.

Nick and Penny lived in an old, rented farmhouse not far from Falls Lake. The house was off a rarely used paved road with few other houses, and then about a quarter mile down a dirt path. Secluded. Just the way Nick wanted to live. The Tahoe had been hidden inside an old barn on their property, and the van parked down yet another long-forgotten dirt path not far away, deep in the woods around the lake. Penny drove Nick in the van to the Tahoe. Nick drove the van to Lake Pine while Penny headed to a rendezvous spot in the Tahoe. Nick then returned to their house, hiding Ray's truck in the barn.

After clearing up Ray's room, removing any evidence that Ray had Donna and the others with him, Ray and Rose had hustled Donna into the van and headed to the rendezvous with Penny. Donna was now safely bound and gagged in the rear of the Tahoe, terrified and wondering what fate awaited her next.

Ray turned from the rear of the Tahoe, shaking his head. Too damn many moving parts to this deal he thought. Something was going to break on them and bring it all crashing down.

Penny exhaled a cloud of smoke from her cigarette and stared at him. "Whatcha shaking your head for, Ray? There a problem?"

Ray stared back. "The whole damn things a problem, Penny. Wouldn't you agree?"

Penny laughed and threw her cigarette on the ground, grinding it with her heel. "You want me to take her down there, Ray? Losing your nerve?"

"Don't you worry about me, Penny. I'll see this through. Me losing my nerve is the last thing you need to be concerned with."

"What about her?" she said, nodding at Rose.

Ray looked at Rose. "She's going back home for now. Drop her off after you drop the van."

Penny nodded. "Come on girlfriend. Let's get the hell out of here." She looked back at Ray. "Nick says call him when you get there."

"Yeah. Will do. Ya'll delivering the ransom note today?"

"Yep."

"Good." He turned to Rose. "Keep a low profile and keep your mouth shut. I'll check in with you while I'm away. Okay?"

Rose nodded. "Don't forget about me on this Ray."

Penny and Rose watched him drive away before getting into the van. Penny started the van, easing it into gear and pulled out onto the road. She lit another cigarette and looked over at Rose. "Hard to watch your man leave with another woman, sweetheart?" she asked, laughing as she reached to turn up the volume on the radio.

Rose didn't reply, choosing instead to look out her window as the landscape sped by. He's not my man, she thought. She would put them all in her rear-view mirror just as soon as she got her payout. Then she might just head back down to Florida. Find her a real man.

CHAPTER 16

The Outer Banks of North Carolina lie about three hours east of Raleigh. Ray had taken Highway 98 east after leaving Penny and Rose early that morning. There were two primary roads to take if you wanted to drive to the Banks, Highway 64 or its close cousin highway 264. 64 was a fairly straight shot and was four lanes almost the entire way. 264 was the southern route, meandering through a lot of small towns and lying not far off the Pamlico River and Pamlico Sound for the last half of the trip before it reconnects to Highway 64 just before a small hamlet called Manns Harbor. Ray chose the southern route because it was more isolated, and he liked the flat lands along the water with their forests and sections of open fields choked with vegetation.

His destination was a few miles south of Manns Harbor, down a dirt road off 264 in an area known as the Alligator River National Wildlife Refuge. The Refuge is home to parks and one of the highest concentrations of black bears on the east coast of the United States. It also has sections that most humans just don't care to venture into, overrun with dense brush, thorny bushes, and snakes of more than one species.

Deep in one of these sections was a cabin owned by a group of duck hunters from New Jersey, one of which had been in Ray's unit in Iraq. The group came down to hunt ducks a couple of times each year, but that was always later in the fall and winter. Ray had joined them once or twice before. The cabin would be empty, and best of all, secluded, this time of the year.

After about four hours of cautious driving, Ray found the turnoff he was seeking. There were no other cars in sight, ahead or behind, as he left the pavement of the highway and felt the tires bite into the gravel and red dirt of the road to the cabin. A few yards in he had to stop the SUV and deal with the metal barrier blocking further access to the road. The barrier had arms coming from either side with heavy logging chain and a padlock holding them together

Although he had to pee like a racehorse, Ray ignored the urge and moved quickly to limit the possibility of being seen by someone driving through on 264. He opened the door behind the driver's seat, pulling more chain and another padlock from the floorboard, along with a pair of heavy-duty cutters that would slice through the chain already on the barrier.

The cutters did their work as planned and the chain dropped from the barrier onto the ground below. Ray pushed the arms open on each side, then scooped up the fallen section of chain. Throwing it on the floorboard of the rear seats, he glanced into the back of the SUV at Donna. Wide eyed but silent, she just looked back at Ray flatly.

"We're driving down to a cabin," he said. "No one around here, so yelling won't help you. If somehow you manage to get away from me, there are more bears in these woods than you can imagine. Not safe for someone to thrash around out there. You hear me?" Donna nodded, her face still without expression. "Not going to hurt you," he said. "Just cooperate with me."

With that, he closed the rear door and got behind the wheel. After driving just past the barriers, he stopped the vehicle and used the chain and padlock he had brought with them to lock the arms back across the path. He got back into the Tahoe and started slowly down the path to the cabin.

The pine trees were thick on both sides of the path. An occasional limb in the roadway, or deeper rut forced him to navigate around a bit, but thankfully there were no trees fallen across the path. The Outer Banks got more than their share of hurricanes, tropical storms, and nor'easters, and the shallow root structures of pines made them an easy target for strong winds.

Around a half mile in, the trees gave way to an open field on the right side, full of brush and tall grass. He remembered the cabin as being tucked back a ways into the field. A few more yards and then he saw it. The driveway, if you could call it that, was overgrown, but no problem for the Tahoe and he pulled off the path and down the drive to the cabin. Ray didn't expect anyone to be in the cabin, but he was a cautious man, so he grabbed his 9mm from beneath the seat and eased it out of its holster. "I'm going to make sure it's just us, then I'll come get you out of the back of this truck."

Holding the pistol down by his side, Ray walked to the right side of the cabin first. It was a simply designed structure. A large open area in the front for the kitchen, eating and social area, with large bedrooms sandwiching the lone bathroom in the back. He made his way quickly around the sides and back, peering into each window carefully as he went. No sign of life.

Ray felt underneath the corner of the front porch, locating the key he expected to be there. It was. He walked up to the front entrance and knocked on the door. One last precaution. No sounds in reply from within, so he unlocked the door and stepped in. The stillness inside was welcoming, the musty smell of a long unopened building less so. He glanced inside the bedrooms, which had bunks on each of the walls. Then inside the bathroom. Nothing.

Back at the SUV, he opened a side door to reach for the couple of bags of food he had brought. Enough to feed them for a couple of days, then he would need to go for more provisions. Who knew how long this might take, he wondered. Looking at Donna, he said "Need to put these inside. After that you go in. Quietly," he emphasized. Donna nodded her head.

After Ray walked away, Donna sat up in the rear of the SUV. She looked out the windows, photographing her surroundings in her mind. Pine trees surrounded the cabin in every direction, save the path back out to the road and a narrower footpath that led in the opposite direction. She wondered where that went. Probably down to a field or pond. She realized this was a hunting cabin of some sort. She also knew Ray wasn't bluffing on the snakes and bears. Given the terrain and length of time they traveled to get there they were likely down on the coast of North Carolina somewhere. Maybe at the Outer Banks, she thought. Wilmington wouldn't have taken this long to get to.

Despite her predicament, this place seemed wonderfully peaceful. And Ray, something about him was trustworthy and made her feel safe, and this surprised her. She didn't doubt he would do whatever he had to but compared to the rest of her captors there seemed to be a kindness in him, not far from the surface. As long as she didn't do anything stupid, she thought, I'll probably be okay.

She turned and watched Ray make his way out of the cabin and back towards the Tahoe. What kind of life led him to this, she wondered. He clearly wasn't stupid. The other one, Nick, also seemed smart. How do people get themselves into this stuff? They seemed to believe Eddie was involved in something illegal too. Was it possible? Her Eddie? She decided she would play nice with Ray, see what he really knew about Eddie.

"You ready to get out of there?" Ray asked after he opened the rear doors. She nodded and held her hand out for him to help her get down. "Once we're inside I will cut those zip ties off of you. You give me trouble, though, I have a bag full of extras."

Donna nodded again and grabbed his hand as she slid her way out of the truck. It felt good to be standing and not cramped up anymore.

She took in a deep breath of the Carolina spring air, suddenly grateful she was still alive.

Ray stepped aside and motioned for her to walk in front of him. Once inside the cabin, Ray closed the door behind them and slid the deadbolt across. "I imagine you need to pee," he said to her. He pointed to the bathroom. "Should be some toilet paper in there. Yell out to me if there's not. I brought a couple of rolls.

"Oh... Okay," she managed to get out. "I'm really thirsty too." Ray nodded and walked over to one of the counters in the kitchen area, grabbing a bottled water and handing it to her. "Thank you," said Donna, as she turned and walked to the bathroom. Ray watched until the door closed behind her, then he began unpacking the supplies on the counter.

In a few minutes the bathroom door opened, and Donna walked out slowly. "My arm is hurting me a bit. Can I have something for the pain?"

Ray nodded and pushed a bottle of Advil across the counter. "You hungry?" he asked.

"Yeah. Kind of. A little."

"Okay. Have a seat and I'll fix you a sandwich. Turkey. You want cheese on it?"

"Yes."

Ray set about making the sandwich while Donna pulled out one of the chairs at the picnic-style table in the cabin. She blew off the dust that had settled on the chair and was staring at the dust on the table when Ray held out some paper towels to her. After cleaning up the table, she wadded them up and looked around for a trash can. Ray pointed to the counter. "Just leave 'em up there. I'll take care of it later."

She sat down at the table and Ray placed a paper plate with the sandwich in front of her. "You drinking water or you want some pop?"

"Pop?"

"Yeah. Soda. Diet coke."

"Why do you call it pop?"

He shrugged. "Just what it was called where I grew up."

She nodded. "Yes. Some pop would be good."

Ray handed her a Diet Coke, then sat across the table from her. They ate in silence, slowly making their way through the sandwiches. Ray started thinking about what was next. They had enough food for a couple of days, but he was going to tire of sandwiches soon enough. Mann's Harbor was nearby and had a small grocery store. He could probably zip tie her to a bed or a chair long enough for him to make the run to the store. He decided he would do that the next day, or maybe early the morning after. Hard to know how long they would have to stay here, so it was probably best to get enough for a few days and go back later if needed.

He glanced across the table at Donna. She was staring down at her plate while she slowly chewed the food. She looked a bit rough after the ordeal of the last couple of days but was an attractive woman he thought. He let his mind wander a bit, thinking about what life would be like if he had found someone like her and settled down somewhere. White picket fence, kids, all that stuff. Probably too late now, and he couldn't imagine it being with Rose. She was too damn clingy and needy. Someone with an independent streak. That's what he needed.

They ate the rest of the meal in silence, mostly with their heads down or staring off into space without looking at each other. Donna finally broke the silence. "How long will you keep me here?"

Ray drained the last of his Diet Coke, then balled up the paper plate and napkin. He rose from the table, reaching across to grab her empty plate as well. "You done?" he asked.

She nodded and looked at him for an answer to her question. "Well?"

"Don't know. Until it's time to go."

"What kind of..." she started to say and stopped as Ray held up a hand.

"Look, I said I don't know, and I meant I don't know. This is going to get pretty annoying if you keep asking me questions I don't have answers for." He threw the trash in a can nearby and turned back to face her. "I don't like being annoyed."

Donna nodded. "Okay. Can I ask another question?"

"Sure."

"What am I supposed to do all day while we're here?"

Ray smiled. "I can see you're starting to feel better."

"How's that?"

"Cause you're getting a little fire in your belly it seems. Pushing on me for answers and entertainment. Am I right?"

"Maybe."

"Well don't get too fired up. That might annoy me too." Ray looked at her with a half-smile on his face. "There's a small collection of books and magazines in that bunk room on the left. Maybe you can find something there. I need to go outside and check on a couple of things." Donna nodded and turned for the bunk room as Ray went out the front door.

The afternoon sun was getting long by the time Jimmy and Micky made their way back to police headquarters downtown. Micky, it turns out, loved the idea of canvassing the Johnson's neighborhood for doorbell cameras that might have captured the van and the Firebird. The sergeant responsible for assigning a patrol car to do that work, on the other hand, said he couldn't spare the manpower that day. After Jimmy and the sergeant got into a heated exchange, Micky stepped in to cool things down, and everyone remained friends. But the sergeant's answer remained no, and the two of them had done the canvassing themselves.

Jimmy turned the car off after pulling it into their assigned spot in the headquarters parking deck. Before he pulled the keys, he looked over at Micky, who was already smirking at him. "What?" asked Jimmy.

"Nothing," said Micky, barely stifling a laugh.

"No, come on. What is it?"

"Good to see a white man worn out for a change," Micky said with a grin as he opened the door and stepped out.

"I'm not white. I'm Irish."

"Guess that makes me not Black but French, huh?"

Jimmy closed the car door and looked at Micky over the top of the car. "Okay. Maybe the combination of the bike ride this morning and the hundred mile walk around that neighborhood was a lot for one day."

"Uh huh. Maybe," said Micky as he turned to walk into the building.

When they got upstairs to their floor, Jimmy grabbed some water bottles and met Micky in a small conference room equipped with a computer and large wall-mounted monitor that would allow them to view the contents of their meager showing for the day. He passed one bottle to Micky and both men drained them before Jimmy sat down at the table.

"I can't believe we have only two doorbell cameras to look at from all those houses in the neighborhood. Jeez, don't people feel unsafe anymore?" asked Jimmy.

Micky slid the room's laptop in front of him and hit the power button. While inserting the first thumb drive, he replied, "Technically, there were four. One house had no one home and we can get that warrant for the fourth one if you want." Micky said the last part with a sly grin on his face.

At one of the houses, they had encountered an older man who had lectured them on improper search and seizure procedures, universally used by the police, he claimed, to arrest and convict thousands of innocent citizens each year. Jimmy, to his credit, had remained calm and patiently explained to the man that they were asking for voluntary cooperation to help find the criminals who had viciously attacked one of his neighbors. To which the man loudly proclaimed "Get a warrant!" and shut the door in their face.

"We should haul his ass in here as a suspect."

Micky laughed. "I don't think that guy has the strength left in him to walk to the Johnson's house, much less tangle with Eddie."

"Yeah. I know. Just pisses me off."

As it was, they did find two people willing to download and share files from their doorbell cameras. They had previewed the videos at the homes enough to ensure that the vehicles had been captured by their cameras. In the office they could enlarge and better assess what had been recorded. Micky loaded up the first file, hit play, and both men stared intently at the screen.

The video moved forward, mostly with no vehicles and an occasional person out for their morning walk. A few minutes in, a brown van consistent with Rachel's description passed through. Then came a lot more of nothing, and finally a red Pontiac Trans Am rolled by.

"You know," said Micky, "We need to ID these walkers. Track them down and talk to them. See if they noticed anything that morning."

Jimmy nodded approvingly. "You're a damn good detective some days, Mick. I hadn't thought of that. Let's focus on the cars right now though. Roll it back at about one quarter speed and blow it up some."

Micky restarted the video. "This camera was on the passenger side of the vehicles. Might be a little harder to make out the drivers. House sits back a little further from the street too."

The video rolled forward, and they stopped it and moved frame by frame as the van and the Trans Am rolled by. Micky had been right about seeing the drivers less clearly. Jimmy remarked that there was something familiar about the Trans Am driver who clearly looked to be a man. The driver of the van was a woman, as Rachel had noted to them.

They moved the video back and forth several times, zooming in as much as they could, balancing the zoom factor against how grainy the image became the closer in they got. They captured several still photos of the vehicles and drivers for further study in their investigation.

These could also be used to show people they might interview in their search to identify the drivers.

Micky loaded the second video, and they ran the drill all over again. This camera had been from a home on the driver's side. Jimmy yelled stop at the first zoom in on the Trans Am and immediately started laughing. Micky leaned in closer, blew the image up some more, then also laughed when he realized what Jimmy had caught.

"Son of gun," exclaimed Micky. "Want to get that warrant now?"

"He might be too old to walk to Eddie's, but he is surely able to drive there." The man who had lectured them on police tactics was the one driving the Trans Am.

Micky turned back to the laptop and captured a few still images of the man and the car. He moved the video forward to the van and zoomed in closer. "Definitely a woman," he said. "We can get some pretty good images of her. Hard to tell, but she doesn't look dressed to be out painting or doing house repairs. Something about her and the van just don't fit."

"Roll it forward and see if we can get a read on the license plate."

Micky moved the video forward a few frames until the rear of the van was in the picture. He leaned forward again, then got up and walked to the screen. "Pretty grainy," he said with his back to Jimmy.

"Can't quite make out all the letters either. Starts with a D, I think, then maybe another D. Can't make out the next one. A three, I don't know, then a seven, then I don't know on the last one."

Jimmy wrote these down as Micky called them out, then repeated them to confirm.

"That's it," replied Micky. "I'll get Janie to start pushing these through the DMV database to see if we can get a match."

"What about the old dude?" asked Jimmy.

Micky smiled. "You think he's a suspect?"

"Naw. Just itchin' to hassle him a little, though," Jimmy smiled in return.

"Tell you what, let's see what we get back on this van. If it goes nowhere, we go back out there to the house where no one was home, plus we yank his chain a little bit. After all, he was exhibiting non cooperative behavior towards an active investigation."

Jimmy grinned and flashed a thumbs up. "How about the people walking and the other cars in the video?"

Micky sat back down at the table and pondered the question for a moment. "We could have Janie run through the videos and pull any other license plates she can see. She could also look through DMV records for that neighborhood, rule out any that belong to neighbors." Janie Williams was the research technician assigned to their division and often helped them on their cases.

Jimmy nodded. "Sounds good. We could show the video to Rachel. See how many of the walkers she could identify."

"Great idea on the doorbell cameras, Jimmy. It might turn up nothing, but it feels like movement."

"Thanks. Maybe a bike ride every day would help us get this one solved."

Micky glanced at his watch. "I'm meeting Julia for drinks and dinner at Revolution. You want to join us?"

Jimmy looked at his own watch and did some mental math. Should he call Dani Harrington and invite her? This was pretty short notice, a little over an hour from now. "Sure, thanks. I'll meet you there. I'll take the thumb drive with the videos to Janie's desk. Leave her a note for first thing tomorrow on what we need."

Micky nodded as he got up to leave the conference room and headed back to his desk. Jimmy watched him go, then pulled out his phone to try and reach Dani. Why not? he thought. He was on a roll.

CHAPTER 17

Rose had started in on her third vodka and soda by the time Tammy got to the Bull Chute. This wouldn't be so bad if not for the fact that it wasn't her third drink of the day. She had been nursing a drink of one kind or another almost continuously since Penny had dropped her off that morning, leaving her with a strong lecture about keeping her mouth shut. After a double Bloody Mary breakfast, she had napped on the couch for an hour, then had a bottle of wine and some cheese for lunch. She called Tammy and begged her to meet after work for more drinks. So here they were.

Tammy took a sip of her wine. Both women were quiet, looking around the bar. Tammy finally broke the silence. "Not much to look at in here, huh?"

Rose nodded. A tear trickled down her cheek and she wiped it away quickly, head down, staring into her vodka. Tammy gently put an arm around her shoulders. "Rose, what's wrong, baby? You can tell me anything. You know that."

Rose sniffled and pushed her drink away. "I lost my job."

"Oh, girl, we'll get you another one. I'll take care of you until we do," said Tammy, squeezing her shoulders a little tighter.

"It ain't just that," whispered Rose.

Tammy dropped her hands from Rose's shoulders and turned squarely to look at her friend. "Are you pregnant?"

Rose managed to laugh. "Hell no! I wish it was that simple." She reached for her drink and drained the last of it.

"What then?"

Now Rose turned to face Tammy. "I can't say. Not right now. Maybe one day when it's over."

"When it's over? What the hell does that mean?"

Rose just shook her head, the tears coming more freely now. "Tammy, I can't talk about it. With nobody. So don't ask. Okay?"

Tammy turned back on her barstool and reached for her glass. She took a couple of healthy swallows before she spoke again. "Rose, we've known each other a lot of years," she said softly. "I'll do anything to help you. No questions asked. You don't have to tell me anything. Just tell me what you need. You got that?"

Rose nodded, getting up from her stool to wrap her arms around Tammy in a big embrace. Tammy reached an arm back and found Rose's hand. She squeezed it tight and said, "Okay. No talking then. Not tonight. Let's have some drinks and some fun and forget all our problems for a while."

Jimmy paced nervously on the sidewalk outside Revolution, a trendy bar and restaurant in downtown Raleigh that served excellent Cuban food and fresh takes on the Mojito. As he waited for Dani Harrington to arrive, he also longed for his favorite drink at Revolution, the Canchanchara. A simple drink of rum, lime, and honey, but he could never quite duplicate at home the way they tasted at Revolution. Maybe because his walls at home weren't covered with posters of the Cuban independence wars.

When Jimmy introduced friends to the restaurant for the first time, most of them immediately linked the name to Fidel Castro. Most of them, it turns out, were ignorant of the three wars fought in the 1800's to gain independence for Cuba from Spain. In fact, as he reflected on this, he realized most of them were largely ignorant of the history of Cuba and its somewhat uneven relationship with the United States. He wondered if he would have to explain all this to Dani as well, and was so lost in that thought he almost didn't know how to respond when she suddenly appeared, looked up at the sign and asked "Which revolution are we celebrating tonight? Fidel's or the real ones back in the 1800's?"

"Whichever you prefer," he replied, recovering rather quickly, he thought to himself. "Glad you could join us."

"Yeah. me too. You're buying. Least you could do after almost running me over with that bicycle."

Jimmy gave her his smile and swept his arm toward the door. "After you, your Grace." She curtsied slightly in reply and walked up to the entrance. He beat her to the door handle and opened it for her to step inside. After closing it behind them, he stood at the reception stand. The hostess, on the phone, held up one finger to let him know it would be a minute. He nodded and turned to look at Dani.

Dani was looking around the lobby at the various posters and prints celebrating the history of Cuba. She was attractive enough in those hospital scrubs, he thought, but it just wasn't fair how good she looked in that dress. Elegant, yet casual. Stylish without being pretentious. Wow, he thought. She's smart and gorgeous.

The hostess hung up the phone and smiled. "Jimmy," she said warmly, "so good to see you again. It's been a minute."

"Hi, Jackie. Good to see you too. Sorry I haven't been in lately. Glad to be back."

"Glad to have you back. Your table is ready, and Micky and Jules are already seated. Are you and your friend ready?"

By now Dani had walked over beside him. She grinned slyly. "Didn't realize you were such a celebrity, Mr. Quinn." To which Jimmy blushed slightly before taking her arm and introducing her to Jackie, who managed to extract her name and occupation before leading them to their table. She and Dani chatted like long-lost friends on the short walk, Jimmy trailing along behind them.

Jules spotted them coming across the restaurant and stood to greet them as they arrived at the table. Mickey stood as well and moved around towards them. "Hello, Dr. Harrington. Very nice to see you again."

"Please, call me Dani. And you must be Julia," she said, offering her hand. "It's an honor to meet you."

"Julia Reynolds, Dani. The pleasure is mine. Please join us," said Jules, waving an arm towards an open seat. "And all my friends call me Jules. I hope you will too."

Dani smiled and nodded her assent as she and Jules sat at the table. Mickey remained standing as he and Jimmy exchanged further pleasantries with Jackie. After a couple of minutes Jackie gave Jimmy a knowing smile and squeezed his arm as she glanced at Dani, who had her back to them and was already laughing about something with Jules. She silently mouthed "I like her" to Jimmy and then turned back towards the front of the restaurant.

Micky caught this and grinned at Jimmy before taking his own seat again. Jimmy nodded and sat down as well, feeling a little stunned at how right the world was at the moment. Then he noticed the four glasses of champagne, one in front of each of them. He raised his own as he looked first at Jules, then Micky, and finally letting his gaze settle on Dani.

"To new friendships," he said, raising the glass a bit higher. "May you live as long as you want and never want as long as you live. Slainte!"

"Slainte!" replied Dani, as she smiled back at Jimmy.

Out at the Bull Chute, Rose was making good on her promise to Tammy to have a good time and forget all her problems. The local house band, known as The Jakes, had drawn an unexpectedly larger than normal crowd. They had been cranking out country, blues, rock, and even a funk song or two for almost three hours without a break.

Drew had slipped into the Bull Chute about twenty minutes before and it hadn't taken him long to spot Tammy. They knew each other from their time at the bar, occasionally flirting with each other but never making anything serious out of it. He wasn't surprised to see her there. It was Rose that surprised him. Why wasn't she at the motel, he wondered.

He had remained on the far side of the bar, away from the women and hanging back in the crowd while he watched Rose and pondered what might be going on. Maybe she was just out for the night blowing off some steam and would return to the Lake Pine Motel later. Then he thought about the possibility they had some kind of disagreement and either she left, or they kicked her out. This worried him a bit. She had seen him there and could tie him into it. That made him nervous. He thought about calling Ray, then decided against it. Maybe he would just find out what he could from her first.

Drew leaned against the wall, thinking about how to approach the women. He didn't want Tammy to know that he knew Rose, and he hoped Rose wouldn't just blurt out she knew him. That might lead to some awkward lies to avoid how they really met. The crowd was gathering tightly around the stage as the Jakes launched into a Dierks Bentley drinking song. Maybe he could ease up behind them in the crowd and whisper into Rose's ear to be cool about seeing him. Let her know he wanted to talk.

She saved him that trouble when he saw her hand her drink to Tammy and point toward the bathrooms. He pushed his way through the crowd in that direction so he could catch her coming out. He leaned against the bar with his back to the stage a few feet away from the door to the ladies' room and took another pull on his beer.

Rose had her head down as she came out, still fumbling with the belt in her jeans. Drew stepped into her path, and she stopped as she sensed she was about to walk into someone. It took her a few seconds to make the connection and then a look of puzzled surprise spread across her face. She opened her mouth but couldn't get the words out before Drew pulled her close to him.

"Why are you here?" he asked.

"What?" she replied, unable to hear him over the noise of the band and the crowd.

"I said, why are you here?" This time Drew spoke more loudly.

Rose waved her right arm in the air drunkenly. "I ain't here for a long-time, just a good time," she half-yelled, half-sang with a stupid grin on her face.

Drew shook his head. "No. Not why are you here," emphasizing the word here. "Why aren't you at the motel?"

"That's a long story," slurred Rose. "Maybe I'll tell you one day."

"How about telling me tonight?" demanded Drew.

Rose laughed and put her hand on his chest. "Gonna' cost you a few drinks and a line dance to get that story cowboy."

Drew looked over his shoulder towards the stage. Tammy was still focused on the band. He released his grip on Rose's arm. "Alright. You go back there with Tammy. I'll come over in a few minutes with another drink for you. Don't let on to her we know each other."

"You know Tammy?" asked Rose. "She's my best friend in the whole world."

"I know her. You just remember to act like you don't know me. I'll be over there in a minute."

Rose turned, threw her hand up in the air to wave bye in a backwards fashion and left Drew standing there. He looked around, but didn't see anyone watching them, so he made his way up to the bar to get their drinks. He threw some bills on the bar and told the bartender to keep the change, then he picked up the two mixed drinks and a fresh beer and made his way through the crowd to where Rose and Tammy stood. Both women were waving their hands in the air, singing at the top of their lungs. Too bad the circumstances aren't different, Drew thought. Rose was a decently attractive woman.

He stood behind them and waited for the song to end, which it did about sixty seconds after he arrived. As Tammy lowered her arms and turned to say something to Rose, she caught Drew in her peripheral vision and turned further to see who was behind her. When she recognized him, she let out a little yell of joy and threw her arms around his neck, almost knocking the drinks out of his hands.

"Drew!" she yelled. "What's happening?"

"Hey, Tammy. How's it going? This place is hopping tonight."

The Jakes were firing up the next song, forcing Tammy to lean back in as she was pulling away from Drew. "Yeah! The Jakes are rockin' the house tonight."

Drew raised his right hand, cradling the mixed drinks in it. "I brought you and your friend here another drink. You looked like you could use one," he laughed.

"Hell yeah," yelled Tammy. She reached over and grabbed Rose by the arm, forcing her to turn and join them. "Rose, honey, meet Drew."

Rose accepted the drink offered to her and played her part as Drew had requested. "Thank you, Drew. Pleasure to meet you."

Drew nodded as the Jakes turned it up another notch on the chorus. Both women turned back to the stage, belting out the words along with the rest of the crowd. Drew took a pull on his beer and wondered how he was going to get what he needed out of Rose. He might have to wait until The Jakes were done, he realized. Might as well enjoy the band and the beer until then he grinned, throwing his fist in the air and joining in.

Jules and Dani hugged each other goodbye on the sidewalk outside Revolution and promised to get together soon for lunch. Jimmy looked at Micky and said, "See you in the morning."

Micky nodded back. "You know it. Dani, it was lovely."

Dani replied she felt the same and the couples headed off in different directions down the street.

"That was spectacular," Dani said to Jimmy as they walked away. "I don't know which I liked best, the Mojito or the fish!"

Jimmy smiled. "That Mojito haunts me. I have tried every mixture I can think of at home, and I still can't quite make it as good as they do there."

Dani stopped to look in the storefront window of one of the shops they were passing by. Chocolat was a small, local store that opened a few years before and offered hand-made gourmet chocolates. "This," she said with emphasis," might be the best chocolate in the world."

"Never tried it," replied Jimmy. He stepped up closer. "Looks like this won't be my lucky night either. They're closed."

"Soon," said Dani with a grin. "They open again at 9:00 a.m.."

Jimmy laughed. "That's a little early for chocolate, even for me."

"Never too early for chocolate," said Dani as they continued down the sidewalk.

"Hey, there's a great coffee shop a couple of blocks over that serves a really good homemade brownie. They top it with ice cream made at the creamery at N.C. State."

Dani looked at her watch. "That sounds like a perfectly acceptable substitute for Chocolat. But... I have an early shift tomorrow and need my beauty rest. A rain check?"

Jimmy nodded. "Of course. Not sure you really need to work on the beauty part, though."

"That's sweet. Thank you."

They continued to walk along, silent in their thoughts, comfortable that nothing further needed to be said at that moment. Jimmy broke the silence a couple of minutes later when they reached the parking garage that held Dani's car. "Let me walk you up to your car."

She reached in her purse, pulling out keys and a small pepper spray device. "Thanks, but no need. I'm armed!"

"Okay, but I'm going to stand right here until I see you safely exit the garage."

Dani did a small curtsy. "Thank you, milord," she said playfully. "And thank you for a wonderful dinner with your friends."

"I hope we can do it again. Soon."

"You betcha." She kissed him lightly on the cheek, then turned and entered the stairwell to go up to her floor. As promised, Jimmy stood right there until she emerged in her car. They waved to each other as she turned onto the street. He watched until her car disappeared around a corner a few blocks down, smiled and thanked God for his good fortune, then turned to walk back to his own car.

"Ya'll have been great!" yelled Jake over the roar of the small crowd still screaming for another song. "Be safe getting home...or...," he paused and grinned, "gettin' to somebody else's home." The crowd yelled even more. "Take care of your bartender before you leave. We'll be back next Friday night." With that, the band played a couple more chords, the drummer crashed his cymbals as Jake let out one final yell, and the house lights came on full bright. Time to clear the bar.

Tammy and Rose, hands in the air, were screaming for more. Drew, still nursing his beer from an hour ago, was pondering his next move. Rose made it for him.

"Let's go to The Hatch and have another drink," she slurred heavily, partly to Tammy and partly to Drew. Drew raised an eyebrow to Tammy, signaling he was open to the suggestion.

"Not me, baby girl", said Tammy. "I gotta work tomorrow."

"Come on Tammy," begged Rose. "One more. Just one more." She laid her head on her friend's shoulder.

Drew looked at Rose, then at Tammy. "I'll take you. That is, if it's okay with Tammy."

"Yeah!" shouted Rose, even more drunkenly than before.

Tammy shook her head. "Last thing she needs is another drink. But I ain't her momma. She's a grown woman. Can do what she wants to." Tammy glanced over at the stage where the band was still packing up. "I'm gonna go say bye to Jake. Ya'll stay out of jail. Rose, you call me tomorrow now."

Rose threw her arms around Tammy's neck, told her how much she loved her and then promised to call as asked. Drew nodded at Tammy as Rose grabbed him by the arm and started pulling him towards the door. Time to find out what his friends were up to, he thought as he set his beer bottle down on a table and they walked out of the Bull Chute.

CHAPTER 18

My mouth feels like a desert, thought Drew as he awoke to the sounds of late morning traffic outside the one-bedroom apartment. He laid for a moment with both eyes closed, afraid of having the room spin on him if he opened them too quickly. Then he felt the nausea, rolling through his stomach and up into his mouth and head. Damn! How much did I drink last night, he wondered. He gritted his teeth to fight the bile starting to well up, then reached up to rub his forehead. His hand came away damp, yet his skin felt cold. Immediately he remembered. It wasn't the alcohol. Yeah, there had been that. A lot of that. No, it was the drugs. Must have been laced with fentanyl.

His arm fell limply beside him, hanging off the couch, which he now realized was where he had passed out early in the morning, sometime after 4:00 a.m., he thought. Or maybe 5:00 a.m. The Hatch had closed at 3:00 a.m., and it had taken him and Rose a while to get an Uber and make it back to her place.

What the hell was he doing to himself, he asked out loud. He knew better than to mess with that crap. But Rose had insisted he keep partying with her, even after they both stumbled their way into her apartment. The booze at the Hatch had loosened her tongue and he wanted that to keep flowing until she revealed everything she knew. And did she ever, he thought. Ray would not be happy right now if he knew what a songbird she was.

Drew opened his eyes and looked around him. An empty wine bottle and some half empty beer bottles sat on the coffee table and one of the end tables. The television was still on, but apparently, they had turned it to mute. Or maybe the speakers were broken, he thought.

He glanced at his watch. Just after 11:30 a.m. He needed more sleep, but he wouldn't get it here. Time to get out and get home. He carefully eased himself into a sitting position, felt the nausea start again. Better not move for a few minutes. He thought about Ray and Nick some more, wondered what their next move would be. Rose said it was a kidnapping, and they planned to pressure the woman's husband into coming up with a bunch of cash. He was part of it now, like it or not.

God, he wanted a cigarette. And another drink to knock off the edge of the fentanyl hangover. Was there still some wine in that bottle? He picked it up. Nothing. There was a pack of smokes on the table. Virginia Slims. Good god! How did Rose smoke those things?

He closed his eyes again, thought about the night before. After the drugs they started fooling around a little. Nothing too serious at first, just some kissing and a little groping, like seventh graders at their first party where the parents were upstairs, letting the kids have their fun in the basement. Then the hands started squeezing a little tighter, the breathing getting a little heavier. And suddenly she passed out. Just slumped in his arms. He had half-walked, half-drug her to the bedroom. Toyed with taking her clothes off her, then thought better of it. He didn't want to cross Ray. At least not that far. So, he laid her on the bed and threw a blanket over her, watched her breathe for a minute then turned the light out and closed the door behind him.

That was the last thing he remembered about the night besides collapsing on the couch after he left her bedroom. He opened his eyes and stared at the Virginia Slims. What the hell. He stuck one in his mouth, lit it and took a deep drag. He blew the smoke towards the ceiling and took another. Having quickly satisfied the craving, he ground it out in the ashtray on the end table.

Drew leaned back into the couch, rubbing his temples more to try and relieve the throbbing behind his eyes. He knew their next move. What was his next move? Shouldn't he have a payday out of this as well? Without him, the woman would have gotten worse, forcing them to either get rid of her or seek medical help somewhere else.

He pondered how to approach them, debating whether to be straight up that Rose spilled the beans or play it more coy, pretending like he stitched some things together after seeing news reports. He smiled at his own wit. Stitched some things together. Just like he did her arm. If he didn't let Ray know what Rose had told him, what if she eventually confessed? They might not trust him any further and try to keep him out of the deal. Or worse, maybe they would decide they needed to get rid of him. He mulled that for a bit, wondered if Ray would really try to kill him if it came to that. Probably not, he thought. With Nick, though, he couldn't be so sure. Could Nick kill him? Best not to have to find out, he thought.

So, he had to give up Rose. But how to do that without looking like he was moving in on Ray's woman or looking like he had set her up to talk. Shit, he thought. Too damn early, and too damn hungover to plan all that out right now. A little more sleep was what he needed, so he stretched back out on the couch. In less than three minutes he was out.

Drew woke again, unsure of how long he had slept. He glanced at the television. It looked like a soap opera, so maybe early afternoon. Looked at his watch. 2:00 p.m. He reached a hand up and felt his forehead. Not clammy anymore. It felt normal. This is good, he thought and decided to sit up. A little dizzy, but not terrible. Perhaps the gods would wink at his behavior last night after all.

He listened for movement. Traffic still rolling along outside, but nothing moving in the apartment. Was Rose still sleeping it off? He got up slowly and quietly, walking into the cramped kitchen. Time to hydrate. He opened the refrigerator door. God bless her, she had two Powerades! He took one, unscrewed the cap and drained half of it as he leaned into the still open fridge door. After closing the door, he turned the bottle up and finished the rest.

After finishing the drink, he started thinking about his next move. Whatever it was, it had to be with Ray. He couldn't tell him everything, though. Just that he knew about the kidnapping and the ransom plan. Rose's other secret confession was safe with him. For now, anyway. He wasn't sure it really gave him any leverage, and it didn't quite feel right to betray Rose's confidence.

Time to go, he thought. Should he just let himself out or should he let her know he was going? Did it really matter? Probably not, but he decided to let her know and see if she needed anything before he left.

He walked softly down the short hallway, past the half-bathroom and stopped at the door to Rose's bedroom which stood slightly cracked. He leaned an ear towards the crack but heard nothing. He hesitated for a moment then gently pushed the door halfway open. He could see that Rose was lying on her stomach, partially covered by the bed sheets. He stilled himself again, listening for her breathing. Nothing. Wow, she must really be out of it, he thought.

He watched her for a couple of minutes, straining to see if the sheet was moving up and down with her breathing. Again, nothing, and now Drew was getting a vibe that something was off. He pushed the door open all the way and walked up to the bed, looking down at Rose. Her face was turned to the opposite side, so he walked around the bed. Her eyes were closed, as was her mouth, but something about her face looked wrong. He pulled the sheet back from her body and watched for breathing. She wasn't moving.

Oh fuck, he thought. No. No! He reached for her neck quickly, checking for a pulse. Nothing. She wasn't breathing and her skin was feeling cool. Drew had the sense that he should immediately be freaking out, and yet he was possessed of an eerie and sudden calm. She was dead. That he knew for sure. How, was something he couldn't quite be sure of, but likely she had overdosed on the fentanyl. The fentanyl that he gave her.

He sat down in the chair next to Rose's bed, staring at her body. Now what, he thought. Should he leave her there lying in the bed for someone else to find? Tammy perhaps? Whether Tammy found her or not, she knew they had left The Bull Chute together the night before. Last known contact. And the Hatch after that. Would someone remember them leaving there together?

He closed his eyes and tilted his head back against the chair. He had to remain calm. To think clearly. No way to avoid him being tied to her the night before. Too many witnesses, especially Tammy. But the fentanyl couldn't be directly tied to him. This left him an opening.

He opened his eyes, this time avoiding her body on the bed. The kidnapping and ransom were another puzzle for him. Where would her death, and perhaps a police investigation, leave Ray and the others? He wondered how much she might have told Tammy, then pondered how he might use this to his advantage in cutting himself into the deal.

Drew closed his eyes again, stealing his body into an even further calm. He slowed his breathing as he worked through the options in his head. Like tumblers in a padlock, the pieces began to fall into their places. One final long exhale and he opened his eyes. He knew what to do next. Time to get started.

Nick breathed deeply and looked at Penny as he slipped the burner phone out of its packaging. "No turning back once I make this call. Agreed?"

Penny nodded and placed a hand on his shoulder, looking deep into Nick's eyes. "No turning back, baby. For your boys."

He threw the cell phone packaging on the beat-up kitchen table and took one more deep breath. Penny held the yellow Post-it note up so he could see the numbers to reach Johnson Auto. After mis-keying one of the numbers he cleared it and started over, slower this time.

After a few rings on the other end, Lila's cheery voice sounded in his ear. "Johnson Auto. It's a great day to buy a car. How can I help you?"

"Eddie," he breathed out.

"I'm sorry. What was that again?"

"Need to speak to Eddie Johnson." Clearer this time.

"Yes sir. Who may I tell Eddie who is calling?"

"Raleigh Police Department. News about his wife."

"Oh my god! Hold on. I'll get him right away."

Lila sprinted a few feet across the office to Eddie's doorway. Eddie looked up from some paperwork as she skidded through the doorway, breathlessly letting him know the police were on line two with news about Donna. He stared for a moment at the blinking light for line two, then looked up at Lila.

"Close the door and go back to your desk. I need to be alone with this." Eddie took a deep breath, then picked up the handset and pressed the blinking light, willing himself to remain calm even as his legs had turned into dead weight. He exhaled and said hello.

"Eddie Johnson?"

"Yes, this is him."

"Are you alone?"

His legs got even heavier. "Yes. Who is this? Detective Quinn?"

"No. You don't need my name. The first thing you need to know is we have your wife."

Eddie felt a rush of relief, followed by fear mixed with anger. "Where is she? You better not hurt her!"

"We're not going to hurt anyone as long as you do exactly what we say. Are you listening carefully?"

"I'm telling you…"

Nick cut him off. "Don't talk. Listen. Do what I say, and you get her back. Do something else, no one, especially you, ever sees her again. Tell me you're hearing me, Eddie."

Eddie was quiet a moment, mind racing.

"Eddie, tell me you're hearing me, or I drop this line and Plan B kicks in."

"No, no. I mean, yes, I'm hearing you. Just don't hurt her. Please!"

Nick breathed out forcefully again to release some tension, looking at Penny as he nodded his head. "Good, That's a good answer Eddie."

"What do you want? Why are you doing this to us?"

Nick laughed on the other end. "Come on, Eddie. Think. Why does anyone do this?"

"Money?"

"See. Smart man. Money. Of course."

"How much?"

Nick's turn to be silent a moment. "Two million." Penny's eyes got wide. She mouthed a giant What! to Nick. They had all agreed on one million. Nick held up a hand to Penny. I got this, he mouthed back to her.

Eddie sputtered back, "Two million! Are you fucking kidding me? I don't have two million dollars!"

"We know about your other revenue stream, Johnson." Nick was getting impatient now.

Eddie didn't respond.

"Eddie? Are you still with me?"

"Yes, I'm here. Two million. That's a lot of money. I need some time to come up with that."

"Three days."

"I'm gonna need more..."

"Three days. No one knows about this but you. I will call back with instructions on the drop."

The line went dead, Eddie holding the phone, starting to panic. Oh my god, he thought. Otto! He's in on this. He told them about the rollback scheme. That asshole. Two million. He was trying to do the math in his head, how many cars they would have to rig to get two million. That would take months, maybe a couple of years.

He placed the handset in its cradle. Where was he going to get that kind of money? And that fast. He leaned back in the desk chair, eyes closed and started totaling what he had stashed away in cash. Plus, his retirement funds. Could he get a loan? He heard a soft knock on his office door.

Without looking he knew it was Lila, ready to ask what the police said. He couldn't open his eyes and look at her. He knew she would sense something was wrong, even more wrong than the fact his wife was missing. "Come in," he said, keeping his head back and eyes closed.

"Eddie, what did they say? Have they found her?"

Eddie sighed. "No news. Just an update to tell me there was no update."

"You okay? Can I get you anything?"

"No. Thanks, Lila. I just need a few minutes alone."

"You got it. We're right out here." She softly closed the door, leaving him to his racing mind.

Now what, he asked himself. He decided to do what he always did when there was a problem. Pulling a legal pad from his desk drawer, he grabbed a pen and started to write down his options. An answer would come to him. It had to.

CHAPTER 19

Drew's phone buzzed in his back pocket. He knew it was Tammy. Again. She had already left two voice mails for him. He decided to answer this time. Better than having her call the police next. He pulled out the phone and punched the answer button.

"Hello."

"Drew! What the hell? Why haven't you been answering my calls? I can't reach Rose. Where is she? Do you know?"

"Hold on, hold on," said Drew. "Slow down a minute with all the questions. How should I know where Rose is?"

"I don't know, shithead," spat Tammy. "Maybe because you were the last one with her?"

Drew paused for a moment before replying. "Did you go by her place?"

"No!"

"How about where she works? Try there."

"She doesn't have a job right now. I've called her about a hundred times. No answer. What time did you leave her place?"

"What makes you think I was at her place?"

"Come on, Drew. She was drunk when you two left for Hatch.

Drinking all day. She doesn't shut down until she falls down. You had to have at least made sure she got home okay, right? You didn't leave her at the Hatch or just put her in an Uber. Did you?"

Drew was quiet again, carefully considering his reply. A lot of people might have seen him leaving Rose's apartment. Not to mention all the damn security cameras they probably had there. "No, I didn't just put her in an Uber. We went to her apartment together."

"Did you stay?"

"Yeah, but it's not what you're thinking."

"I'm not thinking anything other than I can't reach my friend and she always answers my call," Tammy said tearfully. "Please tell me she was okay when you left her!"

"Yeah. She was okay, I think."

"You think? What does that mean?"

Drew took a deep breath and exhaled it slowly before answering. "Look, we were pretty smashed when we got back to her place, but she wasn't... what did you call it?... falling down. We stayed up a couple more hours drinking and, you know, just shooting the shit. It was too late, and I was too drunk to try and get home, so she told me I could sleep on the couch. She went to her bedroom and that's the last I saw of her. I think she was still asleep when I left."

What time was that?"

Drew paused again. Better to be close to the actual time he left than too far off. "I don't remember exactly. Maybe 12:30 p.m., 1:00 p.m. Something like that."

"Okay. Then what?"

"What do you mean, then what? That was it. I left."

Tammy's turn to be silent a moment. "I'm worried Drew. She just lost another job and she's been running with this guy who seems a little shady. I'm scared she's gonna do something stupid."

"Stupid like what?"

"Start using again."

"Yeah, she didn't do that around me last night, but she talked about it. Being afraid of going there again I mean. She talked a little about that guy too, I think. The one you mentioned."

"What did she say?"

"Not much really. Just said she had been hanging out with him a lot lately," Drew said. Seeing an opportunity to cover his tracks he kept going, "She said something about maybe hooking back up with him. She was missing him maybe. And his friends too."

"Tammy, you there?" asked Drew, after the line went silent for a minute.

"Yeah. I'm here. Just thinking. Did Rose say anything else about them?"

"Nope, not really. But maybe she went somewhere with him."

"Maybe," agreed Tammy. "Drew, there's something else I should tell you, but man, you gotta swear to me you don't breathe a word on this. Especially Rose. She can't know I betrayed her confidence."

"What is it, Tammy?"

"Swear to me Drew."

"Okay. Damn. I swear."

"She thinks she might be pregnant with Ray's baby."

"Shit," sighed Drew. "Does he know?"

"She didn't say for sure, but I doubt it. If you hear from her, please tell her to call me right away."

"Yeah, of course," said Drew. "She'll turn up soon I bet."

"I hope so. Bye, Drew. I gotta go," said Tammy, punching off the call.

Drew shoved his phone back in his pocket, then picked up the shovel he had laid on the ground. Before he threw another shovel full of dirt into the hole he looked down at Rose's half buried body. "Sorry, girl, that it ended this way. You rest in peace now." He dropped the dirt in, then turned for more.

Day two at the cabin had been a long day of nothing. Ray had decided to wait until the following day to go for more food and supplies. After a simple breakfast of coffee and granolas bars, he muttered something to Donna about needing to be active. He started cleaning inside the cabin. Everything. Wiping down cabinets, sweeping the floor, shaking out the rugs. If he could find a spot of dust or dirt, he attacked it.

Donna sat on the couch wondering why he was so busy and working her way through the magazines she could find in the cabin. Occasionally she said something to Ray, asking for Tylenol, or if it was okay to go outside for a while - he said no very quickly to that. Her arm ached a little, but she was feeling better. Once or twice, she put her magazine down and napped for a few minutes. Sometimes she pretended to read but was actually pondering her situation and whether escaping was possible. Ray kept the door bolted, his gun on his hip, and physically looked like someone you didn't want to tangle with. Her odds seemed long.

She also pondered again why they had targeted Eddie. The other guy in the group had said something about some business Eddie was in that apparently produced a lot of cash. Not the car business, she thought. Had they made a mistake? Or was Eddie involved in something she didn't know about? If he was, he didn't do at their house. They were almost never apart when he wasn't at work, and she knew every square inch of that house. Cleaned it herself because no one else could do it as well. He wasn't hiding anything there.

Was he doing it at the car lot? Could one or more of his employees be involved? No way it could be Lila. Too sweet. Bill? Too honest. Otto? He kind of gave her the creeps anyway. He was always polite with her the few times she had been around him, but he seemed shady. She could see it in his eyes. Yeah, if it was anyone, it had to be Otto.

Then she caught herself. What was she thinking! This had to be a mistake. No way her dear Eddie could be involved in some kind of criminal activity like... drugs. It came to her at that moment. Drugs and cash go hand in hand. Okay, she thought, Eddie didn't even drink that much, and he always spoke out against drug use. A younger brother of his overdosed a few years back and she remembered how

Eddie had sworn he would never end up like that. Plus, there was no evidence he was living a big lifestyle from a bunch of drug money. So, they targeted the wrong guy. But how? Why? Donna put her magazine down. Too much to consider right now, she thought, and closed her eyes for another nap.

Ray reached a stopping point and looked at his watch. Middle of the afternoon. Time to check in with Nick. He looked over at Donna. Napping, so he decided to step out on the porch and make the call. Walking quietly to the front door, he eased the deadbolt back, closed the door softly behind him and moved to a far end of the porch. It had warmed up nicely and the coastal breeze felt refreshing. Maybe he should just stay down here, he thought, then sighed and pulled out his phone. One day.

Nick picked up on the third ring. "Ray, how's it going?"

"It's boring, but that's good. No drama to worry about. How about there?"

"Okay. Made the call to Johnson yesterday. Gave him three days."

"What did he say?"

Nick laughed a little. "About what you would expect. Don't hurt my wife. Why are you doing this? I don't have that kind of money."

"A million dollars is a lot of money."

Nick was quiet for a moment. "Yeah. It is. So, I told him the price was two million."

"Two million," Ray said back. "That's a nice chunk of change. Be nice to get twice as much as we were thinking."

"I thought you might say that!"

"The problem is, you didn't talk to me before you did it."

"Yeah. I thought you might say that too."

"What the hell, Nick? Is this a partnership or not?"

Nick let out a heavy sigh. "You're right. Of course, you're right. I got caught up in a moment and acted compulsively. Again. I'm sorry, Ray. Shouldn't have done it."

"No, you shouldn't have. But you did, and here we are. Just don't do that shit again."

"I won't," promised Nick. "So, you're all settled in down there?"

"Mostly. I'm gonna' need to make a food run tomorrow but won't need much if you gave him three days, I guess. How are we doing the swap?"

Ray paced up and down the porch while Nick laid out his ideas for exchanging Donna for the money. He occasionally asked a question, but overall, he thought Nick's plan was fine.

"You thought about where you are going to go," asked Nick, "you know, once this is done?"

"Got some ideas. Not locked down yet. How about you and Penny?"

Nick took a deep breath. "After we drop off the money, gonna' head south. Way south. Live out my last days with this death sentence disease where it's warm."

"You deserve that, my friend," Ray said softly.

"Promise me you keep tabs on my kids, Ray. Make sure their momma is treating them good."

"I will, Nick. I'll do whatever I can."

Take care, Ray. Talk soon."

Ray put his phone back in his pocket and leaned against a porch column, staring out towards the lake in the distance. He had known Nick a long time, been through a lot with him. This was probably the end of the road for them. A botched robbery turned kidnapping with a payday at the end of it. He hoped. Not enough money to retire forever, but his half of the two million would keep him fed a very long time. Maybe the rest of his life if he played it smart.

Where to go after was the question. It had to be somewhere he could disappear reasonably well. They shouldn't have to worry about the cops coming after them. Donna would show back up alive, Johnson would make up some kind of story to satisfy her and the police, and soon enough the trail would go cold, or the cops would lose interest.

Rose might be their one loose end. And maybe Drew, he thought. He could carve out a little cash to keep her quiet. Nick might be willing to do the same for Drew. He would mention it next time they talked.

Movement at one of the windows caught his eye and he turned to see Donna backing away inside. How long had she been standing there, he wondered. He thought back on his call with Nick. Not much she could have overheard that was risky. Nonetheless, he had better go inside and see what she was up to.

She was sitting on the couch again when he walked back into the cabin, not even looking up when he closed the door. He paused by the door, staring at her. After a few moments, he said, "Okay."

Donna looked at him now. "Okay? Okay what?"

"Okay, as in, you're pretending I didn't just see you by the window trying to overhear my phone call. Yeah?"

She put her magazine down and stared back at him, some anger starting to rise. "First of all, I don't 'pretend' at anything. Second, yes, I was by the window and trying to hear what was being said. What would you do in my position?"

Ray ran his hand across his scalp. He didn't know whether to be pissed off or to laugh out loud at her boldness. He softened his tone a bit. "If it was me, I'd make damn sure I didn't piss off my captor, first of all. Are you trying to piss me off?"

Donna shook her head.

"Good. What did you hear me say out there?"

Donna sighed and picked her magazine up again. "Unfortunately, nothing. Couldn't make out anything you said."

"You sure about that?"

"I did hear what sounded like 'million', but I couldn't make out what came before that."

"That's it?"

She nodded. "Yes. That's it. I swear."

Ray turned and bolted the door back before replying. "For the record, it's two. Two million. And that's all you need to know."

Donna nodded again and quickly held the magazine up as if reading. Two million! Where would Eddie get that much money? Everything they owned wouldn't fetch that kind of cash. What would they do to her if he couldn't come up with it? Her mind was racing and her breathing getting more and more shallow. Escaping suddenly became her best option. Wasn't it? Breathe, she told herself. Breathe. Calm down. You need a steady mind. So, she did. Just sat there for a few minutes, eyes closed, focusing on her breath. In. Out. In. Out. Gradually she got calmer. Still frightened, but calmer.

She opened her eyes. Where was he? Not in the room anymore. Had he slipped back outside while she was calming herself? She looked at the door. No, it looked like the bolt was still turned from the inside. Then she heard him back in the pantry/storage room, going through something. Could she get out the door without him hearing her, then run to... where? She remembered what he had said earlier about bears and other creatures. Maybe she could get down to the highway before he realized she was gone. But what if no cars came by that she could flag down? It was getting late in the afternoon, maybe there was less traffic now. Should she risk it?

Ray gave her the answer by emerging from the pantry, something from its tiny freezer in his hand. He looked at her, an odd smirk on his face. "Weren't thinking about running, were you?"

Donna shook her head, her stomach tumbling. Damn, was he a mind reader too?

"Good. Found some venison in the freezer. Got any problems with that for dinner?" Again, she shook her head. Ray nodded and walked to the sink to start thawing out the meat.

Back in Raleigh, the investigation wasn't moving much. Their research technician, Janie, had spent most of the afternoon working on their case, laboriously scrolling through the DMV database looking for a hit on the license plates from the doorbell videos they had secured. Most of the plates they were able to make out were traceable to nearby residents. Some belonged to companies of some kind, probably in the neighborhood for a service call or a resident worked for them. A few belonged to addresses elsewhere in Raleigh and Wake County, and she was pulling background on those.

The one that had intrigued Jimmy the most was the brown van with the female driver. They hadn't been able to fully see the numbers on the plate and the combinations tried so far had not produced anything helpful. More of them were tied to cars of some kind. Micky was out in the neighborhood with a patrolman, knocking on doors, showing pictures, looking for anyone who could connect anything. So far, nada, and he and his colleague were getting frustrated.

Steve Mauro was the young patrolman that had been at the scene the day of the break-in. "Detective Bondurant, what now? I think we have hit every house in a three-block radius. Not looking good."

Micky took a long pull from a bottle of water and leaned against his car. "Nope. It's not. Any ideas? And call me Micky please."

"Well, maybe," he said. "I know you got videocam footage from that day, but what about before that? Maybe they had scouted the location before that day to see what they were dealing with."

"Had not considered that. Good idea. Got anything else?"

"Just that. For now," smiled Steve.

Micky finished his water, then smiled back at Steve. "It's a start. Nice work. Let's go see what else we can find at the videocam houses."

Darkness had fallen at the coast of North Carolina. As always, there was a breeze from the ocean winds, and the night air had the cool of early spring still riding with it. The clouds had moved on out to sea for the night and the stars were on full display, dotting the universe in a wondrous pattern. Ray had found a couple of old folding chairs and put them out on the porch. He and Donna sat there silently, each lost in their thoughts of the situation they were in.

Donna decided to try the 'more flies with honey' approach and see if she could gain any more insights into what they had planned. "I have to say, the venison was very good."

"Thanks," said Ray.

Donna waited for a couple of minutes to see if he had more to say. He just kept staring at the stars. "How did you season it?" she asked.

Ray took a sip of his bourbon. He turned to look at her. "This the part where you play nice, not be a smart-ass?"

Donna sighed. "Yes, I suppose it is. Should I go back to smart-ass?"

Ray chuckled. "No. Makes all this a bit easier when you're nicer."

She waited again and this time she waited him out.

"Salt and pepper. Little bit of garlic powder. Sautee' it in some olive oil."

"Simple. Often the best."

"Yes, it is."

She looked up into the same sky he was staring at so intently. "The moon looks kind of odd tonight. Has a sort of halo around it."

"Cold moon," Ray responded.

"Excuse me? Cold moon?"

"Yeah. Cold moon. My grandfather used to tell me stories about the moon when I was a kid. How it meant different things when it was different sizes or shapes. A cold moon supposedly comes only in the early spring. It's a sign that change and new growth are coming next."

"Huh. That's interesting. I hope it's true."

Ray turned to look at her. "How's that?"

"Well, the change part anyway. From being a hostage to being free."

Ray just grunted and they sat in silence for a while. Donna shifted in her chair, fighting the nervous energy of what she was about to say next. "I think you made a mistake targeting Eddie."

"Yeah? How's that?"

"We have been married a long time. He hardly spends a moment away from me when he's not at work. The car lot has given us a comfortable life, and things have got even better lately, but the kind of money you're asking for? We just don't have it."

"That so?" asked Ray. "You spend a lot of time out at that car lot?"

"No, not much", she replied. "Not anymore."

Ray let her reply hang in the air while he sipped more bourbon. "I suppose things could be going on out there you don't know about. Think that's possible?"

It was the way he said it that tickled some part of Donna's alarm system. There was something about the way this man said things sometimes, she thought, that was so full of matter-of-fact confidence that it almost felt like the voice of God speaking to you. All the courage and determination she had mustered earlier in the day in support of how they had the wrong guy was suddenly teetering on collapse. But she wasn't done with the fight yet. "So, what's going on out there? You think Eddie's some kind of drug kingpin?" she asked with a nervous laugh.

Ray turned and looked squarely at her this time. "Don't know about the kingpin part, but yeah, it's something like that."

Donna shook her head. "I refuse to believe that."

"Refusing to believe doesn't make it any less true. Sometimes there's things you don't know about people, even the ones close to you. The ones you're married to. Secrets they keep." He turned back to stare off into the night sky, remembering the time someone he loved had kept secrets.

They sat for a few quiet minutes, listening to an orchestra of the wind in the trees, crickets making their outsized contribution to nature's song, an occasional owl and sometimes a frog. So utterly peaceful, she thought. And yet here she was, a hostage for ransom, wife of a man her captor claimed was a drug runner. She looked at Ray. "How do you know it's true? About Eddie."

"Anyone work for him you ever had doubts about?"

She felt the chill as she said his name. "Otto!"

Ray nodded.

Otto had always given her a creepy feeling when she was around him. Not because of anything he did or said. It was just because… well, because he was, she thought. He just emitted creepy vibes. She began remembering the times Eddie and Otto huddled together, talking quietly away from others. And the odd occasional phone call from Otto to Eddie at night, or maybe on a Sunday when the lot was closed. She thought nothing of them at the time. Just work stuff. My god, could this be true? Eddie and Otto partners in the drug business?

"Tell me more. Please!" she begged him.

Ray shook his head. "Nothing more you need to know."

"Please!"

He stood and stretched. "No. Getting a little late. Best we get inside for the night."

Donna was angry. Desperate now. She lashed out at him instinctively. "She's pregnant, you know."

"Who?"

"Your girlfriend. The dark haired one."

Ray moved a few steps closer. "What the hell are you talking about?"

"I could tell," she said with a bit of a sneer. "At the motel."

"You're bullshitting me. Go on inside. We're done here."

Donna did as he said, going in the cabin, letting the door close behind her. Leaving Ray standing on the porch. He drained the last of the bourbon. Now he was the one with doubts. He would call Rose tomorrow. Ask her himself. Then he went inside.

CHAPTER 20

Morning came like most early spring days in Carolina. Bright and hopeful. New and cheery. A little on the cool side. It did not match Eddie's mood. He sat in his office, door closed, working on his third cup of coffee. Bleary-eyed, he had gotten very little sleep the night before. Everything they owned did not come to two million dollars. He had done the math on that four times. Thought about a fifth time and then hurled the calculator across the room.

He had nodded off, sitting upright in his home office chair while staring at a photo from his and Donna's wedding. Woke up around four. After one last shot of bourbon, he spent the next two hours working over the legal pad now lying on his desk in front of him at the car lot. He had gone through every option he could think of. Twice. Pros and cons. Cons and pros. There was only one that stood a chance of happening at the speed the kidnappers were demanding.

Eddie picked up the phone and punched the intercom line to the shop out back. Otto answered on the fifth ring. "Yeah?"

"Otto, you alone out there?"

"Yeah."

"I'm coming out. We need to talk."

"I'm here," said Otto as Eddie hung up the phone on the other end.

Otto put the receiver back on the hook and laid the wrench in his hand on the workbench. As he wiped off his hands on a nearby rag, he pondered what Eddie might be up to now. Their last conversation had gotten a bit heated, Eddie accusing him of telling someone - presumably the kidnappers - about their rollback scheme. The chat had ended okay, though, with Otto seemingly having convinced Eddie no one else knew about their activities.

Eddie came through the door in a rush, slamming it behind him. "Damn it, Otto. You lied to me!"

Otto was leaning against the workbench, smoking a cigarette. After blowing a cloud of smoke to the ceiling, he looked at Eddie and calmly asked him, "What did I lie to you about, Eddie?"

"Telling someone about what we're doing on some of these cars," an exasperated Eddie shot back at him. "Who did you tell? Donna's life is on the line here, Otto. I don't have time for a bunch of bullshit."

"Something else happen with Donna?"

"Yeah, something else has happened. Something serious."

Otto took a pack of cigarettes out of his shirt pocket and offered one to Eddie. "How about you have a smoke and calm down some? Tell me what's going on. Maybe I can help."

Eddie looked at him for a moment, then stepped forward and took the pack. Hands shaking, he managed to get a cigarette out and put it in his mouth. Otto flicked his lighter and Eddie took a long draw off the cigarette, then another before he spoke. "You swear to me, on your dead mother's grave that you have said nothing to anyone? You swear it?"

Otto dropped his cigarette butt on the concrete floor and ground it out with the heel of his shoe. "Yes, Eddie. No one. You want my help or are we done here?"

Eddie eyed him for a long moment, drawing more on the smoke. "I don't know how you can help me, Otto."

"Try me."

"If I bring you into this you can't let it go past you. Not the cops, not anyone."

Otto snorted. "The cops? Come on Eddie. Me and the police aren't on friendly terms. Hell, they think I might be in on whatever happened at your house."

"Why would they think that?"

Otto shrugged. "Who knows. Cops don't like me. Never have. Must be my outgoing personality, rubs them the wrong way."

Eddie leaned against a nearby car, taking one last drag on the cigarette. "You don't have an ashtray out here?"

Otto pointed at the floor. Eddie shook his head, then dropped the cigarette on the floor. He glanced nervously at the door before clearing his throat to speak. "They want two million dollars before they let her go."

Otto whistled. "Wow. That's a lot, Eddie. You got that kind of juice?"

"Hell no."

"How close can you get?"

"Nowhere near it in the three days they gave me, and this is day two."

"So now what?"

"Shit, Otto, you said a minute ago you could help me. You have that kind of cash?"

Otto wiped his hands on the rag again and leaned back against the workbench. "What about the police, Eddie? Think they can help you?"

Eddie ran his hands through his hair, shifting his weight against the car. "They said I better not tell the cops. Plus, the more they get involved, the more they dig. Maybe they dig a hole big enough to ship me and you off to prison for running odometers back."

"Yeah. There's that."

"Shit," said Eddie. "I have no idea what to do."

Otto shook another cigarette out of the pack, offering it to Eddie. Eddie shook his head. After lighting it, he folded his arms, cigarette hanging from one hand and said, "I know where you can get the money, but you're not gonna' like the price tag."

"Where's that?"

"Rezaviks."

Otto had been carefully thinking through the what ifs of Eddie's, and now his, situation. He hadn't known for sure a kidnapping had occurred, but he knew it was a possibility. And he knew if that happened Eddie wouldn't involve the police because he wouldn't want them digging around for the reasons they had just discussed. If Eddie did go down that path, Otto knew he would have to act and run, or make sure Eddie never let the cops get close enough.

So, Otto had a choice to make. Let it all unfold with him as a bystander and hope it all went well - and the Rezaviks never found out. Or he could get involved and control the narrative with the Rezaviks. Two million was a big ask to go to them with. They would need a significant payday for that. Plus, there was always the risk they just said no and put him and Eddie in a place no one would ever find to cover their tracks. Yeah, he had choices. None without risk, though.

"Rezaviks?" asked Eddie." Why would they fork over two million? And what's the price tag you are talking about?"

Otto looked long and hard at Eddie before answering, doing his final risk calculations. Should he just take Eddie out himself and hit the road now? No, he decided. But that could remain an option. "Remember what you asked me a minute ago? About not letting your situation get beyond me?"

Eddie nodded.

"Well, what I'm about to tell you goes that times about ten. It won't be just Donna's life at stake. It will be mine," Otto paused a moment, "and yours too."

"What the hell are you talking about Otto?"

Otto moved a couple of steps closer, close enough to make Eddie uncomfortable. "You want to see Donna alive again?"

"Of course, I do."

"And you'll do anything to make that happen?"

"Yes. Yes! I will," said Eddie.

"There's more going on here than just rigging the miles on a few cars, Eddie," said Otto. "A lot more. I'm here because the Rezaviks planted me here. To work for them while I work for you."

Eddie replied quietly, a puzzled look now across his face. "Work for them? What do you mean?"

"They move a lot of products. Not all of them are legal."

It dawned instantly for him then. "Drugs?" breathed Eddie.

Otto nodded. "You got it, Edward. Drugs."

Eddie leaned against the car, then managed to eke out a reply, "What... how long... Oh my god. You have been running drugs through my car lot?"

Otto nodded again, taking some pleasure in watching Eddie's reaction to the news. Confused and clearly shocked, Otto knew Eddie would find the silver lining soon enough.

"This is unbelievable!" yelled Eddie, anger starting to replace the shock. "How long has this shit been going on Otto? I should just go to the cops now. Tell them I don't, I won't, have anything to do with this."

"Yeah, you could do that," Otto said calmly. "Bye-bye Donna. She goes first since there's no money to pay the ransom. Then it's bye-bye Eddie when the Rezaviks send someone up to get rid of you."

"And what about you, Otto? When do they get rid of you?"

Otto laughed. "Me? Not me Eddie. I tell them you and the police are coming for them and then I disappear."

Eddie looked stunned, his breathing shallow, palms sweaty. Otto could see him wrestling internally with the options he had just laid out for him. Finally, he spoke, barely more than a whisper. "What are you thinking, Otto?"

Otto smiled, then walked over and put an arm around Eddie's

shoulder. "Nothing's foolproof. But I think they may like what you can offer them." So, he told him.

Ray was sitting at the table drinking coffee when Donna called out to him from the bedroom where she lay with one leg cuffed via a long chain to the bed. Ray didn't like the idea of having to chain another human, but liked her escaping while he slept, or whacking his head with a frying pan, even less. Neither of them spoke while he unfastened the padlock and slipped the cuff over her foot.

She waited for him to leave the room before pushing back the sheets and sitting up. Another day in prison, she thought. What would it bring and how would Ray be towards her after last night's confrontation? She had gotten deep under his skin. She knew that. But she wasn't lying to him. She was certain Rose was pregnant. Would he be angry about it? Or happy? He would probably be indifferent, she thought. It didn't seem like he cared that much for her anyway.

She slipped her jeans on - God, how many days had she been wearing these things? - and stood up. After pulling on the blouse she had also been wearing for several days she opened the door to the bedroom and walked into the main area of the cabin. Ray glanced up from his phone but said nothing to her, so she went into the bathroom.

Looking in the mirror at her tangled mess of hair, she vowed to ask Ray to bring back a hairbrush from the store this morning when he went for supplies. She stared deeper into the mirror. And some lotion. God, her face was dry! She zipped her jeans up after taking care of biological needs, quickly washed her hands, then once again walked into the big room.

"Listen, about last night...", she started.

Ray cut her off. "Yeah. Forget it. We both were getting kind of hot there."

Donna nodded and walked over to the counter for coffee. Ray went back to his phone, scrolling through something. "I didn't make that up. I really do think she's pregnant."

Ray sighed and put his phone down. "I hope you're wrong," he said flatly. "Last thing I need right now."

Donna sat at the table across from him. "What about Eddie and the drugs? Did you make that up?"

Ray shook his head. "No. I didn't. Does it make sense to you that we just randomly chose your house to break into?"

"Maybe you were after money from the car lot."

"I may be a criminal, but I'm not stupid. Car lots don't operate with big cash transactions."

Donna was quiet again, processing what Ray had said. As much as she desperately wanted to believe he was lying, it was somehow resonating with her. And making her feel nauseous. Was she married to a criminal? A drug-dealing, two-faced lying criminal? If it was true, and if she survived this, how could she go back to Eddie?

Ray got up from the table and pushed a notepad and pen over to her. "I'm going in for some food. Something you want, write it on that pad. Keep it short and simple. This ain't Amazon."

She nodded and picked up the pen. "Am I going with you?"

"No chance of that."

"Then I guess..."

"Right," Ray cut her off again. "I don't like it, but I'm going to have to lock you up while I'm gone. Store's not far. I shouldn't be gone more than about 30-45 minutes."

Donna nodded again. No point in protesting. She thought for a moment, then scribbled down a couple of things on the pad. Too nauseous to eat or even finish the coffee, she asked him, "Where do you want to put me?"

He pointed to the bedroom. She got up and walked in there, Ray following behind her. "Don't bother trying to yell for help. Nobody will hear you and you'll just wear yourself out." With that, he snapped the padlock shut to secure her to the bed frame, closed the bedroom door and walked out.

Ray had three routes to consider for his supply run. North on 264, just a few miles away, was Manns Harbor. This was the last stop before taking the long bridge over the Croatan sound to Roanoke Island and the town of Manteo. West of Manns Harbor a few miles lay East Lake, a very small hamlet just over the Alligator River. And the third option was to head south a bit to Stumpy Point.

As he came off the logging road the cabin was on, Ray's cautious instincts overcame his initial choice of Manns Harbor, and he turned right on 264 to go south to Stumpy Point. Manns Harbor wasn't much, but Stumpy Point was even less and had only three buildings - a seafood business, a plumbing outfit, and Bill's Trading Post. He knew he could get what they needed at Bill's and see a lot less people doing it.

The three-mile drive went quickly, and he turned left on Bayview Road and followed it all the way to its end where the inlet to Stumpy Point Bay was. He glanced at the fuel gauge on the Tahoe as he made the left into the parking lot. Probably best to go ahead and fill it up now, he thought, although he didn't relish the idea of the additional few minutes that it would take. The longer he was visible with the Tahoe, the more risk there was.

As he filled the tank his mind wandered back to the decision to drive the Tahoe anyway. His small pickup wasn't feasible. The van they had taken to the Johnson's house was questionable mechanically for a multi-hour drive to the coast. Nick had nothing that worked. Sort of left them with no other options. Then the debate on the license plate. They guessed that having a dealer's plate on it was safer than stealing someone else's plate for it.

So here he was, standing beside the two pumps at Bill's, driving the stolen car of a man whose wife he held hostage for ransom. He shook his head. If they got out of this one, he thought, he was done with criminal activity. As the meter ran at glacial speed it seemed, he looked toward the building that was the Trading Post. A cheap metal structure with plate glass windows across the front side. He could see the checkout counter to the right of the entrance, a man standing behind it, gazing out at him, the lone customer for the moment. As their eyes met, the man waved enthusiastically at him. Must be Bill, he thought, as he gave back a half-hearted wave in return. He finished fueling the vehicle and pulled it over to one of the parking spots to the left of the structure, then opened the door and walked inside.

"Howdy friend. Good to see you again."

Ray looked quizzically at the man behind the counter. Did this guy really remember him from the one or two times he had been here? Those would have been a few years back from his duck hunting days at the cabin. And he never came in alone, always a few of them together coming in for supplies. Play it safe he thought. "Hi. Sorry, but this is my first time here. You must be mistaking me for someone else."

Bill's turn to have a quizzical look. "Hmm. Sorry, friend. Thought I recognized you as one of a group that used to come this way for some hunting."

Ray shook his head, eager to end the conversation. "Not me," he said as he walked deeper into the store. Bill called out to him, "Must be your long-lost twin brother, then," chuckling as Ray walked away. Ray looked back out the window as a flash of an automobile pulling in caught his eye. A sheriff's deputy pulled his cruiser up to the building on the opposite end from where Ray had parked the Tahoe.

"Billy-boy, what's shaking?" the deputy asked as he walked through the door.

"Mornin'," smiled Bill. "Nothing shakin' but the bacon!"

The deputy shook his head. "That's pretty lame, Bill. Keep working on those jokes of yours."

Ray looked toward the counter where the two men stood bantering. Great, he thought. Now I get a deputy to go along with the overly friendly store owner. Get in, get out, he thought. Make this shopping trip a quick one. He looked for the first time at the list Donna had given him. Tampons, lotion, a hairbrush, and a bottle of wine - Sauvignon Blanc or Pinot Grigio - written in parentheses. Seriously? he thought. She was a prisoner being held for ransom, not his girlfriend who needed a few things from his Target run. As he stood contemplating her list he glanced back towards the counter. The two men had lowered their voices, heads closer together. Don't be paranoid, he told himself. Why would they be talking about him?

The deputy was headed out the door as Ray walked up to the counter with his basket of supplies. The deputy was leaving, so maybe he could breathe easier now. He realized suddenly that Bill was talking to him. "Uh, sorry. What's that again?"

"I asked if you found everything you needed."

"Yeah. Yeah, I'm good."

Bill started ringing up the items from the basket - bread, cheese, wine, and a few other things. Ray hadn't seen any hairbrushes, but he could have sworn Bill raised his eyebrows a bit at the tampons. Ray looked out the front window as Bill continued his work. and almost dropped his wallet on the floor.

What the hell? The deputy hadn't left. He was standing behind the Tahoe and it looked like he was writing something down. The license plate number? Now he was definitely paranoid. He willed Bill to go faster while his mind raced with thoughts of what to do next. He watched the deputy walk across to his patrol car and get in, leaving the door open. So, he's not going anywhere, thought Ray.

"$74.50", said Bill.

Ray snapped back to attention and laid four twenty-dollar bills on the counter as Bill pushed the paper sacks with the goods across the counter to him. "Thanks," he mumbled as Bill handed him the change, then pushed his way out the door and into the parking lot.

The deputy looked up as he came out, smiling and raising a hand in greeting. "Take care, friend," he said through the open door of his cruiser.

Ray nodded in return, bewildered a bit by the friendly farewell on top of the apparent license plate check. Go over and see what he was up to or just get the hell out of there? Get the hell out, he thought. If he was running the plate, it would not end well. He opened the door of the Tahoe and put the sacks of groceries on the passenger seat, then closed the door. As he backed out, he could hear the man's cell phone ring through the open window. The deputy answered and immediately started laughing and getting out of his car. Good, thought Ray. A distraction.

As he exited the parking lot his mind was racing again. If the deputy was indeed going to check his plates, he would quickly find out the Tahoe belonged to Johnson. That wasn't necessarily a problem unless the deputy had been clued in to the break-in back in Raleigh, or if the plate number had been flagged in the system somehow. Shit, he thought. Of all the damn dumb bad luck to be at the right place at the wrong time. Two choices. Run or hide. If they brought in a helicopter, it would be hard to stay hidden for long. Eventually they would spot the cabin and check it out. Worse, they might set up some checkpoints quickly on 264 and 64, the only roads in or out.

Ray forced himself to drive calmly and carefully as he headed away from the store and back to the cabin. As he drove, he punched up Nick's number and put it on the speakerphone. He answered on the fourth ring. "We have a problem," he said.

"Yeah? What's that?"

After Ray told him what was happening, he replied, "Yeah. That could be a problem. You going to get the hell out of there?"

"That's what I'm thinking. Hustle back and get her, then head out pronto."

"Where to?"

Ray thought for a moment. "The motel or your place. No other good options."

"Motel. Another day or two and this thing's done."

"Call you when I get there," he said, and then ended the call. He had reached the end of Bayview Drive, and the stop sign there at 264. He checked the rear view - no sign of the cruiser - then turned right and headed back to the cabin as quickly as the speed limit would allow.

CHAPTER 21

"One. Just one break to get the ball rolling!" Jimmy pleaded as he leaned back in the chair. "All we need."

It was day six of the crime and after some promising ideas, Jimmy and Micky had spent day five going nowhere. In fact, worse than no progress, they had actually slipped backwards. The license plate on the brown van in the doorcam video was a dead end. Nothing else on any videos or coming out of canvassing the neighborhood again had proven fruitful.

Micky nodded. "Clock's ticking. This better be a hostage situation or she's probably dead."

Jimmy tossed his notepad on the desk and stood up, stretching his arms upward to relieve the tension gathered in his back. "So, what now?"

"We do what all good detectives do at this point."

"Go get a bagel!" they both said in unison, laughing as they said it.

"You're driving," said Jimmy, "that way I am not distracted and can employ my overwhelming deductive superpowers on the way to create the break we need."

Micky just shook his head. "Why don't you just turn those on now and we'll skip the bagel."

"It's not a switch, my friend. It has to be summoned and coaxed into life."

"What a crock of shit. Let's go, Columbo. I need fuel."

Ray pulled up to the cabin. He threw open the driver's door and ran the short distance to the cabin, hurriedly unlocking the door and pushing in. A few steps more and he opened the door to the bedroom holding Donna, who was startled by his sudden appearance. "What's going on?" she said, fear in her voice.

"No time to talk," he replied as he bent over to unlock what held her to the bed frame. "We have to go. Now!"

"But, what…"

"Later!" he snapped. "Time to go." He grabbed her arm firmly to help her stand and then just as firmly nudged her towards the door. As they walked through the common area and kitchen he paused. Did he have time to clean up, remove all traces they had been there? It didn't matter, he thought. He'd be in the wind before they found this place and sorted it all out.

He realized Donna had stopped also, turning to look at him, stress and uncertainty evident in her face. He took a deep breath and released it before he spoke. "A sheriff's deputy was at the store. I think he was checking the plates on the truck. If he was, this place will be crawling with cops and helicopters soon."

As he said it, he realized there was another problem he hadn't considered: if they brought in a helicopter they could be spotted from the air. The roads out were mostly two-lane for a ways. Shit, he thought. Hunker down or run? Could he ditch the Tahoe and steal another car somewhere? Maybe he could hide it in the woods, harder to spot from the air and they could stay inside the cabin.

Ray reached a decision. Run while they could. If the chance presented itself to swap cars he would take it. He looked at Donna. "Let's go," nudging her forward again.

"Are you going to tie me up again?"

He pondered that for a second, weighing the odds of what could happen if he didn't. "Yes. No choice. Go!"

Back in Raleigh, Jimmy and Micky were pulling out of the deck at police headquarters downtown. "Where to?" asked Micky.

"New place off Glenwood just opened up. Let's try that."

"Name of it?"

"Just Bagels."

"Seriously? Just Bagels. That's the best they could do?"

Jimmy laughed. "Well, I've been told they have donuts and breakfast biscuits too."

"So... they named it Just Bagels. Brilliant."

"Yeah. Brilliantly ironic."

After a spirited debate over whether grits were better with cheese or hot sauce - Jimmy voted for both - the two men sat at a table in Just Bagels. Jimmy was first to bite into his bagel sandwich, a creation with eggs, cheese, peppers, onions, chipotle aoli, and bacon. "Splendid," he declared through a mouthful of sandwich.

Micky had, true to form, chosen a healthier route. Skinny bagel, plain, with almond butter. He nodded as he took the first bite.

"That can't have any flavor," said Jimmy as he wiped his mouth. "I've seen shoe boxes that looked more appetizing."

"Arteries. Mine clear. Yours clogging as we speak."

Jimmy laughed. "We all gotta go somehow."

They sat for a few minutes, working on their bagels and coffee, talking about the case, then about sports. Eventually it turned to their dinner outing a couple of nights before. "Did she wise up after dinner or is she planning to keep seeing you?"

"Yeah, she wised up, but she's going out with me again anyway."

"You're outkicking your coverage on this one, bro."

"What? Never heard that one."

"Football analogy. Basically, it means you're dating way above your station."

"No doubt about that," said Jimmy. "She's the real deal. Having dinner again this weekend. Maybe catch a movie or some music after."

At that moment Micky's phone rang. He glanced at the incoming number, then back up at Jimmy. "Dispatch," he said as he punched to take the call. "Bondurant here." He listened for a minute, then spoke again, "Yeah, I'll take it now. Put him through."

Jimmy could only hear one side of the conversation, but it was clear that something had opened up on the case. He fidgeted in his seat for the few minutes Micky was on the call, like a kid at the fair, itching to ride again. Micky ended the conversation with a promise to call back.

"What?" asked Jimmy.

"Nothing. Just some guys coming over to power wash the house."

He threw his bagel wrapper at Micky, who laughed and threw it back. "Might be a break. Sheriff's deputy from Dare County. Was running plates on a Tahoe. Guess whose?"

"Eddie freaking Johnson!"

Micky nodded. "Yep. Deputy was at a store in a little place called Stumpy Point. Guy was in there picking up some supplies."

"Did they detain him?"

This time Micky shook his head. "Nope. He was running them for a bet he had with the store owner about whether he remembered the guy from before. He had pulled away before the deputy checked the plates. He called in a couple of other cars, and they are out cruising to see if they can spot it."

"No sign of Donna Johnson?" Jimmy asked.

"Not directly," smiled Micky. "Apparently the guy bought some, uh, feminine products though. Could be for her. Could be for his girlfriend."

"Did they..." Jimmy started to ask.

"The deputy is at the store now, having the owner run back the security camera footage from outside the store," interrupted Micky. "And before you ask, the camera inside is broken. Been like that for months. He will send footage up here as soon as he can." Jimmy nodded, excited still, but started to get the calm focus of being on the hunt again rather than spinning endlessly.

"We should…"

Jimmy's turn to interrupt. "Have Eddie look at the footage. See if he recognizes the guy."

Micky pointed a finger at him. "Bingo. Time to head back to the office. Could be a very long day."

Traffic was light, so twenty-five minutes later the two detectives were back in their office cubes. As they waited for the video footage to come through, they speculated on whether Eddie would recognize the man in the video. "If she's alive," said Jimmy, "then he knows the guy. There's something going on with Eddie. This is not a random break-in."

Micky nodded. "Agree on the break-in. Agree something's up with Eddie. Those two conclusions kind of go hand-in-hand."

"But…", Jimmy said with his hands open and a shrug of his shoulders.

"Yeah," replied Micky. "There's a but in here somewhere. Eddie is not the criminal mastermind type, so what's connecting a multi-person daylight break-in to a mildly suspicious used car dealer?"

"That, my friend, is the question that unlocks it all."

They sat silent for a few minutes, pondering the question, and were soon rewarded with the ding notification of an email marked as High Importance. They looked at each other, then Micky turned to his laptop, clicking to open the email with the video file link. "Here, or big screen?"

"Here," said Jimmy impatiently. "I can't wait any longer."

Micky laughed and clicked the link as Jimmy hovered over his right shoulder. The video was a bit grainy given the age and condition of the outdoor camera at Bill's, but the images were certainly clear enough. It opened with a lonely shot of the parking lot and gas pumps, then quickly moved to show the white Tahoe pulling in and up to the pumps. Micky paused the video when Ray got out to put gas in the tank.

"Can you zoom in?" asked Jimmy.

Micky nodded and did as requested. "That helps some, but it gets grainier, and he mostly has his back to the camera. Hard to tell much from this angle. Let's move it forward." They watched as Ray finished pumping the gas, turning to look towards the store, even waving in that direction at one point. After he parked the Tahoe near the entrance and got out to walk in, Micky paused it again. The view was a good one and they could clearly see his face as he glanced up at the camera before entering the store. Micky hit the print function to get a photo of the frame. "Just another white dude," he said,

"Yeah. Kind of average looking. Doesn't really stand out in any way."

They watched the rest of the footage, pausing at various spots as the deputy pulled in, came back out and Ray exited the store and left. "He was moving with a bit more urgency on the way out," remarked Micky. "Betting the appearance of the deputy looking at the plates had him spooked pretty well."

"Go back to the part where's he's out of the parking lot and down the street a bit. Hard to see because of the distance, but it looked like he was making a call." Micky rewound and they spent the next few minutes going back and forth in the video. They finally concluded it was impossible to know for sure, but he certainly could have been raising a cell phone up to his ear.

"Question is, who was he calling." Micky stretched as he stood up from the desk. "Second question is, where is whoever he was calling. And where is Donna."

"That's three questions, Padre. Let's get somebody looking at this and trying to find out who he is. Meanwhile, we can pay Eddie a visit to see if he recognizes the guy."

"Also meanwhile," said Micky, "maybe the Dare County cops catch him, and we can ask him ourselves who he is."

"Copy that!" replied Jimmy as they high fived in celebration.

Eddie was out on the lot looking at a car when Lila's voice came over the outside loudspeaker. "Eddie, call on line two. Guy says you're going to want to take this." He looked at Otto, who was on the lot with him. "Guess who," he said.

Otto nodded. "Want me to listen in?"

Eddie shook his head. "Not taking a chance he hears you and knows that someone else knows." Otto nodded again and Eddie walked quickly across the lot and into his office, shutting the door behind him and ignoring Lila's pleading looks to tell her more. He stood beside his desk and picked up the phone's receiver. "Johnson here," he said as firmly as he could muster.

Nick's voice came through from the other end. "Eddie, are you ready to make that trade we discussed?"

"Almost."

"Almost? What if I told you she is almost alive, Eddie? That work for you?"

"No. Wait. Really. I'm almost ready. Two million is a lot of money, man. I need a little more time."

"How much time, Eddie?"

"Another week, tops."

Nick was silent, giving Eddie time to sweat a little. "Why should I wait, Eddie? You agreed to our terms already. Maybe I start taking off pieces of her arms and legs while I wait. Give you an incentive to move faster."

"No! No! Don't do that! Give me five days, then."

"You have three. No more. Don't disappoint me again, Eddie." The line went dead.

Eddie stuck his head out of the office doorway, "Lila, get Otto in here for me," then closed the door and went back to his desk. Lila gave Bill a look, who just shrugged his shoulders, then went out to find

Otto. She didn't have to go far. He was sitting in one of the rockers on the front porch. "Boss wants you in his office."

Otto nodded and rose from the chair to enter the building. Lila stopped him with her question. "Otto, what's going on with Eddie?"

"Need to ask him about that," he replied as he walked around her and inside. She followed behind him, watching him close the door to Eddie's office as she made her way back to her desk. She looked at Bill again. He shrugged once more, and she decided to keep her questions to herself. For now.

Eddie motioned Otto to a seat beside his desk. "Prefer to stand," he said.

"Fine. He gave me three more days. Threatened to start cutting her up if I'm late."

"Ready to make that call?"

Eddie paused a long time before answering, getting up from his desk and looking out to the lot. "How did I get to this place?" he asked. Otto declined to answer him, standing silently against the wall. He breathed out a heavy sigh of resignation, then turned to Otto. "Okay, how do we do this?"

Jimmy and Micky were on their way to the lot and rolled up a few minutes after Lila had retrieved Otto. As he put the car in park, Jimmy remarked, "Kind of dead out here today. Nary a customer in sight."

"Nary? That's actually a word?"

"Yes sir, Mr. Bayou. It is indeed a word. Even had it on our spelling tests in grade school."

"You are so full of shit."

"Uh-huh. That I am. That I am."

Lila looked up as they entered, a big smile of recognition lighting up her face. "Detectives, what a pleasant surprise to see you again. Micky and Jimmy, right?"

"Ma 'am," replied Micky in greeting.

"That's right," said Jimmy. "Good to see you also."

"What brings you out today? Good news, I hope."

"Not yet," said Micky. "Progress though. Mr. Johnson in?"

"He is, but he was on a call. Let me see if he's available. Can I get you some coffee while you wait?" Micky declined, and Jimmy told her he could make it himself. Lila pointed across the room to where the coffee pot was and then went over to knock on Eddie's door.

"Yeah, I saw them drive up," Eddie said before she could get a word out. "Tell them I need a few more minutes and they can come in."

"Yes sir," Lila replied, closing the door again. They had finished the call just before Micky and Jimmy entered the lot. Bruno Rezavik had heard them out, telling them he would discuss the matter with his brother. Eddie was fighting to remain calm. "What do you think, Otto? Will they help me out or kill us both?"

Otto stroked the stubble of beard on his chin. "They might kill you. Me? Not so much. They will make us squirm, especially you, for a while. But Anton will see the dollar signs in this for them and agree to it."

Eddie breathed out a sigh of relief. "Never thought being partners with a drug lord would make me happy, but as long as it gets Donna home, that's all that matters. We'll find a way out one day."

Otto shook his head. "Don't be naive, Eddie. It's not that simple."

"Well, we'll see," replied Eddie. "Right now, I gotta' deal with my next performance. Put on a show for these detectives, act like I'm clueless about Donna's fate."

Otto was thinking it shouldn't be too hard for Eddie to act clueless but decided to keep that thought to himself. "I'll leave now. Tell them you need a couple more minutes."

Eddie nodded and Otto walked out into the office and over to Lila's desk. "Boss says he needs a couple more minutes." Otto looked towards Jimmy and Micky, acknowledging their presence. "Detectives."

"Otto," replied Micky in return, followed by Jimmy doing the same. With that, Otto exited the building. The detectives exchanged a look, then turned as Lila spoke with a forced cheerfulness that covered up her questions, "Just a couple more minutes, gentlemen. More coffee?" Both men shook their heads and settled back into their chairs.

A few minutes later, the phone buzzed on Lila's desk. After a quick conversation, she told Jimmy and Micky they could go back to Eddie's office. They found Eddie seated behind his desk with paperwork spread in front of him. He rose as they entered, shaking hands, and motioning them to the seats at his desk.

Jimmy spoke first. "Sorry to interrupt. Looks like you're busy here," motioning to the mound of paper on the desk.

"Yeah, yeah. Trying to catch up a little, you know. Keep my mind occupied." Micky would remark later to Jimmy that Eddie's mind seemed exceptionally occupied that morning. "What brings you out? Good news, I hope."

"Maybe," replied Micky. "We might have caught our first break." He sketched out the basics of the Tahoe being spotted near the Outer Banks.

"Did they catch him?" Eddie asked, suddenly excited this might lead to finding her quickly without needing a ransom.

Jimmy shook his head. "Not yet. He was captured on a security camera outside the store. Anyone you might recognize?" he asked as he laid the still image of Ray on the desk in front of Eddie.

Eddie picked up the photo and examined it for a few moments. He sighed and passed it back to them. "No. Afraid not."

"You sure?" asked Micky. He passed the photo back. "Look one more time."

Eddie did, then shook his head. "Sorry. I can't recall ever seeing that man."

Micky accepted the photo back from Eddie. "Okay. We have our folks passing this through facial recognition, see if we can get a hit on him."

"Good. That's good."

"How are you holding up, Eddie?" asked Jimmy.

Eddie rolled a bit closer to his desk and propped his arms on the paperwork. "You know, hanging in there. Trying to stay busy, Keep my mind occupied."

"And physically? Feeling okay?"

"Yeah. Yeah. Doing good."

Jimmy and Micky allowed a few moments of awkward silence to pass. When it was clear that Eddie had nothing else to offer, they rose from their chairs, followed quickly by Eddie. After handshakes and a promise to let him know if anything else broke in the investigation they left his office.

Lila rose and followed them onto the porch. The usual sunshine demeanor on her face had given way to dark clouds and Micky quickly spotted it. "Miss Lila, is everything okay?"

"No. Something's not okay, but I don't know what it is, and I don't think I can talk about it right now."

Micky gave her a reassuring smile. "That's okay. Just call the station as soon as you can. They will put you through to one of us."

Lila nodded and thanked them, turning and going back into the office. Jimmy raised an eyebrow at Micky, who acknowledged it with his own quizzical look and slight shrug of the shoulders.

"Talk to me Ray," said Nick, answering on the first ring. "You make it back to the motel?"

"Yeah, we're here. Finally. Took every back road I knew about on the way."

"What about the Tahoe?"

"We gotta' ditch that ride fast, Nick. It's sitting outside my room right now just begging somebody to ask questions. Starting with Bobby."

"Okay. I'll send Penny with your truck to swap it, then we'll dump it somewhere."

"Good. Call me after. And tell Penny to come in the back way. Bobby sees someone else driving my truck he's gonna' ask what's up."

Nick agreed and ended the call. Ray turned to look at Donna. "A few more days and we're done. You'll be back with Eddie."

"Okay," she replied softly, but she couldn't help but ask herself. Did she want to be back with Eddie, the drug dealer? Was it possible Ray had been lying or at least mistaken? She had time to try and figure it out. But not much. The clock was ticking.

CHAPTER 22

The workday was starting to wind to a close for Jimmy and Micky, at least the part where they were on the clock. Being a detective is pretty much a 24/7 kind of job. The day had started with a bang, then settled into the routines of the chase. The Dare County Sheriff's department, with help from local state police had spent the afternoon cruising the roads and highways around the area where Eddie's Tahoe had been spotted. They had even called in a helicopter from the state police regional headquarters, but they hadn't been able to get approvals to get it in the air until the middle of the afternoon. After a couple of hours with no positive sightings, the state police brass had ordered it back home.

Not that they hadn't spotted a white Tahoe. On the contrary, white turned out to be a very popular color of Tahoe for locals and tourists in the area. They simply couldn't send a patrol car to check every sighting. Randy, the deputy who had traced the plates at Bill's originally, had just called Micky with the last scheduled update of the day. All cruisers would remain on high alert for the Tahoe but would return to their normal patrol routines. Micky thanked Randy for all the work and ended the call.

"Well?" asked Jimmy. "Anything?"

Micky shook his head. "Not yet. Something will turn though."

"Love your optimism. We need it."

"Facial recognition give us anything yet?"

"Nope. That's part of why we need your optimism. Positive vibes to move us forward."

Both men started shutting down computers and preparing to leave for the day. Just as he stood to go, the phone on Jimmy's desk rang. He looked at Micky. "Someone always comes in right at closing time."

Micky shrugged. "Might be Lila."

"Great point." Jimmy dropped his keys on the desk and answered. "Quinn here." He listened for a moment, then nodded at Micky. "Put her through," he said. Another moment of silence, then "Lila, it's Jimmy Quinn with Raleigh PD. Tell me what's going on."

For the next five minutes or so he mostly listened, occasionally clarifying or asking a question. "Okay, Lila. You did the right thing by calling us. Could all be just coincidence and nothing to worry about. We'll start checking things out, okay?" He listened for a few more moments, then told her goodbye and that she should stay in touch if she needed to tell them anything new. He placed the receiver down in its cradle, then sat and turned to face Micky, who looked at him with eyebrows raised. "She thinks something's going on with Otto."

"Well, there's a news flash."

Jimmy laughed. "Yeah. No, she thinks it might be related to the break-in and Donna. She says Eddie almost never spends time talking to Otto, but the last couple of days they have been besties. Then today Eddie's acting all nervous and kind of weird, has her summon Otto to his office and they both are on a long call with their finance guy from Wilmington. Rezavik, I think is his name."

"Hmm. So how does she tie that to Donna being missing?"

"She can't directly. Says it's just an intuition she has. And that Otto is even creepier and more smug than usual."

"I don't know, Jimmy. I can buy that Otto and Eddie might be up to something, but scenarios where them plus these Rezavik guys combine to be at the center of this crime? Maybe, but the tumblers don't fall into place for me on that. They are finance guys. What would drag them into this?"

Jimmy pondered this for a few moments. "Yeah, I see what you mean." After a few more moments of silence his face lit up in a grin. "Look on the bright side, though. Maybe we can solve two crimes at once. Get you that promotion even sooner!"

Micky laughed. "You would be lost without me. But a promotion does sound good."

"You go ahead and take off. I'm going to call my brother Tommy. See what he knows about the Rezaviks. They are right there on his turf in Wilmington."

"Sounds good. Call me if anything pops. Otherwise, see you in the a.m."

Jimmy's call rolled to voicemail, but he didn't leave a message. Instead, he texted Tommy to call him back as soon as possible. He was starting to do an internet search on the Rezavik brothers when his phone buzzed. "Bro, what took you so long to respond?"

Tommy laughed. "What do you want? I got people to see."

Jimmy sketched out the basics on Eddie and the Rezaviks. Tommy knew of them, but not much about them. He promised he would nose around a bit locally and see if any dirt on them came up. After a few minutes of chatting about family and sports they said their goodbyes, Tommy promising to call back the next day.

Jimmy hung up the call and thought about what to do next. Not much more he could do on the case right now. It was waiting time again. Maybe Dani is off tonight. he thought. Grab some dinner and drinks. Clear his head. Just what he needed.

Things were quiet out at the Lake Pine Motel. Ray and Donna, both prisoners inside Ray's room, hadn't talked much since getting back to the motel. There wasn't much to say, really. They were waiting out the clock now. Ray had stopped at a small grocery store on the way back, so they had some food. It was risky, he knew, but less risky than leaving her alone in the motel room once they got back.

The remains of their dinner sat on the table in front of them. Frozen meal for her, sandwich for him. They were both reading, a book for him and a magazine for her. He had picked these up at the grocery store with the food. Staring at the walls for two days wasn't appealing and Ray had been a reader since childhood. Donna looked at him for a moment, then commented, "Kind of strange, you know."

Ray looked up. "What's that?"

"I said, kind of strange, you know."

"Yeah. I heard that. What are you talking about? What's strange?"

"You. A criminal. Kidnapper. Reading a book."

Ray sighed and put the book down. "So, a criminal can't be a reader? Be educated? Just one dimension, huh? Criminal."

Donna put her magazine down as well. "No. Sorry, It's just surprising. To me, anyway. I don't know. Never really known any criminals, I guess. Don't know what to expect. TV and movies are my only reference points on criminals. Oh, and the news of course."

Ray laughed. "I'm not a criminal. I just occasionally commit crimes. Think of it this way. Ever told a lie?"

Donna nodded.

"So, if someone says you're a liar, are they right?"

"I see your point, but..."

At that moment, Ray's phone vibrated. He held up his hold-that-thought hand to Donna as he picked up his phone. Drew. "Gotta take this," he said to Donna. "How about going into the bathroom so you don't hear it."

Donna did as requested and Ray answered as she closed the door. "Drew, what's going on?"

"Ray, we need to talk. Can you meet me at the Chute?"

"What's so urgent, Ray?"

"Not over the phone. Better to be in person. I can come to you. You at the motel?"

"No," Ray lied, suddenly uneasy about what Drew had to say. "You have something to say it's gonna' have to be by phone."

"Shit. Well, okay. It's Rose."

"What about Rose?"

"Umm, let's just say she's dropped out of your band."

"What the hell does that mean, Drew? Don't talk in circles."

"She's dead, Ray."

"Dead? What happened, Drew?" he asked in a loud voice, loud enough that Donna clearly heard this part through the bathroom door. Ray suddenly realized how loud he was and dialed it way down. "Did you have something to do with it?"

"No. Well, not exactly."

Ray also suddenly realized there had been no introductions made when Drew came out to the motel to take care of Donna. "How do you even know her name?"

"Ran into her at the Chute a couple of nights ago. She was out there with a mutual friend. We played it cool. Acted like we didn't know each other, which, really, we didn't."

"So, what happened, Drew?"

Drew ran him through a very abbreviated, and well edited, version of events the night Rose died. One that had him begging Rose not to do the drugs. "Nothing I could do, Ray. She was hell-bent on getting high."

Ray knew his friend well enough to know he hadn't been given the full story, but he didn't challenge Drew any further. "Who else knows?"

"Nobody. Her friend called me when she couldn't get Rose to answer her phone the next day, but I convinced her Rose was fine when I left and had been talking about going back to her group of friends."

Ray digested that for a few moments. "Okay. You know where this friend lives?"

"Yeah. Why?"

"In case we need to pay her a visit. Calm her down."

"What does that mean, Ray?"

"Means what I said. We don't need her running to the police with a missing person report."

"Yeah. I'm the first one they come and visit."

"Bingo," said Ray. "Keep me posted on this, Drew. Anything else?"

Drew hesitated. Should he ask to be cut in now? Would he lose his chance if he waited?

"Come on, Drew," said Ray, sensing the hesitation. "What is it?"

"Okay. You lost a partner, Ray. Maybe you need another."

Ray felt the prickle of agitation in his brain. He knew immediately where Drew was headed. He also jumped quickly to the idea that maybe Rose's death was no accident. Had he killed her to position himself as her replacement? "And you're the new partner?" he asked calmly.

Drew swallowed and breathed out his answer. "Yeah. I can do that."

Ray was silent. Long enough so that Drew thought he might have hung up. "Ray?"

"Yeah, I'm here," he replied." Tell me, Drew, what are you bringing to us in this deal?"

Drew chose his words carefully. "Whatever you need, Ray. I'm pretty resourceful."

"What makes you think we need something?"

"Everybody needs something, Ray. Eventually."

Ray sighed before he responded. "Did you kill her Drew?"

"Come on, Ray," he said, his voice rising. "I'm not the type that could kill someone."

Ray's reply sent shivers across Drew's body. "So, if we needed that, Drew, you're saying it's not something you could provide?"

Now Drew was flustered. "Yeah. No. I mean, yeah Ray. I'll do what I gotta do. You know that man!"

Ray ran his hand across his head and breathed out slowly, forcing down the anger that was coming up. "I need to think about this Drew before I take it to Nick."

"Sure. Sure. I get it. Just let me know."

"Text me the name and address of that mutual friend, Drew. Let's start there."

"You got it."

" And Drew..."

"Yeah, Ray?"

"Lay low. Don't do anything stupid."

Nick and Penny had finished their dinner and were sitting outside on the porch, polishing off the bottle of wine they had opened earlier. They weren't talking much. Just sharing the space and listening to the night. Penny laid her hand on his leg. "Where are you, Nickie?"

Nick took another sip of wine. "Just thinking, babe."

She nodded. "What about?"

"The usual."

Penny sighed. The usual meant Nick's medical status. It was not good. A year earlier, when he had a regular job and insurance benefits, he had started having some pains in his abdomen. These eventually spread to his back and became severe enough that Penny threatened to leave him if he didn't see a doctor. So, he did.

After several tests and scans, his doctor called one afternoon with the results. Pancreatic cancer. Stage four. Essentially a death sentence. The icing on the cake for that day was the call he had gotten an hour later. Don't come in to work, they said. We regret to inform you that we have to make some layoffs. Your position has been eliminated. They sent him a check for two weeks of severance. Then cancelled his insurance benefits at the end of that month.

He was in a funk for a few months. No work and the pain wasn't getting any better. A couple of trips to emergency rooms got him something for the pain, but those pills were about gone now. Penny begged him to go see a doctor again, maybe apply for charity care.

Nick refused. He knew where that ended. The same place after months of treatments that would leave him weak and emaciated. Dead.

He hadn't told his ex-wife or their two kids. Only Penny and Ray knew of his fate. Nick didn't talk to his ex, anyway. They both remained bitter about Nick's past. She left the marriage after his second arrest. Took the kids and moved three states away. That was what ate at him the most. Never seeing those kids since. He sent cards - birthdays, Christmas and the like. With a bit of money when he could. Sometimes they wrote back. Not often, and not in over two years.

So, he had decided to die on his own terms. But not before he had a little something to leave behind. For those kids. For Penny. The idea had come to him a few weeks back, on a night when he was feeling particularly hopeless. He had stopped at a place called The Bull Chute for a beer and a whiskey chaser. On the third round a guy sat next to him at the bar. Not a very friendly fellow, but after a couple of beers of his own the guy started talking to Nick.

After an hour of grousing about life and what a shithole the country had become, Nick confided that he needed to find a way to get some money. Fast. He didn't have a lot of time. The guy seemed sympathetic, hinted around at some things. Finally, Nick had enough whiskey, more than he needed, but not so much he couldn't drive, he thought. Said his good-byes, maybe he would follow up. Otto wished him well, said he would see him around maybe.

Nick made it home, thankfully without hurting anyone or himself on the way. He knew it was a bad idea to drive, but he did it anyway. Also, a bad idea to keep drinking when he got home. Did that anyway too. Penny was working an overnight shift and not there to stop him. So, he stayed up most of the night, part of thinking about the things Otto had said. He did his own math and arrived at an answer: Otto and his boss were moving drugs. Drugs meant cash. He needed that. A plan was born.

Penny snapped him back from remembering that night. "Nickie, let's go to bed. I'm tired."

Nick leaned over and kissed her. "You go on, babe. I'll be up in a few."

Penny left him there with his thoughts and the rest of his wine. She hadn't been gone long when his phone buzzed. Ray. "Yeah."

Ray got right to it. "Might have a new problem." He proceeded to fill him in on his talk with Drew.

Nick stood and walked into the yard, pacing now to tamp down the adrenaline of his agitation. "How much does he want, Ray?"

"Didn't say. He probably thinks Rose was cut in for an equal share."

"No way he gets 25% on this," said Nick.

"Agreed."

They were both silent for a few moments, wheels turning. Finally, Nick said, "What do you think, Ray? Do we give him anything?"

"Well, I think the risk he goes to the police is slim. He was with her the night she died. It won't be easy to explain that away. Still, the risk ain't zero. He might be clever enough to concoct some kind of story that works."

"What's in it for him if he does, though?"

Ray thought a minute before he answered. "Good point. Not much. Unless he trades us for a clear name on her."

They talked back and forth a bit longer, Nick wanting to hold the line at giving up nothing, with Ray arguing for something to give Drew. After all, he had helped them out with Donna's injury. Finally, they settled on a flat amount over a percentage cut. Ray agreed to handle it with Drew the next day and they said their goodbyes for the night.

Nick drained his wine and shook his head. Even to the end, he thought, nothing is ever easy. He turned off the porch light and headed upstairs to Penny.

Ray sat quietly after finishing the call with Nick, contemplating how to handle the offer to Drew. He wondered how much they had to give Drew for him to stay quiet and compliant. He knew that Drew could be a little volatile, so it wasn't just the amount. It was also the way it was presented. He needed Drew to feel like they were sacrificing, at least a little, to take care of him. The best way to do that, he figured, was to lie about the total ransom, making his part seem like a more important share than it really was. There was no way he would ever really know, and even if he found out, Nick and Ray would be long gone. A very good plan, he thought. He would call Drew in the morning.

CHAPTER 23

Jimmy woke early, unusual for him. It took a moment for him to realize where he was. He turned his head to look at the woman next to him. She seemed to have a slight smile on her face, dreaming about something. Last night? Him? God, she was beautiful, he thought. And smart. Too smart for him. That was clear.

She stirred a bit, rolling a little more his way. He wanted to reach out and touch her, brush her hair back from her face. Kiss her again. He moved his face closer to hers. He didn't want to wake her, so he stopped short, breathing her in. Remembering last night. Dinner. Laughter. Serious discussions. Kissing her at the front door. Her pulling him into the house. Urgent with each other. Then slower. Learning and giving. Finally, urgent again. Then calm, content, peaceful. Perfect.

She stirred again, more this time. "What time is it officer?" she whispered with her eyes closed.

Now he reached up and brushed her hair back. "Early."

Dani opened her eyes to gaze at Jimmy. He's a complicated man, she thought. But she liked that. Complicated wasn't boring. She didn't like boring. Hard to be an emergency room doctor if you did.

"Why did you become a cop?" she asked.

He thought for a moment, then replied, "My sister is an addict."

"Hmm. Seems an unlikely reason to become a cop."

Jimmy laughed. "That's fair. She's in recovery now. Always will be, I guess. She started abusing alcohol in her teens, after our mom left, then added drugs. Got in a bunch of trouble for all kinds of things. One night she was super high, disoriented and stumbling around our hometown. I was home for the weekend. Local cop, good guy named Pete, brought her home. He could have taken her in, booked her and thrown her in a cell. Instead, he chose kindness and compassion. Then he made it clear to her, and us, before he left, that next time he wouldn't bring her home. First time I realized that compassion and law and order could live together."

Dani stroked his cheek. "So, it inspired you, huh?"

"Not right away. She didn't change her ways. More trouble, more cops. I witnessed a few who were nothing like Pete. Treated her like trash. That's what inspired me. The need to balance the scales. Add more kindness to the world of law enforcement. Plus, I always loved mysteries and solving puzzles."

They lay quietly in bed for a few minutes. Then Jimmy asked, "How about you? Why a doctor? Why emergency?"

Now Dani laughed. "My dad is an addict, too. But not like your sister."

"What do you mean, he's an alcoholic?"

"Oh, no. Far from it. He's addicted to medicine but providing it rather than taking it. He is - was - a doctor also. Oncologist. Had a lab at UNC as well, studied cellular mechanisms, looking for ways to cure cancers."

"So, how is he addicted? To medicine?"

Dani sighed, rolling onto her back, staring at the ceiling. "He worked a lot, even before my mom died."

"What happened to her?"

"The greatest of ironies. Cancer. She was also a scientist. PhD, also with a lab at UNC. She collaborated a lot with my dad, trying to find ways to cure what eventually killed her. After she died, he became even more addicted. Doubled down on his work. He couldn't save her, but he was determined to save us."

"Wow. That's a lot. How old was she, you know, when she died?"

"Forty-six."

"And you?"

"Twelve."

"What about your dad? How is he now?"

"He's good. Mostly retired but still works some in his lab. Determined to find cures." Dani rolled back towards Jimmy. "This is heavy for first thing in the morning. How are we going to lighten it up?"

Jimmy laughed. "Well, I have an addiction, too. It started recently and it's been growing."

"Yeah. What's that?"

He leaned in and kissed her, reaching for her under the sheets. "There's this doctor. I can't get enough of her. Can you help?"

"Oh, yeah. I have something for that." She rolled on top of him and whispered, "But you might need the ER when I'm done!"

Mid-morning and Drew was sipping coffee at his kitchen table, wondering what he would do that day. Without the burden of a full-time job, it was up to him. No wife or kids to answer to. His parents had been dead for years. His only sibling lived in Oregon with her partner. He was totally, and wonderfully from his perspective, on his own.

He was feeling optimistic. He did okay living off his army pension and the occasional odd job or medical services he provided to friends and acquaintances. The modest inheritance from his parents provided a safety net. But more would be nice. Allow him to travel some. Maybe get a small house somewhere, get out of his one-bedroom apartment. This deal with Ray and Nick might do that. He smiled and sipped the last of his coffee before rising to start the day.

Drew's phone buzzed as he was getting up from the table. Ray.

Good news, he hoped. He sat back down and answered with a happy good morning to Ray.

"Drew, you alone? We need to talk."

"Sure, Ray. What's up?"

"I talked to Nick. He sends his regards and his thanks for helping us out."

"Yeah. Of course, Ray."

"First, I gotta' ask again, Drew. Are you willing to do whatever it takes, whatever we ask if we cut you in on this deal?"

"Sure."

"Okay. Here's the deal. We're not going to get as much money out of this one as we had hoped. Guy just doesn't have the juice. And Rose wasn't getting an equal share. So, we do the math and it looks like $25 grand to you."

Drew shook a cigarette out of the pack on the table, lit it and blew out a cloud of smoke before answering. "Well, Ray, I appreciate the offer man. I really do. Just a disappointing number, ya know?"

Ray took a deep breath to calm his irritation before replying. "Yeah, I get it. We're all disappointed with this one, Drew. Next one will be bigger. We'll get you in on that one."

Drew didn't say anything.

"Look, think of it like this," Ray went on. "We probably won't need you anymore on this one, so $25K for some medical services a couple of times is a pretty good payday."

"Yeah, Ray. I hear you, man. But you know, it's more than that. What I've done on this."

"How's that, Drew?"

"Rose ain't gonna' be talking and she won't be found dead in her apartment for the cops to tie her back to you guys."

Ray was getting more pissed off by the moment now, but knew an argument was pointless and would only make it worse with Drew. "Not sure I am fully buying the value on that but tell you what. I'll cut another $25 grand out of my own pocket. Double your take. That work?"

Drew decided not to push it further for now. "Yeah, Ray. That's a little better. Appreciate you bro." Ray told him he would be in touch in a few days and to lay low until then. Drew agreed and ended the call. Better than nothing, but not what he hoped. He needed to think this through.

Drew's day wasn't about to get any better. He had barely hung up with Ray when the phone buzzed again. Tammy calling. He wanted to send it to voice mail but thought better of it. He needed to control her actions as best he could. "Hey, Tammy. Heard from Rose?"

"No. Thats why I'm calling. Have you heard from her?"

"Not a peep." Drew didn't offer more. He could hear Tammy breathing on the other end. He waited.

Finally, "Drew, I'm scared. I don't know what to do," she said.

"What can you do? Nothing but wait her out. Has she done anything like this before?" Please say yes, he was thinking.

"Well, yeah. Once or twice."

"So, she's probably fine. She will call you soon."

Tammy's voice cracked a little. "This feels different. After all the bad things she said the other night about that guy and his friends. It just seems wrong she went flying back to them."

Drew decided to test her a little. "Huh. That's interesting. You know the guy?"

"Nope. Never met him. Just know his first name. Ray."

Drew took a deep breath. "Ray, huh? Know where he lives?"

"No. She never told me. Said he didn't like people knowing where he lives. What if he's some kind of psycho?"

Drew snorted. "Come on Tammy. Wouldn't he have already killed her if he was psycho?"

She reluctantly agreed he might have a point. Drew prodded her with a few more questions, made some comments designed to talk her off her ledge, then promised to call her if he heard from Rose.

They ended the call, and he stood in his kitchen, thinking. First Ray's lousy offer. Now Tammy was on the prowl to find Rose. And she knew Ray's first name. Suddenly he remembered the night Ray met him at The Bull Chute and asked him for help. Tammy had been talking to him when Ray arrived. Did he introduce them? He didn't think so. Huh, he thought. Very interesting. Maybe he could find an angle in that. Pressure Ray for more. Optimistic once again, he crushed his smoke out, whistling as he headed to the shower.

The Rezavik brothers had just finished lunch - a steak for Bruno, fish for Anton - and were pouring the last of a nice bottle of wine as they started on dessert. The dessert was their favorite, King Cake. But not just anybody's King Cake. No. This was a slice from Hayes Barton Café in Raleigh the restaurant had recently begun carrying. Anton took the first bite, then smiled at his brother. "This cake. It never fails to delight, no?"

Bruno nodded as he shoved his second bite in. "Yes, of course." He could be a man of few words. Especially while eating.

Anton took a sip of wine, then got to the main event of their lunch meeting. "This business in Raleigh, what is our plan exactly?"

Bruno held up a finger, motioning for a pause while he finished his fifth bite of the cake. After a generous swallow of wine to wash it down, he responded. "We go. We get the woman. They agree to do as we say for business. I come home. Easy."

Anton laughed. He knew Bruno was playing the simpleton on purpose and had a much more thought-out plan. So, he waited for his brother to say more. Bruno drained the last of his wine, then looked at Anton. "There are two plans. In one, we simply meet the captors, give them what they asked for, we get the woman, and everyone goes home unharmed. One side richer, one side poorer."

"And plan two?"

"More complicated. I will have to assess the variables on the ground in Raleigh to finalize it. But basically, we discover where she is being held, raid the facility in the pre-dawn hours, take her alive. We remain richer. They will perhaps be deader."

Anton laughed again. "Bravo, my brother! Who will assist you?"

His phone buzzed, so Bruno looked at it before answering, sending it voice mail. "Ethan."

"Perfect. Reliable. Tough. A man after your own heart."

Bruno nodded. "Yes. He is one of our best."

"And only him?" asked Anton. "That is enough? I worry for your safety, brother."

Bruno signaled to the waiter for coffee before replying. "No. Otto and Johnson will also be with us. Johnson must have skin in this game, as they say."

"Brilliant. Let us toast to your success and to an expansion of our business!" Anton snapped his fingers for the waiter, pleased with the ingenuity Bruno was displaying.

Tommy rose from his table across the room, leaving some cash to cover his bill. He had been too far away to overhear what the Rezaviks had discussed, but clearly, they were pleased with something. Time to go dig some more, see what he could find for Jimmy.

Back in Raleigh, Jimmy and Micky were taking one more pass through the additional video cam footage they had secured from the days just before the break-in. They had been through it three times already. The brown van had shown up the day prior, but it went quickly by the house that caught it, and they were not able to make out its driver or anything else of use.

"Remind me why we're doing this again," said Jimmy.

"We're professionals," Micky said without taking his eyes off the screen. "No stone unturned."

"There's no blood in this stone, Mick."

"You got something better for us to look at right now, Mr. Impatient?"

"No, but whining makes me feel better."

Micky laughed and continued moving the footage forward. Jimmy settled in and focused on the screen again. They stopped it again at the van and a couple of other vehicles, commenting on various things, but once again concluded there was nothing there that helped them.

The video ended and Micky pushed back from the table. "What about Otto?" he asked.

"What about him?"

"He has a criminal past and gives off strong vibes of a criminal present."

Jimmy nodded. "That's true. Maybe he is reforming and still shedding his vibes, though. What ties him to this?"

"Maybe he knows something we don't know about Eddie. He and some friends planned the break-in robbery. He stays out of the action since he's easier to tie in."

"That's possible, I suppose. Needs to be a pretty big payday."

"Yeah. At least three of them were involved, including Otto. Maybe four."

They were silent for a couple of moments, contemplating possibilities. "Won't hurt to dig in on him a little more, I guess. Tommy knows some shady types through his security firm contacts. I'll put the word out with him to check his network for any Otto intel."

"Great." Micky looked at his watch. "End of another beautiful workday, bro. Lets' check out of here."

"You go. Gonna' call Tommy, do a little paperwork before I leave."

"10-4. See you in the a.m."

Jimmy reached for his phone, had a sudden thought and set it back down. Something in their Otto file to check before he called Tommy. Something about the Wilmington area was coming back to him.

CHAPTER 24

Tammy had just finished the morning shift at The Farmer and was outside at the back of the restaurant, nervously smoking a cigarette. Her hands were shaking a little from the mixture of caffeine, lack of sleep, and worry about Rose. She didn't trust Drew's version of events. Something was off. Sometimes Rose took a while to respond but she always returned Tammy's calls.

Today was the fourth day since she had last seen Tammy at the Bull Chute with Drew. She had been hesitating to go to the police. Not out of fear of Drew. She could take care of herself if needed. Ironically, it was for Rose's sake. She had some minor things on her record already and God only knew what this group she was running with was up to.

Still, four days, she thought. That's too long. She had waited enough and needed to act before she lost her mind. Tammy ground her cigarette out in the gravel lot and headed back inside to tell her boss she needed the rest of the day off. He wouldn't like it, but she had been there a long time, and he owed her some favors.

An hour later, Jimmy and Micky were at their cubes batting around ideas for how to shake their case loose when a desk sergeant named

Peterson showed up. "Pete, how's it going?" asked Jimmy. "You bring us tickets to the policeman's ball?"

"Hell no, 'ya wiseass. No one's gonna' go with you anyway."

Micky shook his head. "I don't know, Pete. He's got him a live one these days."

"She'll move on soon enough," Peterson replied. "You two working that break-in case on East Lane? Johnson. Missing person."

Jimmy nodded. "Someone here to confess?"

Peterson looked at Micky, exasperated. "This guy," pointing at Jimmy, "does he ever stop?"

Micky laughed. "Never."

Peterson turned back to Jimmy. "No, shit for brains. But there is a woman downstairs says she has a friend missing. Friend told her to ask for the Johnson cops."

Jimmy and Micky sat up straight and exchanged looks. "Damn, Pete," said Jimmy, "why didn't you just open with that?"

Peterson turned without a word to go back downstairs, throwing a middle finger back to Jimmy as he walked away. "Love 'ya, Pete," Jimmy shouted. "Be down there in a flash." To which Peterson added the other middle finger before he disappeared around a corner.

"You go get her," said Micky. "I'll clear out the conference room."

Jimmy nodded. "Get that video queued up."

"Duh," replied Micky, and Jimmy left to escort the woman to their floor.

A few minutes later Jimmy led Tammy into the conference room. Micky rose from the table and offered his hand in greeting as he introduced himself. Tammy settled herself at the conference room table and Jimmy quickly returned with a bottle of water for her.

Jimmy got things started. "Ms. Sherrin, we..."

"Tammy, please," she interrupted.

"Yes, of course. Tammy. First, thank you for taking the time to come downtown to share what you know about your friend who is missing." Tammy nodded, taking a swallow of the water. "Detective

Bondurant and I would like to hear your story and then we may have a few questions. Okay?"

Again, she nodded. More water. Nerves creeping in.

"Last thing, we usually like to record things like this. With your permission, of course. Is that okay?"

Now the nerves roared in and were on full display as she replied, "Am... am I some kind of suspect? Do I need a lawyer?" she stammered.

"No, no," said Micky, reaching a hand across the table, laying it on her arm in reassurance. "Not at all. It could help us later in case some small detail you say is critical and we didn't remember it. We can listen again to those details to remind us."

She looked at Jimmy for more reassurance and he smiled and nodded in agreement.

"Um, okay, but can you state on the recording that I'm not a suspect? Will you do that?"

"Absolutely," replied Micky.

"Okay then."

Micky started the recorder, stating who they were interviewing, the date, and other necessary details. He finished with a few words about Tammy being interviewed willingly and having come in as a concerned citizen, not as a suspect. After asking her if she was comfortable moving forward and getting her consent, he pushed the microphone in her direction a bit and nodded to Jimmy to begin.

"Okay. Tammy, please start by telling us why you are here today."

"Well, my friend is missing, and I'm worried something bad has happened to her."

Jimmy prompted her to state her friend's name and then asked her how long Rose had been missing. After replying, Jimmy asked her to talk about what led Tammy to them. "The last day I saw her, actually it was that night, she was really upset and had been drinking most of the day. She said she had been away with this guy she had been seeing and his friends and now they had sent her back home."

She paused for some water and a moment to blow her nose. "She got fired from her job waitressing because she hadn't shown up for her shifts and hadn't called in sick. On top of that this guy, Ray is his name, seemed to be losing any interest he had in her."

"Did she say anything about where they had been?" asked Micky.

"No. Just away. That's all she would say."

Jimmy leaned in a bit. "How long had she been gone before you saw her that night?"

Tammy thought for a minute. "Hard to say, exactly. We don't see each other every day. Five days. Maybe six?"

Jimmy nodded and made some notes. "Okay. What happened that last night you saw her?"

Tammy told them about meeting her at The Bull Chute to have some drinks. How they sat at the bar and talked for a while before the band started playing.

"And this is when she said something to you about contacting the police?"

"Yeah. She was pretty tight-lipped about it, though. She just said if anything happened to her, I should contact the cops handling the break-in at the Johnson's."

"And that's all she would say?"

"Yes. I pushed for more, but she wouldn't budge and wouldn't talk about it anymore."

"Anything else happen that night?" asked Micky.

Tammy told them about the rest of the night, more drinking, watching the band, and eventually getting to the part where Drew had appeared. "When the band quit and it was closing time, Rose wanted to keep partying. I was done and ready to go home. Not her though. So, she and Drew left for some other bar. That's the last time I saw her or talked to her."

"What about this Drew fellow? Maybe he knows where she is," suggested Jimmy.

Tammy shook her head. "No, I called him the next day. He said he crashed at her place on the couch, and she was sleeping when he left that morning.”

“How well do you know Drew?”

“I don’t know. Not that well, I guess. Met him a couple of years ago. At the Bull Chute.” She paused for a moment, thinking about how she first met him. “We met one night when we were both kind of drunk, honestly. He tried to pick me up. I wouldn’t go home with him, but we did trade phone numbers that night.”

“What’s his last name?”

Tammy realized then how little she really knew about Drew. “You know, I don’t even know. Don’t know where he lives. In fact, only place I have ever seen the man is at the Chute.”

Jimmy was making more notes but looked up at her. “But you kept his phone number?”

“Yeah,” she laughed nervously. “He will call me every once in a while, wanting to know if I’m going to the Chute that night. Or he’s drunk and asking me to come over.”

Micky jumped into the conversation. “So, let me summarize what I’ve heard so far. Your friend, who has a history of disappearing, has been gone for 4-5 days. She’s not returning your calls, which is very unusual. Last seen with a man you barely know, who claims she was fine when he last saw her. Her current romantic interest is unknown, other than his first name. She gave you a cryptic message about the police and a local break-in we happen to be investigating.”

He paused for a minute, looking at Jimmy for more. Jimmy shook his head with nothing else to add, so he turned back to Tammy. “Does that sum it up?”

After she nodded, he continued. “Following all that, the question is which one of them has a tie to the Johnsons - Rose, Drew, or Ray?”

“I... I don’t know,” Tammy replied.

Jimmy leaned back in his chair, wondering to himself if maybe more than one of them had a tie. He decided to hold that thought for now. Who knows, he mused. Maybe Tammy was the one with the tie. "So, you've never seen this Ray character, huh?"

"No. I don't think so. She never introduced him to me anyway."

Micky reached for the keyboard. They had agreed earlier to show her the shots they had of the woman driving the brown van and of the man who had the Johnson's Tahoe at the coast. He brought up the van first. The image of the woman wasn't as clear as they would like, but it worked for Tammy.

"Oh my god. I think that's her. Rose."

"You sure?"

"Well, I can't be 100%. Her face is turned and hidden a little. But that could be her. No question. Where was she in this picture?"

Micky ignored her question and clicked to the shot of Ray. "What about this man?"

Tammy stared at the image for a long while. Something about him resonated, but she couldn't place it. "I think I have seen him, but I don't know him. Do you think that's her boyfriend, Ray?"

"Let's not jump to any conclusions. We don't know who he is either. He was picked up on security cams and was driving a missing Tahoe belonging to Eddie Johnson."

"Hmm. You have any other shots of him?"

Micky ran the video back to the shot at the gas pumps. "This one, but it's not very clear."

Tammy stood and walked about three feet from the screen. "Go back to the close up again."

Micky did and she exclaimed excitedly, "Yes, I remember where I saw him." She turned and faced them, a big smile on her face. "He met Drew at The Bull Chute one night."

"Do you remember when that was?"

"Yeah. April 1st. April Fool's Day! Me and a friend have a tradition of playing pranks and going out for drinks each year to celebrate the day."

"The day of the break-in," stated Micky.

"So, he's a friend of Drew's?" asked Jimmy.

"I can't say. They clearly knew each other and seemed to get along okay. Drew didn't introduce him. Just told me they had some things to talk about. I went back to the other side of the bar where my friend was sitting."

Jimmy asked her what happened after that.

She told them they sat talking for a while and eventually got up and left together.

"Did they come back?"

Tammy shook her head.

"Did Drew know Rose before that last night you saw her?"

"No. I introduced them when Drew joined us out on the floor."

They all sat silent for a couple of minutes pondering what they had now connected. Jimmy spoke first. "Ms. Sherrin, is there anything else you can remember that might help us?"

After Tammy said no, Jimmy asked Micky if he had more questions. He didn't. They got the number for Drew from her cell phone, promising to contact her later and asking her to call them if she thought of more or heard from Rose. Jimmy escorted her to an elevator, then returned to the interview room with Micky to debrief.

"Lot of dots that are almost connected here," said Jimmy as he sat back down at the table. "What now?"

"Two things. Search Rose's place. Find Drew."

"Yep. I am thinking the same."

"If the man with the Tahoe is Ray and Rose is in on the break-in, what about Drew? Is he part of it or just a happy coincidence?"

"Well, that's the question, isn't it? Tahoe man meets him the night of the break-in, but Tammy says she had to introduce Drew to Rose at the bar. There's too many coincidences in there it seems."

"Maybe. Maybe Rose and Drew were faking it, so Tammy didn't know they were connected already."

"Good thought," replied Jimmy. "That's why you'll be captain someday. But for now, you're stuck with me. Let's go find some more clues."

Drew had been stewing for 24 hours now over Ray's paltry first offer of $25,000 and his reluctant increase to $50,000. He and Nick must have a big payday coming on this. Drew could wreck it all if he wanted. Or he could stay quiet and keep Tammy calm to make sure their plan was successful. She could connect all three of them - Ray, Rose, and himself. If she went to the cops, they were all screwed. He had a sense that Nick had set a limit on how much to give him with Ray and was refusing to open up his wallet. That's why Ray had committed the second $25,000 out of his own money. Had to be. Ray would only go so deep in his own pocket, however, and that probably wasn't much further.

As he saw it, Drew had two options. Take the current offer from Ray or go for much bigger money by selling out Nick and Ray to Eddie Johnson. Save Eddie a few dollars and tell him where he could find his wife. If it went wrong, though, his life was probably on the line with Ray. He needed to be ready to bolt. Even if it went right, he might need to disappear for a while. Worth the risk?

He pulled out his phone and searched for Johnson Auto, paused a moment before he hit dial, then pulled the trigger. After a few rings he told the perky woman who answered that he was returning a call to Eddie Johnson. Another thirty seconds and Eddie came on the line. "Eddie Johnson here. Who am I speaking with?"

"You don't know me, but think of me as a friend," said Drew.

"I'm sorry. What's that?"

Drew repeated himself, then, "I might have some news about your wife, where you can find her."

"What? Who is this?"

"Like I said, a friend."

"Yeah? So where is she?"

Drew was silent for a few beats, letting Eddie get a little more amped up. "Who the hell is this? How are you connected to this other guy?" shouted Eddie. "Don't screw around with me on this."

"What are you paying them to get her back?"

"Why would I tell you that?"

"For starters, maybe you save some money. And maybe you can surprise them, get some revenge."

"Revenge?" spat Eddie. "Revenge? I just want Donna back. Safe and sound."

"I can help. How much did you promise them?"

Eddie was quiet for a few moments.

"Call me back in an hour. We can talk more then."

Drew considered that. "Okay. One hour. But that's your only shot at this."

"Got it," replied Eddie.

Micky and Jimmy pulled into a space in front of the office for Rose's apartment complex late that afternoon. Before leaving the station, they had given Drew's cell phone number to their researcher, Janie, to hunt down his address. Meanwhile, they started here. As they got out of the car, a young man came out of the office and turned to lock its door.

"Sir," said Jimmy. "Excuse me, please don't close up yet."

The man turned with an exasperated look, which quickly changed to suspicion once he saw who was speaking to him. "How can I help you, officers?" he asked curtly.

Micky laughed. "That obvious, huh?" After the man nodded, he continued, "We're detectives with Raleigh P.D., investigating a missing person report. We need to look in the apartment of one of your tenants. Rose Brown."

"Uh huh. You have a warrant?"

"We believe she may be in danger, sir. It may be connected to another serious crime that involves a second missing person. Your assistance today could help us find them both."

After a heavy sigh and a glance at his watch, the man unlocked the door and motioned for them to follow him inside. "Look, I want to help you, but I have a really important appointment I need to get to, and traffic will be a bitch this time of day. How long is this gonna take?"

"Not sure, sir. Probably 30-60 minutes minimum," Jimmy replied.

"What? Shit man, I can't stay here that long. Can't ya'll come back tomorrow?"

Jimmy shook his head. "No can do my friend."

Micky took a friendlier tone, "Look, sorry, what was your first name?"

The man just pointed to the name plate on the counter. "Okay. Look Chris, we don't want you to miss your appointment. But someone's life may be on the line here. You don't want to be responsible for something bad happening, do you?"

Chris shook his head.

"How about this? Take us to her apartment and let us in. You hang around for a while, then take off when you need to. We'll do our work, lock the place up, and everybody goes home happy. Sound good?"

Chris considered that for a moment, then responded, "Third building on the right, 2nd floor, 3200. Here's the key. Put it in the drop box outside when you're done."

Micky accepted the key with a word of thanks, then he and Jimmy headed out the door to Rose's place. Chris stood for a couple of minutes, watching them walk away through the office window. Rose had been there a couple of years. Not much of a problem, save an occasional late-night noise complaint from neighbors. He hadn't seen her around much the last few weeks. There was that one guy a few days ago, though, who had been picking up a trunk from her. The guy said it was old clothing she was donating to a charity he worked for. Seemed innocent at the time. Tomorrow he would look back through security footage from that day. For now, he better get moving if he wanted to meet his friend on time for dinner.

Over at 3200, Micky knocked on the door and called out for Rose. After a couple of rounds with no response, he slipped the key in and opened it up. "Rose? Ms. Brown?" he called loudly as they stepped inside. Nothing but silence responded, so he closed the door and said to Jimmy, "Okay. Small place. It shouldn't take long. Let's find some clues." He handed Jimmy an extra pair of surgical gloves. "I'll take the bedroom and bathroom. You take out here and the kitchen area. Okay?"

After agreeing and slipping on the gloves, Jimmy started to walk into the kitchen. "The place is pretty tidy," he noted. "Somehow not what I expected."

"Yeah. But you know, women have a thing about coming home to a dirty house after being away for a while. Ours is never cleaner than before we go on a trip somewhere."

"I'm sorry. Am I hearing some gender bias from you sir?"

"As Peterson would say..." Micky walked into the bedroom, throwing up a middle finger to Jimmy as he went, mimicking the way Seargent Peterson had flipped them both off earlier. Jimmy chuckled and started opening cabinets in the small kitchen area. He had barely gotten started when Micky called out for him to come to the bedroom.

"Wow, I guess she didn't have time to clean everywhere," Jimmy noted as he surveyed the unmade bed and piles of clothes scattered on the floor and furniture.

"No time to hide the drugs either, apparently," replied Micky as he motioned for Jimmy to come over to the other side of the bed. He pointed to a small packet of white powder on the nightstand and then in an open drawer in the chest of drawers against the wall.

Jimmy stepped closer and whistled when he looked in the drawer. "Man. She was ready to party, huh?"

"Something seem off to you here?"

Jimmy smiled. "Like the way the kitchen and living area are spotless and the bedroom is a mess?"

Micky nodded.

"And the way the drugs are conveniently visible the moment you walk in the room?"

Micky nodded again.

"Well, maybe she keeps the rest of the house clean for appearance's sake when someone comes over?"

Micky shook his head this time.

"Okay. Maybe she's had enough of the drug life, so she left it behind when she went to meet her friends?"

Micky just looked at him this time.

"Maybe Drew isn't telling Tammy the whole story of that night and something bad has happened to Rose?" he said with a grin.

"Bingo," replied Micky. "Time to get a crime scene crew in here, let them see what they can find."

"Calling it in now," said Jimmy, leaving Micky alone again in the bedroom as he walked out into the living area. Was Drew tied into the same group as Rose, he wondered? Or was this all just coincidence? Micky didn't believe much in coincidence, not when criminals were involved. He pulled out his phone and called his wife. It looked like a long night ahead.

CHAPTER 25

Drew woke from a deep and restful night of sleep. A big day ahead. Two more days in Raleigh, at least for a while. The deal was agreed to with Eddie Johnson. Tomorrow he would meet Eddie, lead them to where Donna was being held, collect his payout, then disappear for a while. A million bucks is what he and Eddie had finally agreed to after Eddie's low ball starting offer. A hell of a lot better than the $50,000 Ray had promised.

He laid in bed for a while, alternately daydreaming about the money, then about his plans for the day. Finally, he rose and stretched. Long list of to do's in his head. Better get started.

Across town, Jimmy and Micky made their way to their cubicles in the late morning hours. It had indeed turned out to be a long one at Rose's apartment the night before. Four hours after he called it in, the crime scene tech finally arrived to meet Jimmy in the parking lot outside Rose's building. The lone tech, Roger, had apologized profusely, explaining how short-staffed they were, and he had just worked another crime scene since 10:00 a.m. that morning. Jimmy quickly climbed down from his perch on the ladder of agitation and thanked Roger for showing up. It was well after midnight when they locked the door and strung the crime scene tape across it.

Jimmy sipped his coffee, then said to Micky, "Dollars to donuts we don't even get a fingerprint back on that kitchen and living area."

"I don't eat donuts," replied Micky.

"No, dumbass. You're betting the donuts. If I win, I get to eat the donuts."

Micky ignored him. "So, what now gumshoe?"

"Let's talk to Janie. See what she found on Drew. Go from there."

"Let's do it."

Ray had become worried about Tammy. If she went to the cops, things might somehow unravel very quickly. They only needed to get through two more days and then they could make the swap, and he would be on his way. He couldn't do anything himself. He had to keep sitting on Donna. They didn't need to get rid of Tammy, just make sure she stayed away from the police. Hell, he thought, Drew was the one with the most to lose. They would likely find him first. Still, even after this was over, he could be at risk because Drew would still be around in case the detectives kept looking. Time to put some pressure on Drew, make him earn that extra $25,000.

He stepped outside the room at the motel, warning Donna first not to do anything stupid. Drew picked up after a few rings.

"Ray. What's up?" he asked.

"Been thinking about your friend Tammy."

"What about her?"

"We need to make damn sure she doesn't run to the cops before this deal goes down, Drew. It might spoil our fun."

"What are you asking me to do, Ray?"

"I'm asking you to earn your damn money, Drew. Keep the woman from screwing this up!" Ray almost shouted at him.

"Calm down, Ray. No need to yell at me."

Ray took a deep breath, exhaling slowly to let the tension out.

"You're right. Sorry, Drew. But look, I need to know if you are all in on this thing."

"Killing someone was kind of theoretical, man. Being asked to do it, that's big Ray."

"I didn't ask you to kill her, Drew."

"Oh. Okay. Good!"

Ray let the line go silent for a few moments. His gut was telling him Drew was a problem and couldn't be trusted. "But would you, if I did?"

"Kill her?"

Ray was silent again, letting things get very uncomfortable. Finally, Drew spoke. "I will do what I need to do, Ray."

"You better mean that brother," Ray replied softly. "How about you give me her cell number and address? As a backup plan."

This alarmed Drew. "Backup plan? What the hell do you need a backup plan for? I told you I got this Ray."

"Can't be too careful on this one, Drew."

"I don't know her address, man."

"Call her and get it, Drew. Text it to me in the next two hours. You hearing me?"

"Yeah, Ray. Got it."

"Good. Talk later. And Drew..."

"Yeah?"

"Make damn sure you take care of this."

With that, Ray ended the call. He stood outside for a couple of minutes longer. He had rattled Drew's cage, but was it enough? He decided to pay Drew a quick in-person visit if that text didn't come through as promised. Rough him up a bit if he needed to. Take care of the problem himself if it came to it. He stuck his phone in his pocket and went back in the room. Not much longer, he thought. Not much longer.

Micky and Jimmy were back in a conference room on their floor. It turned out that Janie hit some roadblocks trying to chase down an address for Drew. They had decided to find him and surprise him with a visit rather than simply calling his phone. They didn't want to risk spooking him and having him disappear on them.

Janie had managed to find an address linked to his cell phone, but the location was now a Walmart parking lot. That did lead her to old utility bills with another address and that address was on file with the DMV for his driver's license. Of course, that location now housed a Chili's restaurant. They at least knew his last name from the DMV files. Baldwin. Drew Baldwin. Janie was working on digging up more, while the guys were discussing a move that would allow them to get Verizon to locate the towers his cell phone was pinging.

"It still won't pinpoint his location," sighed Micky.

"No. But it will give us a narrower area to look in."

"Yeah. Not a needle in the haystack, but it's close. It's going to take some manpower to try and search that area, too. Not going to get that approved."

Jimmy nodded in agreement. "Yeah, but some idea of his location is better than no idea, right?"

After Micky agreed, Jimmy called down to Janie to start the paperwork on the request to Verizon for the cell phone trace. They were contemplating what to do while they waited for that plus a report from the crime scene forensics when Jimmy's phone buzzed.

"Tommy," he said to Micky before answering. "Brother, tell me you found something we can use."

"Well, hello and good afternoon to you too," Tommy replied.

"Sorry, man. We're kind of stuck here. How 'ya doing, Tommy?"

"Much better, thank you. I'm doing well today. Got something you might be interested in." Tommy told him about observing the Rezaviks' lunch celebration the day before, how he had tailed them a while to see if anything interesting came up, and finally about his research and a few conversations with colleagues of his. "Found three things you should know. First, these guys have several business lines that appear to be legitimate."

"Yeah. We know they are the money behind a payment plan Eddie offers to his buyers."

"Right. They wholesale cars also, so they are probably selling some to Johnson. Second, rumor has it they got into the drug business a few years back. Started out small, local, with some weed. Have graduated up the chain. Oxy, fentanyl. Maybe into heroin now."

Jimmy whistled on the other end. "That is truly interesting. Might explain motive for what's going on up here if there are drugs and money tied to this. What's the third thing?"

"There's an outstanding warrant for Otto in nearby Pamlico County from about five years ago. He got caught up in some kind of fight at a bar, was supposed to show up in court related to the charges and never appeared. Local cops there looked for him a while, then gave up but never closed the warrant."

"Well, that could come in handy if we want to shake him down a little," remarked Jimmy.

"Yeah. I thought you might see it that way. One more thing, Jimmy."

"Yeah?"

"These guys are dangerous. A few people who crossed them or got in their way seem to have disappeared. Anton's the brain of the pair, but Bruno's the muscle and a genuine badass. Be careful brother!"

"Will do," Jimmy said. "And Tommy..."

"Yeah?"

"Thanks. You be careful too."

They said goodbyes and ended the call. Jimmy relayed everything to Micky and the two of them discussed what it meant for their investigation. "Drugs would explain why someone came after Eddie for money," said Micky. "But does he seem like the type to be trafficking heroin to you?"

Jimmy shook his head. "Not really. But Otto does."

"Agreed," Micky said. "So, let's recap where we are. Donna is still missing. A guy named Ray has been seen with Eddie's car down east and seems to live in this area somewhere. Ray is a known acquaintance of Drew, last seen with Tammy's friend Rose, who is probably connected to Ray. Eddie is in business with some shady guys from Wilmington who are suspected drug traffickers. He employs an ex-con with possible ties to the Wilmington guys." Micky stopped there and looked at Jimmy.

"And we can't find Ray, Rose, or Drew."

"Bingo."

"So, the only people we can push on until Janie finds Drew or Ray's address for us are Eddie and Otto."

"Double bingo."

"Let's get out of here and go see Mr. Edward Johnson."

Drew was deciding which items from his wardrobe he would leave with when the knock came at the door. He looked out his bedroom window at the parking lot but didn't see any unusual cars. Probably a neighbor or the girl from the apartment complex office, he thought. He walked a short distance to the door and called out to ask who was there.

"It's Ray, Drew."

Drew paused for a moment before replying in his best rendition of being sick. "Now is not really a good time for you to come in Ray. Got some kind of bug. Throwing up. Diarrhea too. You don't want this."

"Open the damn door, Drew."

Drew considered the options for a minute, then reluctantly opened the door. He knew Ray was true to his word about breaking it in. He stepped back as Ray brushed by him aggressively. "You lying to me, Drew?" he asked hotly.

"What do you want, Ray?"

"I had doubts, Drew. Now I have more."

"Doubts about what, Ray?" Drew asked, feeling his anger starting to rise as well.

Ray snorted, taking a step closer to Drew. "What the hell do you think it would be, Drew? Huh? Doubts about whether Rose overdosed, or you killed her. Doubts about whether you will take care of this new situation or not. I don't think we can count on you."

As Ray was talking, Drew looked over his shoulder to the bedroom. The door was standing open, revealing his travel bags and a bunch of folded clothes on the bed. Ray sensed the alarm on his face and turned to look as well. Drew knew what would come next and reached for a large glass statue on a nearby table, intending to hit Ray in the head while he was turned.

Ray caught the sudden movement in his peripheral vision and crouched as Drew harmlessly swung the statue where his head had just been. He launched himself into Drew out of the crouch and drove him into the wall behind. With his breath knocked out, Drew gasped for oxygen and Ray delivered successive punches to his mid-section and jaw. Drew crumpled to the floor, still gasping and bleeding from the mouth.

"Going somewhere, Drew?" Ray sneered down at him. "Running out on us before you ever get your money?"

"Hell no, Ray. I was packing to hit the road for a couple of days after this was over," he said, gasping more and wiping the blood with the back of his hand.

"Bullshit, Drew. Be a man and tell me the truth."

Drew sat up against the wall, looking up at Ray. "Truth? You want truth, huh? Okay, let's start with how screwed you and Nick would be if I hadn't agreed to patch up that woman's arm. Then, that pregnant bitch girlfriend of yours ODs on me and what do I do? Go bury the body so she won't be found and connected to you. And what thanks do I get offered? A measly-ass $25,000." He spat blood out his mouth and struggled to his feet. "That enough truth, Ray?"

"She told you she was pregnant? With my baby?"

Drew nodded.

"And you still let her do the drugs?"

"Come on, Ray! How was I gonna stop her, huh?"

Ray shook his head. "And the clothes you're packing? Thats a lot of clothes for just a few days away, Drew. You're up to something. What is it?"

"Nothing, Ray. It's what I said."

"You're lying to me, Drew. I can see it on your face. Last chance."

"Last chance?" Drew laughed. "Or what, Ray? You gonna' kill me?"

Ray just nodded, icy eyes staring back.

Suddenly Drew realized how serious Ray was and he lunged forward to knock him off balance, hoping to grab the statue off the floor and finish Ray off. Ray was ready, sidestepped it and threw his leg out to trip Drew.

Drew fell face down, hard, into the floor, stunned by the impact. Ray dropped down on him and put him in a chokehold. Drew struggled but Ray had pinned him and kept the pressure on his neck, slowly draining his life away. Finally, Drew stopped struggling. Ray held on for another minute or so, then released his grip, confident Drew was dead.

Shit, he thought. Not what had wanted to do, but Drew left him no choice. He stood up and backed away from the body. Now what, he thought? Search the apartment, see if there was any evidence of what Drew had been up to. Clean up his prints on the door and elsewhere as best he could. He walked into the bedroom, rifled through the clothes and bags on the bed. Found nothing of interest. Spotted Drew's phone on the nightstand beside the bed. Got blocked by the security app, so he walked back into the living area. He rolled Drew over and held the phone close to his face, letting the facial recognition software do its thing and open the phone.

After disabling all the security apps, he scrolled through it, focusing on text messages and the list of recent calls. Nothing interesting in the texts, but one of the outbound phone numbers looked familiar. Two calls were made to it the day before. Ray hit the call button and held the phone to his ear. As soon as he heard the Johnson Auto greeting, he ended the call.

Son of a bitch! Had Drew sold them out? Suddenly he needed to be out of the apartment as quickly as possible. He would contemplate this later. He finished searching the apartment, moving quickly now, cleaning up where he thought he might have touched anything. He considered what to do about the body, then had a thought. Maybe there was a wrinkle he could throw into all this that could prove useful. Ray shoved the phone in his pocket and slipped Drew's wallet from the back pocket of his jeans after rolling the body once more. Satisfied he had done what was needed, he left the apartment, locking the door again as he went out. Security cameras may have picked him up, but no time to deal with that now. He walked quickly to his truck and left the parking lot, punching up Nick's number as he drove away.

CHAPTER 26

It was late morning when Eddie and Otto arrived, separately, at the Hyatt Place hotel near the airport. Bruno and his associate, a very dangerous looking man named Ethan, had checked in the night before. Earlier that morning Bruno had summoned Eddie and Otto to come there to discuss plans for the swap. Eddie, per direction from Bruno, had been keeping a low profile for the last 24 hours, staying in another hotel under an assumed name and avoiding calls to his cell phone from the detectives. He had argued against it, saying it might make Jimmy and Micky suspicious, but Bruno insisted it was better than them picking him up or tailing him right now.

Otto arrived a few minutes before Eddie and carried a large gym bag with him, as though he were headed to a workout. It wasn't filled with sweats and sneakers, though. It was filled with cash, the latest proceeds from the drugs flowing through Johnson Auto. Normally he would never walk in a public place with a bag of drug cash, but Bruno had insisted he bring it in this morning.

Ethan opened the door to the room moments after Otto knocked, then stepped aside to allow him to pass by. Bruno sat on a couch, sipping coffee, watching highlights from Premier League soccer on ESPN. He motioned for Otto to sit in an adjacent chair, then turned off the television. "The money these guys make, kicking a ball, it is obscene, no?"

Otto nodded and placed the bag on the coffee table in front of Bruno. He didn't give a shit about soccer, but never disagreeing with Bruno was a lesson he had learned long ago. He pointed to the bag. "As requested. Everything from the last few shipments."

Bruno smiled. "Good. Our new friend Edward should get the smell in his nostrils, like a new car. Not like the hand-me-downs he sells at his business." Otto nodded again, and Bruno continued. "Also, he needs to see how we are putting our hard-earned dollars out for his benefit. To win back his wife, no?"

Otto smiled in return and right on cue, Eddie knocked on the door. Ethan repeated his doorman act and ushered Eddie in. Bruno rose from his seat and walked around the table to Eddie, who looked mildly alarmed, as though he expected a confrontation. Instead, Bruno smiled broadly and embraced him in a bear hug. "Edward," he said as he stepped back from the hug, "Welcome. Welcome to our new business together."

"Um, thanks," Eddie replied awkwardly. "Thank you. I am grateful she will be home soon."

Bruno smiled warmly, clasping Eddie on the shoulder, then motioning for him to sit on the couch with him. After settling back down himself, he looked around the group gathered, his gaze settling on Eddie. The warmth had disappeared. Business Bruno had returned. "Now, this man who has called and wishes to strike an alternate arrangement for your wife, you do not know him, yes?"

Eddie hesitated for a moment. Bruno's use of yes or no in his questions created double negatives or conflicts he had to sort out. "Yes," he stammered. "I mean, no, I don't know who he is. He claims to be a friend of these kidnappers."

"A friend?" asked Bruno, stroking his chin. "No. No friend, this one. One who betrays his loyalty to others. This is not what friends do, no?"

He let this question hang in the air as he looked at Otto, then back to Eddie. Both men shook their heads in turn. Bruno's message to them was received. "Our friend now?" he asked, smiling again. "Yes! He can be our friend for now. Tell me again what he has offered."

Eddie looked at Otto, who nodded for him to go ahead and speak. He walked through the two calls from the day before, outlining the basics. In exchange for $1 million, the man would meet them and then lead them to where Donna was being held.

"Hmm. I see," Bruno said pensively. "So, this could be dangerous? We must surprise them, perhaps there will be gunfire exchanged. We walk away with your Donna, and I keep my million dollars, eh?"

Eddie looked again at Otto, then nodded, terrified as he began to fully realize what lay ahead. "Yeah, I guess so. Maybe we should tell this guy no. Stick with the original plan?" he asked hesitantly.

"Danger. Surprise. Gunfire," Bruno said gravely, then suddenly burst into laughter. "Yes. Yes. This will be good! We have some fun and we save $1 million. Brilliant!"

Eddie swallowed hard, forcing a smile onto his face. "Um, okay. Good, I guess. He is supposed to call me this morning with the location of a place to meet."

Bruno became serious again and started outlining his thoughts on how to pull it off. He told Ethan he would ride with their new friend to the place Donna was held, while he and Eddie trailed behind with Otto. They were discussing various possibilities for the unknown location itself when Eddie's phone buzzed. He pulled it out and looked at the screen. "It's the original guy, I think."

Bruno told him to put the call on speaker phone and admonished the others to remain silent. Eddie did this and hit the answer icon. "Eddie Johnson here."

"Johnson, it seems we have a problem," said Nick.

"What do you mean?" asked Eddie, concern spreading across his face.

"You got another... wait, am I on speaker phone here? Is someone else listening to this?"

"No. No. I'm shaving. Stuff all over my face and hands. Just me here," Eddie replied, looking at Bruno giving him a thumbs up for his quick thinking.

"You better not be bullshitting me, Johnson. Anyone comes with you, she's dead."

"No one but me, man. I swear. But... you mentioned a problem?"

"Yeah. You got two calls yesterday from an - let's call him an associate. What did he tell you Johnson? He try to make another deal with you?"

Fully alarmed now, Eddie looked to the others for help. All he got was a keep talking sign from Otto. " How... how do you know he called me?"

"Let's just say we have his phone. And he won't be using it anymore."

Otto had leaned forward to hear the voice on the other end better. Recognition was creeping in, but he remained quiet, deciding to keep the revelation to himself for now. He knew the voice on the other end.

"Okay," Eddie replied to Nick, "What do you want me to do now?"

"What did he tell you? And don't lie to me Johnson."

Eddie looked at Otto, then Bruno, unsure of what to do next. Otto mouthed 'don't lie to him' as he leaned back in his chair, then. Bruno nodded in agreement. "Said he knew where she was and would take me there if we gave him a nice payday. He told me he would call back today to set up a plan."

Nick considered this, then replied, "So you and him were gonna' take us down, huh? That arrogant prick. Well, you're on your own again, Johnson. Back to plan A. You get one more call from me, pal. Tomorrow. I will tell you when, where and how it goes down. Got it?"

"Yeah. Got it."

"And Johnson..."

"Yeah?"

"Don't be taking any other calls," Nick said, laughing as he punched off.

Eddie laid his phone on the table, head down, running his hands through his hair. "Now what do we do?" he asked.

"Now, we wait," said Bruno. "Edward, you go back to your hotel. Remain there until tomorrow morning, then return here. Otto, back to work. Our empire must keep running, no? You also must return here tomorrow morning as we make our final plans." With that, he waved them toward the door.

Out in the hallway, Eddie grabbed Otto by the arm. "You knew something in there, didn't you? The way you leaned forward during the call."

Otto shook him off, saying they would talk outside. After a silent and tense elevator ride down, they walked out the lobby door into the brilliant Carolina sunshine. Eddie spoke first. "Okay. What is it, Otto?"

"That voice. Pretty sure I know who it is."

"What! Who is it?"

He shook his head. "No. I need to check this out. Confirm it somehow."

"Shouldn't we tell Bruno? Now? Let him decide?" Eddie asked urgently.

"Not yet, Eddie. You gotta' trust me on how we handle this with him. If I'm wrong, he'll be pissed off and punish me for it. Hell, if I'm right, he still might do that."

"Punish you?" Eddie asked, puzzled by what Otto was saying. "Why would he punish you if you are right?"

"No time to explain now. Go back to your hotel. I'll call you when I know more."

"No. Let me come with you."

"Johnson, just go to your hotel. You can't be with me on this. If it's him, he can't see us together right now."

Eddie reluctantly agreed and the two men parted ways to their own cars. Eddie drove away quickly. Otto sat at the wheel of his car for a few minutes, smoking and planning his next step. Satisfied with his plan, he threw the cigarette butt out onto the pavement, then started the car and drove out of the parking lot, headed east away from the airport. No time to lose now.

Micky and Jimmy were stuck again. Or, still stuck depending on which one of them you asked. Their trip to Johnson Auto the prior afternoon had been fruitless. Eddie had told Bill and Lila he was going to be out for a couple of days, not feeling well, needing to clear his head. They should run things as normal, and he would call them soon.

Otto had taken to coming and going on a random schedule Bill could not figure out. He claimed he had some urgent family business to attend to. Lila, of course, took all this as further proof they were up to something, and it had to be related to Donna's disappearance. Micky and Jimmy tended to agree. Eddie wasn't answering their calls and Otto kept his cell number to himself apparently.

All of this left the two detectives sipping coffee and wondering what to do next. "Be nice to catch a break on where this Drew guy lives, go harass him for a while," sighed Jimmy.

Micky just nodded. "Be even better if the perps just walked in and confessed."

"True," replied Jimmy. "Maybe we can…"

He was interrupted by the ringing of his cell phone. "Janie, what's up? We need some good news," he said after putting the call on speaker for Micky to hear.

"Do I ever call you with bad news?" she replied with mock indignity. "Your request for the cell phone trace has been approved. Cranking that up now with Verizon. Also, for bonus points, I might have a lead on the last known address for Drew Baldwin."

"Hot damn! You are the best," said Jimmy.

"Yeah, you say that now," Janie retorted. "I'll get back to you ASAP on the last known. Still running something. Should have cell phone info in an hour or so."

"Thanks, Janie," said Mickey, and Jimmy ended the call. "What now?"

"Lunch?"

Mickey smiled. "Why not? Could be the last free moments we have for a while. Things are moving!"

Ray threw the last of his worldly possessions into the back of his truck, then slid the truck bed cover over and fastened it down. He and Donna would soon head out to Nick's place. The motel was the one place Drew had known for sure that Donna had been held. Without knowing what Drew had really told Eddie, he and Nick had decided it was best that they abandon it and come to the farm. Ray walked back into his room. Donna sat stoically in one of the ancient chairs at the small table in the kitchenette.

"So, this is it for here, huh?" she asked. "Where are you taking me?"

"Somewhere safer."

"You mean safer for you, right?" she said sarcastically. "Why are we leaving here?"

"Details you don't need to know. I need to make one more call and then we hit the road. You're going to be a model hostage, right? No yelling. No running."

Donna sighed and nodded. "Yes. I would like to remain alive."

Ray nodded and then stepped outside again, pulling the door shut behind him. He looked around to make sure no one was nearby that could overhear his call. Satisfied it was clear he walked over and leaned against his truck. He pulled out Drew's cell phone, powered it up, and pressed the number to call Tammy. She answered after one ring.

"Drew!" she exclaimed. "Where are you? I have been trying your number all morning."

"Drew won't be calling you anymore. Make sure you keep your mouth shut or the same could happen to you."

"What?" she shouted. "Is this a joke? Who is this?"

"Not a joke. Don't be stupid!" Ray said, ending the call.

He looked around the parking lot and adjacent rooms. Nothing stirring, so he opened the door to the motel room, calling for Donna to come out and get in his truck. She did so without any trouble, afraid to cause problems this close to freedom. Ray took one final glance inside, mentally bidding the room farewell, closed the door and got in his truck. Time to go to Nick's farm.

Jimmy had just picked up his second taco and was about to bite into it when his phone buzzed. "Why do people always call me?" he asked Micky, sighing as he put the taco down.

"Maybe because you are always so eager to hand out your number?" he laughed.

To which Jimmy showed him a middle finger in response as he answered. "Quinn here."

"Detective Quinn? It's Tammy," came a frantic reply.

"Tammy, yeah. What's going on? You sound upset."

"Oh my god. I think Drew might be dead."

"Dead?" He looked at Micky and whispered 'Drew!'

"Yes. Dead. I got a call just now. Someone had Drew's phone. I didn't recognize their voice. I bet it was that damn Ray guy! He said Drew wouldn't be calling me anymore. Then he told me to keep my mouth shut or something would happen to me. I'm really scared now, detective," she sobbed at the end.

"Okay, Tammy. You're gonna' be okay. We'll make sure of that. Did he say anything else?"

After telling him there was nothing else said, Jimmy asked Tammy where she was. It was her day off and she was out shopping. She agreed to come down to their office and give them an official statement.

"What about after that?" she asked. "What if this guy is following me?"

"We can keep you safe," Jimmy assured her. "One step at a time. How soon can you get to the station?" After agreeing to meet her in twenty minutes, he ended the call and said to Micky, "Eat up, bro. I'll fill you in on the way downtown. You don't know how right you are about things moving."

Ray called Nick on the way to the farm. "We'll be there within the hour."

"You called her?"

"Yeah. That's done. She will go straight to the cops. That should keep them busy for a while. If they ever find a way to tie Drew to us it will be after this deal is over and we're long gone."

"Good work, Ray. See you soon."

Ray laid his phone on the dash. He felt Donna staring at him, so he turned to look at her. Neither of them said anything. Donna turned to look out at the landscape rushing by. Ray turned back to focus on the road ahead. So close to the end, he thought. So close.

CHAPTER 27

Otto was cruising the roads near the farm where Nick and Penny lived. He had been there just once, to meet with Nick and explore a possible drug business relationship. He hadn't stayed long. It took only one beer to figure out that Nick really didn't have a pipeline to move any serious amount of drugs.

He drove by the narrow dirt path leading back to the farm before he realized it was the one. He wasn't planning to drive straight in anyway. It was a bit back through the woods to the farmhouse as he remembered, with no other way in or out by car. He drove a little further and found an abandoned house about a mile down the road, parked his car behind it and then considered how best to get through the woods to take a look at Nick's place.

There was no way to avoid walking down the narrow two-lane road back towards Nick's place. He could cut through the woods before he reached the driveway, but he had at least one-half mile of open road before he reached that point. There were a handful of houses lining the road on either side, but no one outside and traffic, as one would expect, was sporadic this far outside the city limits. Otto made his way down the road, moving quickly but not so fast he might draw attention from a neighbor looking out their window. He kept his gaze forward, turning once when he caught movement at a window in his peripheral vision. Nobody was there, so he kept moving.

He reached a spot after a few minutes that offered a promising walk through the woods. He stopped and looked around carefully for any prying eyes watching him. Seeing none, he stepped off the road and made his way into the woods.

Once he was in the cover of the trees and brush, he moved more quickly, headed generally in the direction he knew the farmhouse would be. He slowed as he got close, careful to be as quiet as he could. He also considered the light wind rustling the trees, mindful to stay downwind as much as he could in case Nick had an outdoor dog who might sniff him out. He soon reached a spot not far from the house that would work. Heavy brush that would shield him well, but a clear line of sight to the rear of the house and the drive leading in. He settled in and began his vigil, confident he would be rewarded soon enough.

Back at police headquarters in Raleigh, Tammy was once again in a conference room with Micky and Jimmy. They had recorded a formal statement about the phone call from Ray and were discussing what came next. "I think Rose might be dead," she said shakily. "Now Drew. You have to find this guy!"

Jimmy leaned in. "We will. We are doing everything we can, Tammy."

She dabbed her eyes with a tissue, forcing the tears back in, breathing deeply to gather herself. "And what about the woman? The one who is missing from the break-in?"

Micky explained to her how he and Jimmy were investigating all the leads at the same time, slowly pulling the clues together. Tammy nodded but didn't seem convinced they had it under control. "Now what?" she asked. "How will you keep me safe until this is over?"

Jimmy glanced at Micky, who nodded at him to step in. "Tammy, we know you must be very frightened right now. We appreciate the courage it must have taken to call us and come down here." Tammy nodded and he continued. "This guy may be trying to keep an eye on you, but we're thinking he has his hands full with what might be going on with Mrs. Johnson, the missing woman. We think the best thing is for you to continue your activities as normal. We'll put undercover policemen nearby to protect you if he shows up."

"Around the clock?" she asked.

Jimmy nodded. "Yes. Someone will always be close by. You can call them or us if you see anything or get any more calls. Okay?"

Tammy agreed and they concluded the session. Micky rose from the table to escort her back to the lobby, then returned to the conference room. He sighed as he sat back at the table across from Jimmy. "Bodies are piling up it seems. If only we could find one." He looked at Jimmy, who had a huge smirk on his face. "What?"

Jimmy grinned. "Janie called. We have an address for Drew Baldwin." They high fived as they rose from the table.

"Here we go," said Micky. "I told you we were in for a long day."

It didn't take long for Otto to be rewarded for his surveillance efforts. Twenty minutes after settling in he heard the crunch of tires down the narrow path leading to Nick's house. An older model Ford Ranger pickup rolled into view and stopped behind the house. As the man driving opened his door, another man emerged from the house. After a brief greeting and man-hug, the two walked around the front of the Ranger to the passenger door. The shorter man opened the door and Donna Johnson stepped out. Her hands were zip-tied in front of her. He fished out a pocketknife and cut the zip tie, freeing her hands. After saying something to her that Otto could not pick up, the second man turned to the house. Donna and the driver of the truck fell in behind and they disappeared into the house.

Otto sat for a few minutes, contemplating his next move. He could slip up close and try to learn more, but he risked being seen, perhaps caught or shot as well. He decided that just knowing she was there was enough and quietly backed out of the brush he had been hiding in. He would call Eddie first when he got back to his vehicle to let him know she was alive and seemed okay. Then he would call Bruno. They had new options now. Bruno would be pleased.

They had debated the need for backup on the way to Drew's and decided it was a good idea. The squad car was already at the address for Drew when they arrived. Micky pulled in next to it and the two patrol officers got out of their car. "Sheila," said Micky to the driver, "How are you doing?"

Sheila nodded in return. "Just fine, Detective Bondurant. This is Officer Stevens", she said, waving her hand towards her partner. All four of them exchanged greetings and handshakes and then Micky filled them in on the case and how Drew factored in.

"We think he's probably dead, taken out by a member of this group, a guy named Ray," remarked Jimmy. He went on to tell them they weren't positive this was the case and didn't know if he would be in the apartment or not.

"Lot of maybes there, sir," Sheila said wryly.

"Just Jimmy, please. And yeah, a lot of maybes, so let's assume he's in there, alive and well armed."

Micky pointed toward the apartment building, and they talked about their approach. Not a lot of options to consider and they started moving within a few minutes. A couple of residents had gathered outside the adjacent building, talking quietly with looks of concern etched on their faces. The patrol officers had suggested evacuating the apartments around Drew's as a precaution in the event of a shootout, but Micky ruled that out as probably not needed.

They made their way to Drew's door. Jimmy and Micky set up in front of the door, while Sheila and Stevens covered opposite ends of the building. Jimmy looked at Micky for the go sign and then rapped loudly on the door.

"Mr. Baldwin, Raleigh police department."

They were met with silence, and Micky motioned for Jimmy to

repeat, which he did. More silence. After a couple more minutes of that and ringing the doorbell, Jimmy said to Micky in his most serious smart-ass manner, "Detective Bondurant, do you have sufficient reason to believe the occupant may be in physical danger and thus we should enter the premises?"

Micky shook his head at Jimmy's theatrics and then waved Sheila over. "No answer. No one seems to be stirring inside. We can kick it or one of you go see the apartment manager for a master key."

"On it sir," she replied, heading to the opposite end to instruct Stevens. She returned in a couple of minutes and stood with the men in the breezeway outside the apartment.

"How's Laura?" asked Micky. Laura was Sheila's partner, a local attorney and former colleague of Micky's wife.

"Good. Works her ass off all the time."

"Yeah? Good thing you have a cushy job like this then, huh?"

Sheila laughed. "Good point." The bantering went on until Stevens returned with the manager, red faced and out of breath trailing behind him. The man looked at all of them and asked, "Aren't you guys supposed to have a warrant for this?"

Jimmy explained why they didn't need one and the manager reluctantly walked over to the door. Jimmy couldn't resist. "We're pretty sure he's not waiting for the door to open so he can unload on whoever's there."

Micky glared at him while Sheila suppressed a giggle. The manager backed away quickly, handing the keys to Micky. "You guys want in so bad, you open it," he huffed at them as he turned and walked back towards the office.

Micky tossed the keys to Jimmy. "Here you go, smartass."

Jimmy caught the keys, laughing as he walked over to unlock the door. He turned serious before he rotated the key in the lock, turning to look at his colleagues. They had their guns drawn, ready if trouble was waiting. Jimmy counted down from three and then unlocked the door and pushed it open so hard it banged against the wall. He yelled,

"Raleigh Police Department, hands up where we can see them," as they all rushed in.

It took about three seconds for them to stop in their tracks. Drew's body lay face up on the floor in front of them. Micky signaled for the patrol officers to clear the rest of the apartment, then bent down to check for a pulse. He glanced at Jimmy and shook his head. "Looks like we found our first body."

Jimmy nodded as Micky stood back up. They heard the officers yelling 'clear' as they checked the other rooms, then rejoined them in the living area. "Sheila, can you and Stevens go out and tape off the area outside the door, then call in the crime scene crew please?"

"10-4, detective."

"Let's do a walkthrough of the place quickly, then let the crew come in and do their job with the photos before we start digging in too deep."

Jimmy nodded, already pulling on a pair of latex gloves. "Let's hope we find something useful."

"Yeah," Micky replied, looking down at the body. "That would be good."

Bruno was pleased with the news that Otto had discovered where Donna was being held. So pleased that he instructed Otto to return to the hotel immediately and advised Eddie to do the same. Which is why they were all gathered once again in Bruno's hotel room. Empty boxes of takeout Asian food sat on the table. Bruno was giving a toast to their good fortune and insisting they all take several shots of the premium vodka he carried wherever he went. Eddie was becoming more alarmed by the minute.

"To our health," Bruno said boisterously as he drained the shot glass. He motioned for Ethan to refill all the glasses, then held his up once again. "And finally," he said, laying a hand on Eddie's shoulder, "to our success in rescuing your beloved Donna and punishing the evil men who have taken her. Ziveli!"

Over the previous hour, Bruno had laid out their plan with help from Ethan and Otto. After describing the terrain around Nick's farm, along with his best guess at what the house was like inside, an assault for the pre-dawn hours of the next morning had been laid out. Eddie was terrified. Bruno had insisted he would be part of the raid, armed to the teeth like the rest of them. My god, I could die tomorrow, he thought. Or worse, Donna might get killed or badly wounded. This guy was insane. What the hell had he been thinking when he agreed to this partnership.

He glanced over at Otto, who seemed to only be half-listening as Bruno rambled on about their coming victory. Otto seemed almost bored. He sensed Eddie's gaze on him and turned slightly to look at him. He winked at Eddie and raised his now empty glass a little. No turning back now, Eddie realized. He and Donna would be reunited tomorrow. Or never. It was out of his hands, and he vowed to himself that he would do whatever it took to keep her safe.

CHAPTER 28

Eddie was startled when the alarm on his phone sounded at 4 a.m. His heart was pounding, and he hadn't slept well during the few hours since Bruno had ordered them to bed. The time had come to go and rescue Donna. He slipped out of the bed, stood, and took a few deep breaths to steady himself.

As he did, he fantasized that he somehow would take them all out. Bruno, Ethan, Otto, Donna's captors. Rid himself of all he had gotten entangled in and return with Donna to their normal, happy life. No more rigging odometers for a few extra bucks. His life of crime behind him.

A mental image of Anton Rezavik burst into his mind. Anton rushing into his office at the car lot, one arm around Donna's throat, his other holding an automatic pistol to her head. His fantasy was just that, he quickly realized. Bruno would be avenged. There was no escape from this. He reached for the dark colored pants and shirt folded and lying neatly on the chair. Time to meet his fate.

In the adjacent rooms, Bruno and the others were also rising. Bruno was rested, almost gleeful for the activities that lay ahead. He didn't get his hands dirty much anymore and he relished the fight when it became available.

For Ethan and Otto, just another day at the office. They were stoically going about the business of dressing in dark clothing like Eddie's, packing their clothes and gear, brushing their teeth. Ethan had even taken the time to straighten the bed covers.

At 5:30 a.m. sharp they all gathered in Bruno's room for one last, quick run-through of their plan. While he was happy, Bruno was all business as they walked through the steps of their attack on the farmhouse. "And you are certain," Bruno asked Otto, "no dogs that will hear and smell us as we move in?"

Otto shrugged. "Never saw one the time I was there for the party. Didn't see any yesterday."

"Good," Bruno replied. He looked around the group at each man, asking them one by one if they were ready. He looked at Eddie last. "And you, Edward? You are ready to do what you must? To rescue your wife?"

Eddie swallowed hard and nodded, thinking what a psycho this man in front of him was. He was acting like they were some kind of Navy Seal team. Dear God, he prayed to himself for the thousandth time, please keep Donna and me safe. He realized Bruno was still looking at him.

"Edward, you are sure you are ready?"

"Yeah," Eddie said. "I'm ready." No way he could back out now.

"Good! Then let's go. Get your gear and we go down the stairs and out the rear entrance so as not to be seen by the night clerk. May Allah bring us victory!"

The men all picked up their duffel bags and filed out of the room, led by Bruno, Ethan in the rear. They made it down and out without making contact with anyone. They slid all their gear in the back of the panel van and climbed in. Otto was driving since he knew the location. Bruno up front. Ethan and Eddie on jump seats behind them. Otto put the van in gear and pulled out of the parking lot, lights off.

A few hundred yards down the street he switched the headlights on and accelerated up to the speed limit. Eddie sensed Bruno turning to look at him. Nothing was said, but in the dim lights from the dashboard Eddie could see the evil in his eyes. Bruno turned back to the front and Eddie realized he was holding his breath. He let it out slowly and quietly. Here we go, he thought, and closed his eyes as he settled back in the jump seat.

Ray rolled over and looked at the clock. 5:45 a.m. He had been awake for a while, tossing and turning, unable to get comfortable enough to fall back asleep. His mind was working at a very high pace. Big day ahead. Once they made the swap, Donna for the money, a new chapter lay ahead. One with a big enough cash stake that he could make a new start, one that was legitimate.

What he needed right now, though, was to get his body moving. Burn off some of that nervous energy. Running had stopped being a thing for him long ago, but walking was something he enjoyed. Early or late were the times he loved, when the world was either just on the edge of waking or sleeping.

He rolled out of bed and slipped on a hoodie over the T-shirt he had slept in. The shorts would do. It might be a little cool out, but the brisk air would be energizing. After lacing up a pair of old running shoes he stuck a ball cap on his head and quietly opened the door to his bedroom.

The house was still, no one else moving. He glanced at the bedroom door next to his. Donna was locked in there. He wondered if she, too, had a restless night. Anticipating her freedom and returning to normal life. Well, not as normal as before, he thought. Knowing her husband was a drug dealing criminal would change that.

He walked down the hall and into the kitchen, intending to go out the back door. He paused at the counter, then decided to get a pot of coffee brewing while he was gone. Three minutes later he unlocked the door and stepped out. No idea where the house key was, so he left the door unlocked and quietly pulled it shut. Not much chance of anyone trying to get in a house out here in the country, he thought.

Ray stepped off the back porch and stretched a little before heading off into the woods. Thirty minutes, maybe an hour should do it, and he would come back and drink his coffee on the porch, watching the sun rise. Fifteen minutes later, Ray was almost a mile away from the house. After a brief walk through the woods, he emerged into an area that was clear cut to allow for the towers that carried electric power lines to the area. The clear cut and towers ran in a narrow corridor for miles. It made for an easier walk, so Ray followed the line of towers, moving east away from the farmhouse.

At the same time, Otto was turning off the road and onto the path that led back to the farmhouse. He killed the headlights, then stopped, backed up and turned around to back down the path after Bruno commented they should be parked to head out quickly if needed. Otto took his foot off the accelerator, allowing the van to roll ever so slowly back. The path was lined with woods on both sides and eventually opened up to the yard surrounding the house. He stopped the van short of the yard and put it in park, shutting down the engine.

Bruno quickly and quietly went back through the plan and asked each of them again if they were ready. Eddie was last and just nodded, his stomach churning with acid and adrenaline flying through his body. They opened the doors softly and exited the van, weapons in hand. Otto moved out first, slipping into the woods and emerging again on one side of the house. He stood still, observing the front and back portions of the yard. Nothing was moving and the house was dark, save the small light on the exterior by the rear entrance.

He crouched and swiftly made his way from the edge of the clearing and stood adjacent to the house. Now he needed to check out the far side. He crouched again and slipped around the rear corner of the house, then quickly skirted the porch that led to the rear door. Still nothing moving inside or out. As he got to the far corner of the house he paused, then peeked around to the far side of the rectangular structure. Another cleared area with about one hundred feet to the wooded area. As expected, nothing moved there either.

He hit the button on the walkie talkie attached to his belt three quick times, letting Bruno know it was clear to proceed. Two quick vibrations in return as Bruno acknowledged receipt of the all clear. As Otto turned to move again to the rear of the house, his foot caught on a root from a bush and he fell to his left, catching himself against the side of the house. He froze as he waited to see if the slight noise had woken anyone in the house.

Bruno and the others were moving out when he got the second alert from Otto. Three short bursts with a pause in between each. The signal to stay in place. Bruno turned and held his hand up to Ethan and Eddie, motioning for them to stop. Otto remained frozen in place. One minute. Two. After three full minutes with no sign of life from the house, he buzzed Bruno. Once again, all clear.

Inside the house, in the bedroom at the very corner Otto was crouched at, Penny lay motionless, eyes open and listening intently. An exceptionally light sleeper, the small bump and scrape on the siding had woken her. She waited for more, but nothing else came. Still, her senses were heightened for some reason, and she never ignored that. She gently shook Nick's arm. "Nickie," she whispered, "Wake up baby. I heard something outside bumping the house."

They both got out of bed. Penny was closest to the window, and she cautiously slid one of the slats in the blinds up a bit to peer outside. Nothing at first, then a slight movement by Otto crouched directly below caught her eye. She turned and whispered again to Nick, urgently now. "Someone outside, right below the window!"

Nick nodded and quickly retrieved his 9mm pistol from beside the bed. Penny grabbed hers as well, opening the nightstand drawer softly to take it out. "You stay here. I'm going to wake Ray and we'll check this out."

Penny nodded and racked a bullet into the chamber of the 9mm. As Nick opened the bedroom door, she peeked out again. The man was moving slowly around the corner to the back of the house. She hurried over to the window at the rear and opened the blind there. A second man was creeping from the other side towards the porch with an automatic rifle held in front of him.

"Shit!" she whispered loudly to herself, then yelled for Nick.

Nick was sticking his head back in their bedroom as she turned. "Ray's not in his room," he said.

"Two of them," she replied. "One coming from the other corner. Where's Ray?"

"Don't know. Stay put! Shoot anything that moves through this door that's not me or Ray," he said, closing the door and turning down the hall. He got to the end of the hall and stopped at the corner before moving any further. The blinds were up on the window to the right of the rear door. With the light from the outside bulb shining he could see the second man, looking to his left. He turned to his own left to look towards the front door, contemplating whether to go out and circle around back to surprise them. A shadow moved across the two narrow windows on either side of the door. Damn, he thought. Are there more or did the guy on the side move to the front porch?

Penny's 9mm went off at that moment in the bedroom and as he whipped his attention back, he caught sight of the guy with the rifle going down in the back yard. Shit! Penny must have shot him through the window. Now he moved quickly towards the front and into the living room. He could clearly make out the shadow of someone standing on the porch, a perfect silhouette for a shot. He ripped three quick shots through the window, and the body fell.

Penny yelled from the bedroom. "Nickie, you okay?"

"Yeah, yeah! One down on the front porch," he yelled back.

Then shots fired from the back, and he heard Penny scream. He ran back to the bedroom, hearing Donna from the locked bedroom across the hall yelling to ask what was happening. Penny was down by the rear window. He rushed over and knelt beside her. She had taken two slugs, one in the chest and the second in the temple. She was gone even as he looked at her. Where the hell was Ray? He grabbed his phone off the table and hit the speed dial. Ray picked up after two rings.

"Nick. What's up?"

"Shooters! They got Penny. We got a couple before that. Don't know how many more. Where the fuck are you?" he screamed into the phone.

"Shit! Walking. Coming back now!"

"Be quick! I'm pinned down in the house."

Ray was already sprinting back, jamming his phone in a pocket as he ran.

At police headquarters in downtown Raleigh, Janie sat down at her desk, first cup of coffee in hand. Almost 6:00 a.m. and the floor was deserted except for her. Not her normal start time, but she was headed out on vacation the next day and wanted to wrap some things up before she left for two weeks.

She had been puzzling off and on the last two days over the partial plate numbers from the brown van in the Johnston case. They had given her the numbers they could see and a couple they guessed at. Three complete unknowns. Seven numbers in total.

She had exhausted all the combinations she could come up with the day before. Actually, she thought wryly, the software had done that. No hits in the DMV database. Then last night as she closed her eyes in bed she realized she was only searching for active plates. What if the plate was no longer registered? Less than an hour later she had her answer. Two answers really. D-D-M-3-3-7-9. The plate was no longer active. And she had an address from when it had been active years before.

The plate had been registered to a man named Louis Slagle, with an address off Carpenter Pond Road, north of the city of Raleigh. It had been tied to a 1973 Ford F-100 pickup truck, blue in color. A far cry from the brown van Jimmy had shown her in the door cam video. More research revealed Mr. Slagle had died some years back and the property had been left to children who now lived in another state.

Janie debated whether to call Jimmy now or just hold the info until he came into the office. It was still early, way early for him to be up. She could call Micky. He was probably up. But what were the chances this information was that urgent, she wondered. Well, let them decide. She punched up Micky's cell phone.

"Mornin' sunshine," he greeted her. "You're on it early today."

"Yep. Getting out of here for a long, much needed vacation."

"What's up?"

Janie filled him in on what she had found. Micky asked a couple of questions, and she promised to drop all the data in a network folder he could access from home. "Thanks, Janie. Great work."

"No problem."

"And Janie..."

"Yeah?"

"Next time feel free to call Jimmy. It would be good for him to be rousted out of bed this early," laughed Micky.

Janie just snorted at him. "Later, Detective Bondurant."

Micky looked at his watch. He would hit the greenway for his morning run, then look at the stuff from Janie before he took a shower.

CHAPTER 29

Nick moved back into the hallway. Donna heard him and yelled out again. "Stay down on the floor!" he yelled back at her. He was thinking quickly now, completely amped up. Ray was on the way back. Could he hold out until then? Two of them down so far. At least one more at the rear. Could there be others? He decided to move back into the living room by the front door and try to get a look out front. As he moved, he caught sight of Otto on the back porch and snapped off three rounds through the window of the rear door. Not much chance of hitting him, but it should keep him pinned down a couple of minutes. He prayed Ray had locked that back door when he left.

He got to the front and slid the blinds open a fraction on the window, careful not to silhouette his shadow as an easy target. The guy he had shot was still down on the porch, not moving. A second man was in the yard, slowly moving towards the cover of the house. Probably circling to meet with the other one at the back. He couldn't see any others out front. Just the two of them left. How far away was Ray, he wondered. Maybe they could catch them in a crossfire in the back yard. Wait, Ray probably didn't have his pistol with him. Shit!

He could slip out the front door. Circle around to the back himself and catch them by surprise. He stepped through the doorway of the living room into the hallway. A quick glance to the rear showed no movement yet from the back yard. Turning back to the front door he rotated the locking mechanism and opened the door inward. Now the screen door. He unhooked the latch and silently pushed it open far enough to be able to look towards the corner. He waited for a beat before he looked to see if there was a response to the door opening. None came so he stuck his head out. Porch guy still down, no sound or movement from him.

He looked left. The second guy was standing at the corner, looking toward the back yard. As Nick was raising the 9mm to take the shot, the man suddenly stepped around the corner and out of sight. "Damn," he swore silently, then gently pushed the screen door all the way open. The spring squeaked loudly just at the end of the opening. Nick swore again, momentarily distracted. Bruno heard the screen door and popped back around the corner, snapping off shots when he saw Nick at the door.

Nick took two of the shots, the first in his right shoulder, the second to the chest. He managed to fire a couple of rounds back, then he stumbled back into the hallway, slamming the door shut and locking it. Blood was starting to soak through his shirt. The shoulder was on fire. The chest wound, oddly enough, wasn't hurting much. But it was bad, and he knew it. Where the hell was Ray?

Outside, Bruno eased up to the front door. He saw blood on the door handle, so he knew he had scored a hit. There were narrow six-foot windowpanes on either side of the door. If he stepped over to try and open the door he would be exposed. Time to circle to the back and talk to Otto and Ethan. He hit his radio button, two short then one long to let Otto know he was coming.

Otto heard the shots exchanged and was considering the next steps when his radio buzzed. He stepped against the side of the house, then ducked and shuffled to the corner to meet Bruno. Bruno almost ran into him at the corner and each man raised their weapon instinctively.

"They got Ethan," whispered Otto.

Bruno shook his head. "Edward also," he replied. "Just us now. I wounded one of the men at the front door."

"I think I took out one of the women. She fired at me through the window. Couldn't see who it was."

"It matters not now, my friend. With Edward dead, what is his wife to us?"

Otto thought for a moment. "Better she's alive than dead. We need that car lot to move product through. Maybe we can make a deal with her?"

"Hmm. A very excellent point, Otto. Let us keep her alive then if possible. The second man, he is in there?"

"Don't know for sure, but it seems maybe not."

They talked quietly for a couple of minutes about their next move. There was a risk that the gunshots might be heard by a neighbor who would call in the police. Speed had to be their friend. Get in, eliminate Nick, rescue Donna.

Micky was less than a half mile into his run and was thinking about the call from Janie. He was feeling a bit guilty. Donna Johnson's life, if she was still alive, was on the line and he was out running. What if the information from Janie unlocked it all for them? He stopped, turned, and started sprinting back to his house. On the way he punched up Jimmy on his cell phone.

"Micky, what the hell man?" came the sleepy response from Jimmy.

"Get... out of... bed, bro," he huffed as he was running. "Janie found an address for the plates on.... that brown van. I... I got a feeling this.... might be the key."

"Dude, are you running right now?"

Micky stopped as he got to the back door of his house. "I was.

Sprinting back to the house. Throw some clothes on. I'll text you where to meet me."

"Yeah, yeah. I'm on the way," said Jimmy, ending the call.

Micky took a couple of deep breaths to get his wind back, then opened the door and went to his laptop. He scanned the info from Janie quickly. Carpenter Pond Road. He could cut across Norwood Road from his place off Six Forks in Coachman's Trail. Ten minutes max. He texted Jimmy:

CVS at Norwood and Creedmoor. Meet me there.

He got the thumbs up response from Jimmy, then grabbed a shirt, his badge and gun just as Jules came into the kitchen.

"Where are you headed so early?"

Micky leaned over and kissed her on the forehead. "Break in the case. Meeting Jimmy to check it out."

Jules laughed. "Must be big if you got Quinn out of bed this early. Stay safe."

"Always," came his reply as he closed the door behind him.

In the edge of the woods, Ray crouched in the brush. He was too far away to hear the two men outside Nick's house clearly, just the murmuring of their voices as they talked. A third man lay out in the yard, assault weapon next to him where it had fallen. No chance Ray could get to it without being seen and mowed down.

Nick said they got two, he thought. Maybe the other one was lying in the front yard, and Ray could retrieve his weapon. He backed up quietly, then started to move through the woods and around the house. In less than a minute he was there. Bingo! Second body on the porch, gun lying on the ground.

He glanced at both sides of the house. No one came around. Deep breath, then he sprinted from the cover of the brush to the house. Grabbing the rifle, he prodded the body with the end of the barrel.

No response. He looked at its face. Eddie. Immediately felt sympathy for Donna.

Ray snapped himself back into gear and considered what was next. He could ease around the corner, perhaps take them both out before they could react. A safer bet would be to circle back around through the woods, using the cover of the brush there to take them out sniper style. Of course, if they stormed the house before he got them, he would be useless as a sniper. Worth the chance he concluded, so he ran quickly across the front yard and back into the woods.

Ray was almost around to the back when he heard someone shouting. Muffled at first, and then clearer as he made it back to where he had first been positioned. One of the men was yelling to Nick. " ... no chance you're getting out of this Nick. We got you pinned. Send her out and we leave you alive."

Ray was puzzled. They knew Nick's name. What the hell? Then Nick's voice drifted out the shattered kitchen window. "Fuck Off, Otto. No money, no hostage."

Ahh, Ray thought, this was the guy Nick had met from the car lot. The one who worked for Eddie. He chuckled a bit at Nick's bravado. Of course, Nick knew Ray was on the way back to the farmhouse and those guys didn't.

"Last chance, Nick," shouted Otto. "We're coming in."

The two men started to move. Otto sprinted to the corner and turned to go to the front of the house, out of sight before Ray could line up a shot. The second man moved closer to the door and appeared ready to step up onto the porch. He leveled up the rifle and squeezed off several rounds. The weapon was not all that accurate at this distance. Still, one of the rounds caught Bruno in the leg. It buckled and he fell off the porch on the far side, shielding him from further shots from Ray. Otto heard the shots and appeared at the rear of the house, cautiously peeking around the corner.

"Bruno, you hit?"

"Yes. Leg," he replied, panting from the pain.

"How bad?"

"Bleeding is not bad, but I don't think I can walk on it."

"Where's the shooter? Must be Nick's partner."

Bruno pointed to the wooded area behind the house at about the same time Ray fired towards the corner where Otto was. Otto stepped back as several slugs whizzed by and embedded into the siding on the house.

"Bruno, I'm going back to the front. Gonna' kick in the door and see if I can get in and take out Nick. You good here for now?"

Bruno gritted his teeth and flashed a thumbs up. "Go, Otto. Allah will bring us victory on this day!"

Otto turned, shaking his head as he went. What a nut job, he thought. I gotta' find someone new to work for when this is over.

Ray's cell phone buzzed. Nick. "Nick, talk to me. You okay in there?"

"Hit pretty bad, Ray. They got me twice. I'm still moving, though. What's the situation out there?"

"Looks like there are two left. I hit one at the back of the house. Leg, I think. He's holed up next to the porch. The other one just circled back to the front."

"You?"

"In the woods at the rear right now."

"Okay. He's probably gonna' kick the front door and shoot his way in." Nick and Ray talked for another minute or so about what to do next and ended the call.

Otto was by the front porch, assessing the best way to get in. Tricky because of the front windows and the panes on each side of the door. Easy shot for Nick if he crossed by them. The steps up to the porch were directly in line with the door. He could crawl beside the porch to the steps, then bolt straight up and into the door.

He started to move, then had another thought. He could create a diversion by smashing in the window of the front bedroom. Maybe

Nick would think that he was coming through there, leaving the doorway unguarded. He crawled around the porch and got to the far side. Careful not to make himself a target there, he crouched, then flipped the rifle in his hands and rammed the butt into the window above his head. He lunged to the side to avoid falling glass, hearing the screams of a woman inside as he moved. Must be Donna in that room, he thought.

"Donna!" he said from just below the windowsill. "Donna, it's me, Otto. Can you hear me?" He was trying to be quiet enough to keep Nick from hearing inside the house.

"Otto?" she replied. "What... what are you doing here? Where's Eddie?"

Otto glanced at Eddie's body lying on the porch and decided not to tell her yet. "Donna, we came to rescue you." Inspiration came to him. "Donna, can you open this window? I can help you crawl out."

"No. They nailed it shut. I..." and then she screamed again as Nick threw open the bedroom door and fired a round through the shattered window. The bullet sailed harmlessly over Otto. Seeing that his diversion had worked, he took two steps and leapt onto the porch. Back against the house, he stood next to the closest of the narrow windows next to the front door. He risked a quick glance into the house, then moved in front of the door once he saw the hallway inside was empty. Nick was still in the bedroom.

Otto grabbed the front door handle. Locked as he expected. He stepped back and fired several rounds into the area around the handle and lock, shattering everything there so he could easily kick the door in. Inside the hallway he moved quickly. He stepped inside the living room to his left after a glance that way. All clear in there. He heard movement in the hallway that led to the bedrooms.

Nick called out into the hallway. "That you out there, Otto? You're a dead man."

Otto laughed. "Not me, Nick. You're the one holding the bullets right now. Bleeding pretty good aren't 'ya?"

"I won't die before you do, asshole," Nick yelled as he fired a round towards the end of the hallway before moving across the hall to his bedroom for more ammo. He yanked the bedroom door closed as he went, locking Donna back in.

Outside, Ray was circling back around through the woods to the front of the house. Once there he sprinted to the side closest to the driveway, crouching and moving quietly to the rear corner. Bruno would be an easy target. The porch had shielded him before, but this side offered him no protection.

He was smart enough to realize the vulnerability on that side. When Ray peeked around the corner, briefly exposing his head, Bruno was ready and fired towards the corner. Ray pulled back and the slugs sailed by. He stuck the rifle around the corner and blindly sent a few rounds towards where Bruno lay against the porch foundation.

He heard a grunt and a gasp, and more shots came whizzing by the cover. Ray repeated the blind fire at Bruno. No response this time. He counted to twenty, then risked another peek. Bruno was sitting up, back against the porch foundation. When he saw Ray, he tried to speak, but blood trickled out as he opened his mouth. He attempted to raise his gun, but the life in him was spent and he only managed a few inches before his arm collapsed.

Ray stepped around the corner, walking over to Bruno. "You're done, asshole," he said as he put one more bullet in the center of his forehead. He reached down and grabbed Bruno's rifle, discarding the one he held. He yanked two clips off the vest on Bruno's body. He thought about it, then yanked the 9mm from the holster at Bruno's side, jamming it in his waistband at the small of his back.

One more to go. He could hear the muffled shouts of Nick and Otto inside. Surely Otto had heard the shots exchanged between him and Bruno and had probably guessed how that ended. Would he press on in the house, Ray wondered, or make a break out of the front door to get away?

Otto was inside pondering that same question. Bruno was probably dead now, he reasoned. The van and the money were maybe two hundred yards away. He could disappear with the money in the van, somewhere Anton could never hunt him down. An easy choice. He began slipping back towards the front door, hoping Ray was still out back. He might be coming through the back door at any moment, so Otto had to move. Now.

Micky had time to grab two coffees from the small convenience store across from the CVS. Jimmy had at least a twenty-minute drive from his place. Unless he came with lights flashing. Which he did. They were still going when he rolled into the parking lot and up to Micky's car. Micky slid in beside him, handing Jimmy one of the coffees. "Thirteen minutes to get here," he said triumphantly. "And gracias for the coffee."

"You know it. How about you kill those lights and let's go low profile to this address?"

Jimmy nodded. "Yep, was planning to do that."

As he pulled to the exit of the lot, they both heard a police siren coming their way. Seconds later, a Wake County Sheriff's Deputy crested the hill on Highway 50, slowing as he reached the intersection where they were. The light was red, so the deputy had to stop long enough for the traffic moving across to register his lights and siren and move aside.

Jimmy looked at Micky. "Do you think…"

Micky shook his head. "Naw. Too big a coincidence. Probably headed to a car crash."

They watched as the deputy turned left onto Norwood Road, accelerating as he made the turn. Jimmy waited for the traffic to clear, then pulled out on Norwood as well, following the path of the deputy. "I don't know," he said to Micky. "I got a feeling."

Micky snorted. "Just drive, maestro. We'll find out soon enough."

Ray had reversed course and was back at the front corner of the house by the time Otto started to emerge. He shrank back, knowing Otto would look that way. He figured Otto would either creep to the corner he was at to get a look towards the back before heading to the van, or he would do a full sprint across the yard into the woods for cover and then cut through to the van.

Ray got his answer when he saw Otto moving across the yard. He fingered the gun to full auto and yelled at Otto. "Stop! Drop the weapons or I mow you down."

With fifty more yards to go before the woods, Otto quickly calculated his odds. Not good. He stopped, dropped the rifle he was holding, then slowly raised his hands. "I'm gonna' turn around now," he yelled back at Ray.

Ray stepped around the house and into the yard, the rifle centered on Otto's chest. "Now take the pistol out and drop it on the ground. Move slowly. Use your left hand. My trigger finger's kind of itchy right now."

Otto nodded and did as instructed. After raising his hands again, he said to Ray, "Look man, we can make a deal here. We all walk away. No one gets hurt."

Ray laughed. "No one gets hurt? Look around asshole. Already a few dead bodies. My partner's wife, dead inside. He's hit pretty bad, probably bleeding out thanks to you."

Otto swallowed hard. "Look, Ray. It's Ray, right? I'm just a worker bee on this man. The boss is around back. He called the shots."

Ray laughed again. "You mean the guy propped against the porch? The one who was using this gun?" He waived the rifle in his hands towards Otto. "His last words were 'Otto's in charge'. Or something like that."

Ray moved a few steps closer. "Besides, it doesn't look like you've got much deal-making power right now."

"Look man, you let me go, the cash is all yours. I hit the road. No one ever sees me again," said Otto, desperately searching for a way to keep Ray from pulling the trigger.

"And this cash," Ray asked, "it's in that van parked down the drive?"

Otto instinctively glanced over his shoulder in the direction of the van. When he turned back Ray was smiling. "Turn around asshole. Walk to the van."

Otto again did as instructed and they quickly made their way to the van. Ray motioned for him to open the rear doors. Several duffel bags lay in the rear of the van. "Raise your right hand high and keep it there. With your left, pick up the bags with cash and place them on the ground between us. And Otto, if your hand ends up with a gun in it you die right here."

Otto nodded and turned to the van again. He picked up the two bags with cash and placed them in front of Ray, who crouched and unzipped both bags. Each was gleaming with stacks of bills. He zipped them back up.

"You gonna' let me go, Ray?"

Ray shook his head.

"You gonna' kill me then?"

Again, Ray shook his head.

Puzzled, Otto shook his own head. "Then what, Ray?"

The faint sound of police sirens wafted in, still far away but likely headed for them. Both men realized it at the same time. "Cops will be here soon, Ray. What's it gonna' be?"

Ray glanced into the back of the van. "Better you rot in a cell than in a grave," he said. "Grab a handful of those zip ties out of the van. Hook yourself to that fence over there!"

Otto looked at the fence, then back at Ray. "You gotta' be kidding me!"

The sirens were getting louder. "Ticktock, Otto. Move now and you live. Keep yacking and you die. We're out of time."

Otto moved over to the fence, securing one arm and an ankle to the fence. Ray decided the van was his best exit option and threw the bags of cash back in and quickly shut the rear doors. After checking to make sure the keys to the van were up front, he returned for one last word to Otto. "I really should just shoot your ass right now, but I'm going to spare you. Good luck in prison Otto!"

"Fuck you!" Otto screamed as Ray got in the van, started it and roared down the drive.

At the end of the drive, Ray turned left, knowing the police would likely be coming from the right. He needed to put some distance down quickly, then find a place to hole up for the day and a new ride. Otto would describe the van and soon enough they would be looking for it.

He pulled out his cell phone and hit the speed dial for Nick. No answer and it rolled to voice mail. "Nick, it's Ray. I fear you are not picking up because you can't. You may never hear this message. The cops are almost there, so I'm on the run now. If you're still alive, your best chance to get to a hospital quickly is with them."

Ray paused, took a deep breath to settle the emotions that suddenly came on, then continued. "But I hope you're not alive my friend. That you slipped away peacefully to be with Penny. To not have to face the end that damn cancer inside you promises. It was a good ride, Nickie. I have a bunch of cash those assholes had with them. I'll take care of your kids, just like you wanted."

He paused one more time, then went on. "Farewell. Until I see you on the other side. I love you, brother."

CHAPTER 30

Two weeks after the shoot-out at the farm, Jimmy and Dani lounged on the patio behind her house. It was a gorgeous spring afternoon and the first Saturday either of them had off work in a few weeks. After sleeping in late, Jimmy had gone for takeout sandwiches from Steve's, their favorite local deli. That was followed by a bloody mary and a retreat to the bedroom. Now they were perched on a couple of chaise lounges, mimosas in hand, soaking in a sun that hadn't become a summer inferno yet.

Dani reached over and laid a hand on Jimmy's arm. "Details, please," she said. "You promised to tell me how this whole car lot caper ended."

Jimmy laughed. "The car lot caper. Clever. You should be a writer."

She raised her glass in salute. "My next career."

Jimmy sat up a bit straighter and took a generous swallow of his drink. "Okay. Where shall I start?"

"When you and Mick got to the farmhouse. I know the basics up to that point."

"I had met Micky at a CVS not far from the farm. Janie had gotten a hit for the address of an old license plate they had put on the van they drove to the Johnson's house on the day of the break-in. Also stolen, by the way. As we were pulling out, a Wake County deputy came flying up, full dress mode, and…"

"Wait! Full dress mode?"

"Sorry. Lights and siren going."

Dani nodded. "Continue."

"We figured he was headed to an auto accident or something. Turns out he was also headed to the farm. Neighbors had reported multiple gunshots nearby. We were two to three minutes behind him. When we got there, he was out of his cruiser, gun drawn and questioning Otto."

"Otto?" queried Dani.

"Otto was the mechanic at Johnson Auto. He was zip tied to a fence, loudly proclaiming he was a victim of the whole thing. The deputy was about to cut him loose when we rolled up." Jimmy paused for another sip of his mimosa. Dani did likewise and he continued the story. "I hit the lights on the car to alert the deputy that we were the good guys. We convinced him it was best to leave Otto tied up while we checked everything out at the house."

"Poor Otto," Dani said wryly. "That close to freedom before you show up!"

Jimmy laughed at her sarcasm and continued. "We didn't know who was alive or not, so we quickly agreed on an approach and made our way to the house. Eddie Johnson was dead on the porch. Two dead in the backyard. More on them in a minute. Nick and his wife Penny, dead inside. Donna Johnson was alive and unhurt, locked in a bedroom."

"Damn, that was quite a shootout. How did it all start?"

"We didn't know for a while," Jimmy replied. "Otto clammed up right away once we outed him to the deputy. A couple of days later he spilled it all. The offer for some leniency for him in return for giving up the drug traffickers was just too good to refuse."

"Drug traffickers? Were he and Eddie dealing drugs from the car lot?"

Jimmy shook his head. "Nope. That was all Otto, in cahoots with the Rezavik brothers. Bruno Rezavik and his compadre Ethan were the ones dead in the back yard. The other brother, Anton, was safe and sound at his home in Wilmington when it all went down."

"So, Eddie was clean?" Dani asked with a puzzled look. "Why was he at the farm that morning?"

"No, he wasn't clean. He just wasn't quite as dirty as the rest of them yet. He and Otto had been running a scam where they rolled back the mileage on a few cars, making some extra cash when Eddie was able to sell them for a higher price. That started not long after Otto was planted there."

"Planted there?" she asked as she drained the last of her mimosa and pointed to the pitcher beside Jimmy for a refill.

"Yeah. Eddie was buying a lot of his car inventory through the Rezavik brothers. His mechanic left a few years ago and Anton saw a chance to plant one of their guys in Raleigh and start another hub in their growing drug network."

"Drugs hidden in the cars in Wilmington and Otto takes them out in Raleigh?"

Jimmy nodded. "You got it."

"And Eddie never knew?"

"Not until after Donna was kidnapped. Nick and friends - his wife Penny, his pal Ray, and a local named Rose - engineered a forced break-in at the Johnsons. They were convinced Eddie was the drug king and he had a bunch of cash stashed there."

"So, they never intended to kidnap her?"

"Nope. Eddie came home early and surprised them. There was no money at the house, so they saw a way to get some through a kidnapping. They pressed Eddie for $2 million. He couldn't come up with it and was afraid to go to the police for two reasons."

Jimmy paused to refill his own glass and Dani jumped in. "Nick told him if he went to the police, Donna was a goner. Reason number one."

Jimmy gave a thumbs up while sipping his mimosa.

"Reason number two," she continued, "Eddie's already a criminal with the mileage scheme and doesn't want to risk the cops snooping around in that."

"Right again, Sherlock," replied Jimmy. "So, Otto and the Rezaviks recruited Eddie into the drug business in exchange for the ransom money."

"So, the swap went sideways at the farm and ended in a bloodbath?"

"Wrong this time. The Rezaviks decided they would save themselves the $2 million in ransom and go with a Navy Seal style raid on the farm to rescue Donna."

Dani laughed. "Well, that didn't end well."

"Nope."

"So how did you get Otto to talk?"

Jimmy smiled. "My brother had given us the lowdown on the Rezaviks and their rumored side business in drug distribution. After a day or two of hinting that we knew more than we really did about things, Otto was ready to make a deal to give up Anton."

Dani was quiet for a couple of minutes, reflecting on all the players involved. She was curious about what happened to the rest of them. "Okay, first of all you didn't mention what happened to the other woman. Rose?"

"Last seen alive with apparent friend of the gang Drew. He's the guy we found dead in his apartment. Drew was telling Rose's friend Tammy that she had gone back to be with Ray, Nick's compadre. She - or at least her body - hasn't been found yet."

"Let's see," mused Dani. "Who's left? What about the other Rezavik, the one who wasn't killed? I guess he was arrested when Otto came clean, huh?"

Jimmy shook his head. "We were too late. Found dead in his office with a bullet hole in his forehead."

"What?" exclaimed Dani. "Who did that?"

"We don't know, but we have a suspicion."

"Ray," they both said at the same time.

"Yep. Anton had a safe in his office. The door was open when the local police found him. Some papers were still in there, but it had been looted. Probably had a bunch of drug cash in it."

Dani drained the last of her mimosa. "A revenge killing by Ray for Nick."

"And an insurance policy for Ray. One less person to worry about coming after him."

"Any idea where he is yet?"

Jimmy set his glass down and stared off into the distance. "No. I'm betting we will never find him."

EPILOGUE

Cristina Flanagan was in the kitchen of her modest town home in Richmond baking cookies on a Saturday afternoon. A rainy afternoon, which meant the kids were inside, yelling at each other over the television channels.

"Jenny. Nick Jr.," she yelled. "Pipe down in there."

The doorbell rang and she set the mixing bowl on the counter. After wiping her hands on a towel, she walked to the front door. She could see through the locked storm door that a FedEx driver was waiting with a small envelope. After greeting him and signing for it, she walked back to the kitchen.

The package was from some bank in the Bahamas. That's odd, she thought. She set it down and went back to the mixing bowl. Two minutes later her curiosity won out and she opened the package. There was an official looking document of some kind, several pages long, and a brief handwritten note. She read the note first.

Cristina,

You don't know me, but I was a close friend of Nick's. You may have already found out, but Nick died a short while ago. He wanted you to know that he hoped your life had turned out well and that he loved the kids fiercely. It wasn't how he died, but he had stage four pancreatic cancer and knew his time was short. He spent the last weeks focused on leaving some money behind for their future. The documents included will tell you more about that.

Cristina set the note down, already thinking of how to break the news of their father's death to the kids. She picked up the document and started to read it, then gasped and dropped it on the floor when she realized what it was saying. An account, in the names of the kids, with her as administrator. A balance of $2 million. The tears came quickly, followed by soft sobbing. For Nick. For the memories of what he had been when they met, and for what he was at the end.

That same day, back in Raleigh, Donna Johnson was in her yard, yanking at the weeds that had taken over her flower beds in the last few weeks. Eddie had been laid to rest in a quiet, private ceremony at a nearby cemetery. Donna had been grateful to learn via Otto's confession that Eddie had not yet become a drug dealer before he died. The rollback scheme was bad enough. She missed him every day.

While she worked, she thought about the car lot and the conversation next week with Bill. She had to sell it - what did she know about used cars - and she wasn't sure Bill could raise the money to buy it from her. She was so lost in her thoughts she didn't hear the FedEx truck pull up to the curb. She was mildly startled when the driver spoke to her from a few feet away. She signed the electronic pad he carried and looked at the label on the package. A bank in the Bahamas. Odd. She read the note first.

Donna,

So sorry about what happened to Eddie. Really, I'm sorry about it all. It wasn't what we planned. You deserved better. I hope what's in the document helps.

R

She quickly scanned the document, stunned at what she read. $1 million in an account in her name. She too dropped the letter and cried.

Ray was sitting in coach class on an Aegean Airlines flight headed overnight to Athens, nonstop from the Robert L. Bradshaw International Airport in St. Kitts. After the battle at the farmhouse, he had made his way to Wilmington to pay a visit to Anton Rezavik, who happened to have quite a bit of cash close by.

From there he drove to Miami and in a couple of days hopped a few charter boats to reach the Bahamas. An old friend helped him get a phony passport and some new identity papers. After completing his banking visit, he took a flight to St. Kitts and had spent a quiet week or so in a house on Mosquito Bay. Now he was headed to Europe. He had read about some houses for sale for one euro in Zungoli, a small town close to the Amalfi Coast in Italy. The $3 million he had kept from the drug money would go a long way there.

He was staring out the small airplane window at a faraway moon, remembering childhood stories his grandfather had told him about it when the flight attendant handed him the glass of prosecco he had ordered. He set it briefly on the tray table while he consulted the Learn Italian! book he had bought in Nassau. He raised the glass and whispered softly, "A to Vecchio amico. Riposa in pace, Nick."

AUTHOR'S NOTES

Writing this book has been a journey. The initial pages were written over a decade ago. While the first thing I can remember wanting to be was a writer, my choices in life took me down other paths. I kept reading though, a pastime I can't remember ever being without, and I rarely go a day without reading part of a book.

I have read more authors than I could ever recount at this stage, but I want to acknowledge three whose work has been particularly satisfying for me. Robert B. Parker, writer of the Spenser for Hire books, was perhaps the first one that got me to intentionally become a repeat buyer. John Grisham came next, and I always remember the story of how he wrote A Time to Kill one page at a time. Lastly, and perhaps, most importantly, is John Sandford, writer of the Prey and Virgil Flowers novels. His style has been an inspiration for me in completing this book and thinking about how the plot should flow.

When I started this book, I already had two others under my belt, both of which remain to this day mostly in my head and not on paper. The length of time it has taken to complete it is the product of many things, but probably mostly due to how I used to approach the process of writing. In a word, it was unstructured. Two things changed that, and I want to give credit for those here.

I was fortunate enough to meet David Routh during his tenure at UNC-Chapel Hill. David knew John Grisham and told me a story one day of how Grisham apparently approaches the process each year for his newest book. I am also a collector of quotes that speak to me, and Stephen King has one of my all-time favorites: "Amateurs sit and wait for inspiration, the rest of us just get up and go to work." What I learned from both of these enormously successful authors is the most important thing of all. Give the writing the dedication it deserves, and good things will happen.

The inspirations for all the parts of this novel are numerous, and I won't try to list those here, but will simply give thanks for all the people and events in my life that contributed.

I will bring this section to a close with acknowledging the people I am most grateful for during this journey. It begins with Celeste Webster, my earliest reader and cheerleader. She was there at the start. Debbie Carter came along in the last few years and stepped right into the role Celeste had played. Thanks to William Boggess for the excellent editing he provided once my manuscript had reached its first draft conclusion.

Finally, to my wife Ginny and our children Kerry and Haley. Nothing compares to the joy and inspiration you bring me in all aspects of my life.